THE UNKNOWN SEA

FRANÇOIS MAURIAC

THE
UNKNOWN
SEA

(*Les Chemins de la Mer*)

Translated by
GERARD HOPKINS

LONDON
EYRE & SPOTTISWOODE

Les Chemins de la Mer was first published in 1939
First English translation, 1948

*This book, first published in 1948, is produced
in complete conformity with the Authorized
Economy Standards and is made and printed
in Great Britain for Eyre and Spottiswoode
(Publishers) Limited, 15 Bedford Street,
London, W.C. 2, by Billing and Sons Ltd.,
Guildford and Esher*

F 8427

"*FOR most men the road of life is a dead-end, leading nowhere. But there are some who, even in childhood, realize that they are moving towards an unknown sea. At the very beginning of their journey they are amazed by the bitter violence of the wind and taste the salt upon their lips. On they go until at length, when the last dune has been surmounted, they find themselves in a world of spume and blown sand which seems to speak to them of an infinity of passion. That is the moment when they must choose their path. Either they must take the final plunge, or they must retrace their steps.*"

I

DENIS REVOLOU was pretending to revise his lecture notes. But in fact his whole attention was centred upon his mother, who was pacing up and down the room. Her long train dragged over the carpet with a sound that partook both of softness and solemnity. Her face had that "official" look which was the product of Monsieur Tardy, the hairdresser from the Cours des Fosses, whenever he came to prepare her for a ball: the same look that she assumed when sitting for her photograph. Her white waved hair, still with a faint hint in it of yellow, was built up into a fragile architectural structure, protected by a gossamer veil and topped by an emerald crescent. Her daughter Rose, whose hair, like her own, was grandly "done," was still in her dressing jacket, because her dress, which had needed a few last-minute alterations, had not yet come back from Habrias.

"If your dress is not here in five minutes I shall begin to feel seriously perturbed."

Denis tried, unsuccessfully, to stifle a faint giggle.

"Not gone to bed yet, Denis?"

"I'm waiting to see the dress," he said.

A tall standard-lamp threw light upon his hair, which he wore parted on the left-hand side. His large hand was resting upon a *Manual of Psychology*. Behind his rather heavy-looking head long folds of faded silk hung from a velvet pelmet. He was devoured with impatience to have a look at Rose's dress which one of the under-servants had been sent to fetch from Habrias. It would, he supposed, be like all dance-frocks—frankly immodest. He stared at Rose's rather babyish face, but did not return her smile. In less than an hour's time she would be standing in a drawing-room doorway, offering to the common gaze the spectacle of her throat and shoulders, of her back, and even of those childish breasts that were set a shade too high. She would allow herself to be clasped, thus stripped, in the arms of the first man who might

3

care to ask her for a dance . . . though perhaps, now, it was not that hypothetical "first man" who was most to be feared. What about Robert Costadot? . . . Weren't they all but engaged? Very soon their life together would be an established fact. She might, at least, have married someone with whom she was not in love. Women in novels are scarcely ever in love with their husbands. . . . Still, even now something might happen to stop the marriage. . . . Old Mother Costadot was doing all she knew to put a spoke in that particular wheel—spreading all sorts of damaging rumours about the Revolou practice—which was worth millions, and was certainly more prosperous than that of any other lawyer in the city. . . . It was women like her who created a dangerous state of mind in the public . . . though if his mother had been really worried, he thought, she wouldn't be making so much of the pimple she had just discovered on Rose's left nostril.

"It's grown!" she was saying at that moment. "It'll be a lesson to you not to stuff yourself with chocolates and to eat more green vegetables!" (She had a passion for pinning responsibility on to those about her.) "With a complexion like yours, you ought to avoid all heating foods. . . . I can't think where you get it from," she added thoughtfully.

"Not from you—that's quite certain!" said Denis to himself, indignant that his mother, whose skin was as coarse as old leather and showed the pores only too visibly, should dare to criticize a surface so delicate that it flushed in response to every fleeting emotion.

Madame Oscar Revolou was moved by a kind of instinctive animosity where her daughter was concerned. She was forever "getting at her," and never minced her words. With her, irritation quickly turned to ill-temper which expressed itself in violent outbursts, though she hurt herself as much as she hurt the girl by her gift of cruel invective.

"You look positive hideous this evening, my poor child! I only hope you won't be a wallflower! . . . It's lucky for you that your parents are who they are. . . . That's right! turn on the

waterworks! . . . as if there wasn't enough trouble without
that. . . . You'll have a puffy face and a nose like a potato! . . .
Run along, do, and bathe your eyes in cold water!"

Rose hurried sobbing from the room, though Denis shouted
after her that she "needn't bother," because she'd be the prettiest
girl in the room—as usual.

Madame Revolou protested that she was speaking only for the
girl's good. "It's odd," thought Denis, "how much fonder she is of
Julien and of me . . . of Julien, who's a fool, and of me . . . poor
me!" he muttered in a low voice, gently stroking the soft down
on his cheek.

The butler came in to say that Monsieur Landin, their father's
senior clerk, would like to have a word with Madame. His
mistress seemed to be both surprised and indignant. . . . What! a
word with her, at nine o'clock at night? Monsieur Landin must
have taken leave of his senses! Besides, didn't he know that she
never interfered in business matters? Her husband would be back
from Léognan tomorrow evening. If things really couldn't wait
the senior clerk would just have to go out there (the Château of
Léognan was only about seven miles from town).

Denis found himself wondering whether this unusual request
of Landin's mightn't, perhaps, be causing his mother some
anxiety. Abandoning his *Manual of Psychology*, he slipped out of
the room in the wake of Louis Larpe, the butler. Like a half-
starved dog, he wormed his way through the door before it
could be closed, hot on the scent of—as his best friend, Pierre
Costadot (the younger brother of Rose's Robert) was fond of
saying—"bis destiny."

Monsieur Landin was standing in the hall. He was coatless,
and held a wet bowler-hat in his hand. His legs, encased in a pair
of grey and black striped trousers, were set slightly apart. His
short jacket had a rather exaggerated "waist." A very full black
beard which sprouted just below his eyes did little or nothing to
conceal the flabby contours of his cheeks. His sloping shoulders,

which Oscar Revolou loved to compare to those of the Empress Eugénie, his stoop and his prominent paunch, invariably moved the Revolou children to mirth, though not so much as his shining, knobbly, shapeless head, which reminded them of some old saucepan on a refuse dump. Landin was, in their eyes, the most abject of creatures. He was probably the only human being in dealing with whom their father—always so courteous to inferiors—was guilty of quite inexcusable outbursts of violence. It was as though he were forever trying to see just how far he could go with the man, as though he were indulging some mood of bitter dislike. But if anyone had said: "Landin is the lynch-pin of the practice . . ." none of the family would have dreamed of uttering a protest, or, if they had, the denial would have sounded hollow. The whole city knew that the bulk of the work was done by Landin. Time and time again the children had heard their father say with his familiar drawl: "Oh, ask Landin . . . Landin's certain to know where the file is. . . ." They knew nothing about him beyond the fact that he was the son of one of the janitors at the Faculty of Letters, that he had been at school with their father, and that he lived with an old unmarried sister who was not considered worthy of being invited to the house. None of them had ever set foot across his threshold. The great lawyer said, as though it were the most natural thing in the world: "Landin has got no private life."

The strangest sentiments, once they have become habitual, lose all power to surprise us. The fact was that the Revolous were living cheek by jowl with a perfect miracle of love. But how can one have any feeling about a miracle that has lasted a lifetime? It may be that Oscar Revolou's harshness in his dealings with Landin was an outcome of that irritability which we all of us feel when we know that we are the object of an indefinable and extravagant passion—especially when we derive advantage from it. The contempt which he openly showed towards his senior clerk was fed from sources of which the rest of the family knew nothing, sources which must have had their origin many years earlier in the gloomy school building where the janitor's son had been the trembling slave of the rich middle-class boy.

"If it's urgent, you can always take the early tram," said Louis Larpe, in the mocking tone which even the servants used when talking to Landin: "though the master doesn't much care about being disturbed when he's at Léognan."

The butler could not refrain from adding: "Can I offer you a drop of something, Monsieur Landin?"

"Are you sure Madame won't see me—really sure? . . . in that case, if it is absolutely impossible . . ."

He seemed relieved to know that the problem of this interview had been taken out of his hands. Louis Larpe had failed to notice what Denis had seen at the first glance. The fringe of hair round the knobbly skull which shone in the light of the ceiling lamp, that thin, silky hair which, so Oscar Revolou always said, reminded him of a poisoned mouse, was soaking with sweat. The wretched creature had dyed it, with the result that the drops, which were the colour of black coffee, had left long dark streaks on his pasty face.

He began muttering, like someone talking to himself:

"I must try to find a cab or a taxi. It won't be easy at this time of night, especially with the Fredy-Dupont ball on. . . . Should anyone happen to want me, say I've gone out to Léognan. . . ."

At that moment he became aware of Denis. There was something almost tangible about the expression of his eyes, some quality of *weight*. It was as though once his gaze had been fixed on anyone he found difficulty in at once removing it. Tonight he ventured to lay his hand on the boy's head. It was a permanently damp hand, a hand that had become a byword in the Revolou household, so that whenever one of the children was caught biting his nails someone would be sure to say: "If you're not careful, you'll have hands just like Landin's!"

Denis made a movement that was expressive both of impatience and disgust.

"Really, Monsieur Landin! . . ."

But the hand, like the glance, seemed to adhere to his forehead. It was a leaden hand, and apparently beyond the power of its owner to withdraw. Landin's viscous blue eye, forever swimming in the moisture of an unshed tear, was eloquent of feelings too vague for definition—perhaps of pity? Suddenly the man spoke:

"You must go to your mother, Monsieur Denis, and tell her, as gently as you can . . . but no, perhaps on second thoughts you had better say nothing. . . ."

He turned on his heel and opened the door. The boy remained where he was, rooted in amazement, listening to the sound of Landin running down the steps. He sat down on the wood-chest in the hall. The gas whistled noisily in its old-fashioned glass globe. There were Spanish mirrors on the walls, panoplies of savage weapons brought from the South Seas by a Revolou uncle, panels of painted silk, framed engravings. To Denis it always seemed that these things must have been there for centuries.

A young footman passed him, going towards Madame Revolou's room. He was out of breath, and carried a cardboard box under one arm. He winked as he hurried by.

"It's the dress!"

Denis followed him, and at once, while Rose was opening the box, sidled up to his mother.

"Landin's trying to find a cab or a taxi. He's going straight to Léognan."

"Much good may it do him."

Denis knew that the phrase bore no relation to his mother's anxiety at that moment. She turned to Rose, who had just slipped on the dress.

"Turn round . . . yes, it hangs all right now. . . . Show me the back. Good! . . . You'd better do your hair again."

"That was the front-door bell," said Denis suddenly. His was the only ear sharp enough to catch the distant sound.

"Who on earth can it be at this time of night!" asked Madame Revolou.

The two children were to remember, later, that there was already a strange, unrecognizable note in her voice. Denis reached the hall just as Louis Larpe was opening the door. The visitor was Léonie Costadot. She looked enormous in her short astrakhan coat, and she was breathing hard. Though on terms of intimacy with the Revolous, she had never before made so late a call. . . . She was the mother of Robert and Pierre. . . . Denis's first thought was that she had come on her elder son's behalf to ask for Rose's hand.

"She raises all sorts of difficulties," Oscar Revolou had said, "but I know her. Once she's made up her mind to the inevitable she'll get them married off in a fortnight."

"Is your mother in her room?" she shot at Denis, hurried past him into the passage, and pushed open the door without knocking.

Madame Revolou had already thrown a skunk wrap over her ball dress, and was busy enveloping her daughter's nose in a final cloud of powder.

"Just off to the dance, my pet?"

Rose smiled and offered her cheek to Robert's mother. Her mind, too, was running on thoughts of a proposal. Denis noted the sudden appearance on his mother's left cheek of the yellow patch which always showed when some strong emotion had drained the blood from her face. It was the forerunner of disaster. Her words, when she spoke, tumbled over one another:

"This *is* a surprise! . . . What lucky wind! . . ."

"Would you very much mind if the children left us alone?"

Denis was conscious of Rose's shining eyes. But he was under no illusion. He knew well enough that the visitor had not come to discuss marriage plans. Poor little Rose! . . . the question of marriage would never now be raised—or not in connexion with Robert Costadot. . . .

She drew him into her own room which opened out of her mother's.

She sat down on the bed. Denis, his back turned, could see her reflection in the mirror which hung over the mantelpiece. Her thin, rather round shoulders rose from a full frill of spangled tulle. She was leaning forward so that the bodice gaped a little above the diminutive breasts. Hope had set her cheeks on fire. Watching her in the glass, he could see the change in her expression as Léonie's Costadot's opening words reached their ears. The woman had a way of raising her voice even when there was no reason for her to do so, with the result that her interlocutors were compelled, in self-defence, to shout back at her. On this occasion, she made so much noise that Rose and Denis failed to catch everything she was saying. But they heard enough to realize the nature of her errand.

"You *must* listen to me, Lucienne. There's nothing to be gained by mincing words—the matter's far too serious for that. *Do* you know where Oscar is?"

It was only by making an effort that the pair could establish a connexion between their mother and the childlike, obsequious voice which came in reply. Of course she knew . . . her husband was at Léognan. . . .

"Well, if he is, then I can assure you it's through no fault of his own. . . ."

There was a confused, unintelligible murmur which Léonie Costadot interrupted:

"You're just pretending not to understand what I'm getting at!"

It had been the talk of the whole place for the last three days— so Lucienne went on—and she had good reason, she added, to know that what was said was true!

The next sentence came in a low voice. The children heard their mother give a low groan, and caught the words, "By what right! . . ."

The other was speaking now about "four hundred thousand Costadot francs" which Oscar had invested for them. "He'd squeeze the last drop out of them"—was the way he had put it, adding that there was no relying on real property these days, and that mortgages were worth just nothing at all. . . .

"I'll keep this pear ripening," he had said, "until you're really thirsty" . . . until *he* was really thirsty, was what he meant.

From this moment the whole of Denis's attention was concentrated upon the sobs coming from the sprawled young body on the bed. He could see it in the glass, but dared not turn round. He took a few steps backward until he reached the bed and sat down beside his poor little Rose. He was too shy to put his arm round her because her shoulders were bare. "Don't cry," he kept on saying: "Nothing's lost. I'm certain of Robert, he'll never give you up. Only last Thursday, his brother Pierrot was saying . . ." He babbled on, trying to smother in a spate of words the thought that was in his mind. . . . Madame Costadot's character was known only too well. She wielded complete authority over her sons, especially over Robert. To the eldest, Gaston, her favourite —popularly referred to as "the handsome Costadot"—she had always delegated some part of the independence which was his by right, as being the head of the family. She delighted in his good looks, in his success with women, in his racing triumphs . . . but it wasn't Gaston who was in love with Rose, and over the weak-willed Robert her sway was absolute. At this moment, when their family fortune was about to fall in ruins, their social position, perhaps even their honour, Denis was sharply conscious of one thing only, that Rose would never marry Robert. This thought stood out clear-cut and unshaken among the piled rubble of their lives. But he dared not look it boldly in the face. Instead, he put it aside, buried it for later examination. Once more he concentrated his mind on the high words coming from the further side of the door.

"Give me some proof. . . . You *have* no proof, Léonie. You've been listening to a lot of gossip, and you've believed it. You always get into a panic where your children are concerned. See, now, you're hesitating . . . you can't produce a shred of evidence. . . ."

"Because I'm sorry for you. . . ."

The voice with which Léonie broke in on her victim's outburst was calm and determined. She had made up her mind to do what she had set out to do, no matter what the cost. Her children's patrimony was at stake. She began again. To Denis and to Rose it was as though someone were raining heavy blows upon a prostrate body. Their mother had abandoned all resistance. Rose clasped her brother's arm. She was no longer crying. "Poor mummy," she said: "We must go to her." But neither of them ventured to make a move.

"It hurts me to have to cause you pain. . . . If it wasn't for my children. . . . But you'd have had to know sooner or later. . . . Regina Lorati let the cat out of the bag to my son Gaston . . . the dancer at the Grand Theatre, you know. . . . What has she got to do with it? Are you serious, my poor dear? You can't tell me you didn't know? . . . What's the use of *pretending* you're sur prised . . . though I *do* understand how you must be feeling. . . . But, darling, you did, surely, realize that Oscar was *keeping* the woman . . . on a princely scale, too. . . . You *can't* not have known . . . why, it was common talk—her carriages, her liveried servants, her villa at Mouleau, her house in the Rue de Pessac furnished from floor to attic with antiques. . . . Do you mean to tell me honestly that you *didn't*? . . . For Heaven's sake, don't faint! Now, if ever, you've got to keep a level head. . . . What's that? . . . I've got no proof? . . . You *will* go harping on that . . . as though I should *want* to wish you harm! . . . My dear, I *am* so sorry for you, really I am. But don't you see, as I told you before, the Lorati creature showed Gaston your husband's letters to her. . . . He wanted her to run away with him to South America, if you must have it. . . . It's awful, I know, for you to hear such things, but it's still more awful for me to have to tell you. It must be done, though . . . and now you know the truth about Oscar. *Of course* Gaston's her lover . . . *that's* no news to me! . . . A fine state of affairs, you say? . . . What on earth does it matter? You don't suppose I thought that my son was a disembodied angel?. . ."

Denis and Rose, pressed close up against the door, were listening to what sounded like the whimpering noises made by a complete stranger.

"Please go away, Léonie: I can't stand any more. . . ."

The cool, the passionless executioner, now that the blow was delivered, now that the duty had been accomplished, had become milder. The moment had gone for loud words. No longer was the voice raised and angry. It spoke now with an obstinate, a patient insistence.

"I am not going until you have given me the four hundred thousand francs which belong to my sons. . . . Don't talk nonsense: of *course* you've got authority—full authority. I've already taken counsel's opinion on the point. . . . What you brought to your husband as dowry is your own. Your father was a shrewd, far-seeing man. But even if the settlement had provided for the joint holding only of property acquired *after* marriage, the situation would be precisely the same. Your personal fortune is intact, and I want you to sign a deed in my sons' favour. I've got the draft here with me. It was drawn up by Maître Lacoste and merely requires your signature . . . here, in the margin . . . initials will do. . . . I know you think I'm being very hard, Lucienne, but what I'm doing, I'm doing for my children's sake. . . . You'll feel *so* much easier in your mind when the whole thing's settled. . . ."

"But it's not *my* money . . . it belongs to my family. I am sure that what you're asking me to do is quite illegal. . . ."

"Don't let that worry you. Maître Lacoste knows precisely how matters stand. . . . If you like to take me to court, that's your affair. The important thing at the moment is that you should sign. . . . You'd much better make up your mind to do as I say. I'm sure you don't want to compel me to call your children as witnesses. *They'd* realize soon enough how things stand. . . . What's that? . . . a lot of baseless rumours, you say? Possibly. But if it turns out that there is no truth in what people are saying, your husband has only to give me back the money and we'll never mention the matter again. But don't forget, Gaston has actually *seen* the letters. . . . Besides, for the last few days *everyone's* been talking. Sit down, do. This is no moment for fainting: here, at your desk. . . ."

"I must take advice. . . ."

"From whom? From your husband? He's at Léognan, waiting for the Lorati woman. But she won't turn up for the very good reason that she is at Monte Carlo with Gaston. . . . Why not go and *see* Oscar?—there is no risk of any awkwardness. . . ."

"Give me time at least to talk things over with Julien . . . he's at the Fredy-Duponts'. . . ."

"I am not going to wait until he comes back. You've *got* to sign. What harm will it do you? The money would melt away quickly enough in Oscar's hands . . . I'm under no illusions about him! It would merely go to other creditors, and it is a great deal better that my sons should get the benefit of what's left. . . . You'll sign all right in the long run, so why waste time?"

Léonie paused for breath. She hesitated before playing her last card, but finally realizing that Oscar's life might be at stake: "You ought to be on your way to Léognan at this very moment," she said: "My poor dear, what are you waiting for? Surely you know there's nothing a man won't do when he's got his back to the wall?"

"What do you mean, Léonie? Oh, heavens!—here we sit talking, while . . ."

Rose and Denis could hear nothing now but the sound of sobs and a single phrase repeated over and over again with urgency, almost with supplication and a persuasiveness that verged on tenderness: "Come now, sign: *please*, sign, my poor, dear Lucienne . . . get it off your mind. You'll feel so much better, and you'll be free then to go straight off to Léognan. . . . It's not too late even now to save him. . . . But you must sign first . . . there, and *there*: initials will do. . . ."

The sobs grew less frequent. There was the sound of a chair being dragged across the carpet. The bureau creaked. They could hear a shuffling of papers. In the ensuing silence, Léonie Costadot's voice was plainly audible.

"*That's* done. . . . I'm afraid the business isn't finished yet, but the hardest part is over. . . . Who knows?—I may be quite wrong, after all. . . . Perhaps Oscar's just been playing a trick on Regina Lorati, or perhaps she was lying to Gaston so as to frighten him into doing something . . . one never knows with creatures like that . . . in which case the signature will commit you to nothing. . . ."

Her mind was at rest now. The tension had slackened. She stuffed into her bag the document which for years to come Oscar Revolou's creditors were to attack unsuccessfully. She put her arm about her bruised and battered friend.

"My poor, poor dear . . . are you *sure* there's nothing I can do for you? . . ."

II

LÉONIE, on leaving the Revolous' house, walked quickly, in spite of her corpulence, along the deserted Cours du Chapeau Rouge. Her state of mental intoxication was unaccompanied by any sense of shame. She clove her way through the fog, revelling in its smell, and clasping to her body the bag which contained the deed. She had won back part of her children's patrimony, and gloried in her victory. The document, duly signed, was there. With that in her possession—said Maître Lacoste—the battle was as good as won. True, the struggle had been horrible, the duty hard. . . . Poor Lucienne, what dreadful times lay ahead of her!

It was only by dint of making a considerable effort that she could achieve a softer mood, could induce in herself a mood of compunction which was far from being spontaneous. The thought that once, as a young girl, she had been heartbroken because she could not marry Oscar Revolou, made her shudder.

She might so easily have been in Lucienne's shoes tonight . . .
' though it's true that if *I'd* been his wife, I should have been able
to exercise *some* control, could have staved off the worst of the
blunders. With me beside him he would have steered a straighter
course. . . . All the same, a business-man of genius. . . . I knew perfectly well what I was doing when I entrusted all that money to
him. . . . He was more than capable of "squeezing the last
drop." . . . The greatest mistake he ever made was when he married Léonie Willy-Durand. With her high and mighty airs she
antagonized everybody, and yet, poor dear, was such a little bore
that he started deceiving her almost at once. . . .' Oscar. . . . She
could see him in imagination waiting out there at Léognan for
Regina Lorati, only to be confronted by Lucienne at the very
moment that Regina and Gaston were on their way to Monte
Carlo. . . .

She was ashamed of the pleasure that the thought gave her and
drove it from her mind. She despised herself for the pride she
took in her son's successes with women, but, in spite of herself,
could not altogether resist the temptation. Gaston . . . he, at any
rate, would have been proud of her this evening, would have admired her pluck. . . . Unfortunately, though, it was not that
dearly beloved figure that she would find waiting for her at
home, but the other two—Robert and Pierrot.

She began to walk more slowly, not only because she was
slightly out of breath, but also because she was no longer anxious
to reach her goal. She began to wonder how best to explain what
had occurred, and the mere fact that she had got to find an explanation made her angry. That really was too much! Here she
was, having saved their patrimony at the cost of a hideous, a
harrowing scene, and she'd got to trump up some excuse, behaving as though she were a criminal! She knew them only too well
. . . or did she? No, perhaps, on second thoughts, she did not
know them at all.

It was not difference of outlook that poisoned her relations
with the two younger boys. Gaston and she never agreed about

anything, but there was an instinctive sympathy between them Rake though he was, leading a life at odds with all that his mother held sacred, he understood her, she him. The other two were serious and hard-working, but somehow she could never feel certain of what their reactions would be.

At this moment, for instance, she had the consciousness that she was safe from all attack. The money she was taking back with her was money left by their father to his sons. She felt pride in the fact that she had been true to a sacred trust, had fought hard, and had won. The money would, in any case, have been lost to Lucienne, for it would have gone to other creditors: 'Far better that my children should get the benefit of it. I'm not blind to the element of horror in this expedition of mine at dead of night and in such circumstances. But there is nothing to be afraid of. I shall just tell them what is perfectly true, that I've probably been instrumental in saving Oscar Revolou's life. . . . Thanks to me, Lucienne has gone to Léognan. . . . I only hope she won't be too late. . . .'

Yes, the more she thought of the business, the less did she see what effective answer the two boys could possibly make to her representations. Her best course would be to feign amazement. "What!"—she would say, "don't I get so much as a word of thanks?" That they would be indignant she did not for a moment doubt . . . for there was one element she was deliberately leaving out of account—Robert's feeling for Rose Revolou, and Pierrot's friendship (though that was less serious) for young Denis. . . . Less serious? . . . well that remained to be seen. Robert was flabby, spineless . . . but Pierrot was capable of acting like a lunatic in moments of crisis. She was often quite genuinely frightened of him . . . with his head stuffed full of sick fancies, and those ridiculous poems he was for ever scribbling. . . . Robert must realize that, in any case, this idea of marriage would have to be abandoned. Quite apart from the possible disgrace and the certain ruin of the Revolous, it would be years before he could qualify as a doctor, finish walking the hospitals and get through all his examinations. . . . He wouldn't be making a living before he was thirty. . . . If he really cared for the girl (yes, that was the line to take) it was his bounden duty to leave her free and not to compromise her future.

Léonie Costadot and her family occupied the ground and first floors of a large house. It occurred to her suddenly, as she was going upstairs, that Robert, too, would almost certainly be at the Fredy-Duponts' Ball. . . . 'But as soon as he notices that Rose isn't there, he'll come back. . . . This afternoon, he was already worrying about some of the rumours that were going round.'

No, Robert had not yet returned. She did not wait to take off her hat and her fur coat, but went straight to her desk, opened it, and took out the key to the safe which was built into the far end of the bed, "disguised"—as Pierrot was fond of saying—"as a night-table." A range of sham drawers hid the heavy steel door. She made the "combination" which acted as an "open-sesame," and put the deed which Lucienne Revolou had signed on one of the shelves. Then, taking a lamp, she went along the passage which led to the boys' rooms.

A light was showing underneath Pierrot's door. She entered as, always, without knocking. Pierrot had fallen asleep while reading in bed—a by no means unusual occurrence. His book had dropped from his hand on to the coverlet. He lay propped against the pillows in an uncomfortable position. With his head thrown back and his neck extended, he looked as though he were about to have his throat cut. A pencil, a pile of papers, and a large open notebook, handsomely bound in leather, lay beside him. A low standard lamp shone on the page which was covered with the careful, copper-plate handwriting in which he made his fair copies. Raising a pair of lorgnettes, Léonie read the verses. The expression on her face was one of hostility. The words seemed simple enough, but their sense escaped her.

> "He sleeps! . . . I'll force the Gods to hold their peace.
> About the dreaming Atys I will make
> The world a nothingness. So shall deep slumber take

Life's fret from him, and all his limbs at ease
Shall lie like serpents aping death, nor wake
From their long clasp of earth." Shaken she stood
While he slept on, as free from crime and passion as a God.

"What *is* he trying to say? What *does* it all mean?" she wondered. Why should she be so conscious of a sense of irritation?

"The muted flies shall turn their dozing hum
To a soft lullaby made noisy by the crow
Of some far-distant cock. Into his sleep has come
No thought of lowering skies, nor can his slow
Senses heed my rain-drenched fragrance. Dumb
To his ears are all the dripping leaves.
The nymph Sangaris whom he now receives
Moves in dim waters that no slumber charms.
What formless thing am I whom Ocean frets,
Who cannot in the circle of my arms
Contain him?—A queen about whose forehead wide
Dark weeds and coloured ooze are left by each sad murmuring
    tide?"

Whence rose in her this deep fury, this shameful longing to destroy and tear in pieces the notebook in its handsome English binding? She did not know—nor yet that this barely controlled violence was similar to that which moved her son. Little did she realize that now, when what she felt was almost hatred, the two of them were most alike, not in the movement of the head or heart, but in that impulse to destroy which, at this very instant, she set herself to counter by moving from the table and pressing her face for a moment to the window-pane.

"Who's there?" cried Pierrot in a waking panic.

"It's only me. . . . Isn't Robert back yet?"

"He can't be long now. . . . I expect he just looked in for news and came away again at once . . ."

Pierrot yawned, showing his wide-spaced teeth.

"Have you got any, mother?"

"Yes, I've just left them."

"D'you mean to say you've actually been to the Place de la Bourse?"

Wide awake now, he fixed her with a baleful and mistrustful stare.

"It was my duty to go."

'What a hypocrite!' he thought to himself.

Yet his mother had never felt so certain of having performed a duty, the duty of a watchful administrator with her sons' interests at heart . . . to say nothing of the fact that she had been able to warn Lucienne.

"And it was just as well that I did. You'll hardly believe it, but the poor creature had absolutely no idea. . . . She's been desperately worried for weeks, of course, but it had never occurred to her that the crisis was actually on top of them . . ."

"What did you say to her?"

Already, Léonie Costadot was on the defensive. What right had he, she asked, to question his mother in that tone of voice? Anyone would think that he suspected her. . . .

"Not at all, mother: I was merely asking . . ."

"I refuse to give an account of my actions to a graceless young puppy. . . . I shall speak to your brother as soon as he comes in. Go to sleep, and don't let me hear another word from you!"

She left the room, taking the lamp with her. It was not anger that prompted the move. She realized that she had much better see Robert alone, out of hearing of this high-spirited young fanatic.

Scarcely had she got into her dressing-gown than she heard the sound of Robert's hesitant fumbling with his latchkey. She coughed so as to let him know that she was still awake and waiting. He was carrying an overcoat on his arm. She made a mental note, as always, that dress-clothes suited him, that his slim figure gave him a far more elegant appearance than Gaston, who was inclined to be dumpy. Though she preferred the type exemplified by her elder son, she could not, in justice, deny that Robert had an air of greater refinement and breeding. . . .

"Naturally," he said, in the slow, uncertain tones that always got on his mother's nerves, "she wasn't at the Ball. I saw Julien

Revolou in the distance, but couldn't get a word with him. I gather that some of his friends had made it pretty obvious that he wasn't wanted. . . . So I hurried round to the Place de la Bourse, but they had just left."

At this moment Pierrot entered the room in his pyjamas, barefooted and with tousled hair. Madame Costadot turned on him.

"I thought I told you to go to sleep. . . ."

"I don't sleep just because you tell me to."

Robert pulled him up short: "There's no need to be rude, Pierrot. . . ."

The boy broke in on him:

"I don't mind betting she's afraid to tell you where *she's* come from, where *she's* been tonight. . . ."

"I won't have you saying 'she' like that when you are discussing me in my presence!"

But Pierrot pressed his point. Unknown to them, he said, she had been spending the evening at the Place de la Bourse.

Robert turned to his mother, a look of consternation on his handsome face.

"That's not true, is it, mamma?"

"Why should it not be true?" she asked defiantly.

"Did you see Monsieur Revolou?"

"No, he has gone to Léognan. I knew that, and I knew why, though Lucienne did not. . . . Now do you understand? I warned her. It's entirely owing to me that she has gone to him. . . . He may have been contemplating suicide, in which case I have probably saved his life."

Robert heaved a sigh.

"Then, since Monsieur Revolou was not there, you weren't able to talk about the money. . . ."

Léonie Costadot made no reply. Robert heard his brother mutter:

"You don't think she did herself out of that treat, do you?"

"Say that again, louder, so that we can all hear."

"I said it was unlikely that you'd done yourself out of the

pleasure of discussing the money. . . . That was the only reason you went there. . . ."

Things were going just as she had been afraid they would. Robert and Pierre stood confronting her like judges on the bench. Had Gaston been there he would have been filled with admiration of what she had done, would have thanked her. Well then, war was declared: impossible now to avoid it. At least she had justice on her side.

She took the initiative and attacked at once. "It isn't a question of *my* money, but of *yours*, of your father's. Had it been mine, I might have been generous. . . ."

Robert interrupted her. Since the money was theirs, theirs, too, was the right not to claim it. . . .

"You are forgetting Gaston—to whom your motive does not apply. You are forgetting that Pierrot is only eighteen, and that until he comes of age, I, his mother and trustee, must protect his interests even in the teeth of his wishes. . . ."

"What it amounts to," Robert was obdurate, "is that you tortured them unnecessarily, since Monsieur Revolou had gone away . . ."

She turned pitying eyes on him. Was there ever such a fool? There are no more helpless creatures in the world than young men who think they have the wings of eagles.

"There is no need for you to get in such a state. Lucienne and I discussed the situation in a perfectly amicable way."

Robert wanted to know whether Rose had been present. Madame Costadot shook her head.

"What about Denis?" asked Pierrot.

No; both the children had left the room. She was trying to find some way of explaining how well she had succeeded. It really was incredible that she should have to wear gloves in her dealings with these two young idiots, that she should have to go to all this trouble just in order to announce the perfectly simple fact that their man of business was faced with ruin, but that, thanks to her, they would not be a penny the worse for it.

"Lucienne, I must say, behaved very well, and with great dignity. She saw at once that her husband had a very special obligation in the case of orphans . . ."

"What orphans? *we're* not orphans"—protested Pierrot.

Ever since his childhood he had detested the words "orphan boys"—"orphanage"—"orphan girls."

"She volunteered the information that the sum in question, the money due to us, was just precisely the amount of her private fortune, to do with as she likes—four hundred thousand francs."

"How extremely convenient!" exclaimed Pierrot. His mother took no notice of this piece of insolence. The consciousness that she had been led by imperceptible degrees into a lie was causing her acute embarrassment. It was not in her nature to tell lies. But she had been forced to do so by this pair of "simpletons," as Gaston called them.

"Four hundred thousand francs!" there was a strange note in Robert's voice. "She can't have had that much in the house, surely?"

He really was too innocent! Léonie Costadot answered with a shrug:

"Of course she hadn't . . . not ready to her hand. All I wanted was her signature. . . ."

"But it wouldn't be legal . . ."

"You can set your mind at rest on that score. We may be taken to Court by the other creditors—we probably shall be. . . . I'm prepared for that, and we are bound to win."

He said nothing, and she was beginning to feel that her fight was as good as won.

"You don't suppose I acted without first taking advice, do you? I thrashed the whole matter out with Maître Lacoste. Everything that can be done has been done. . . ."

Their silence was beginning to get on her nerves. An ocean separated her and them. What good would it do to carry on a shouted conversation across that sundering flood?

The two brothers were seated side by side on an ottoman at the foot of the bed. Both were leaning forward, and the lamplight caught their reddish hair, Pierrot's with the hint of a wave in it, and all rough from recent sleep, Robert's carefully smoothed and parted, and curling slightly at the nape of his neck.

"As soon as I get my share," said Robert, "I shall just give it back."

"Not so quick," replied Léonie. "You get nothing but the residuary right to the capital. The life-interest is mine."

"You don't say so!" sneered Pierrot. At that, her temper burst its bounds.

"This contempt of money is all very fine, but how, may I ask, do you think you live? Have you the slightest idea, Robert, what that very becoming dress-suit cost? As for you, Pierrot, who do nothing but grumble when there is only cold meat for supper, has it ever occurred to you to look at the bills I have to settle with your bookseller and binder? Gaston costs me a pretty penny, but at least he knows it, apologizes and is grateful. He doesn't presume to sit in judgment on me. I suppose you think of me as a woman completely without ideals, a woman who thinks of nothing but detaching dividend vouchers and getting in her rents, while you stalk through life with your head in the clouds, and pay Heaven knows how much for a lot of rubbishy books. . . . All *I'm* good for is to fill your stomachs, warm your bodies, light your rooms, find you in clothes, and provide wages for the servants without whom you would be lost! You ought to be ashamed of taking this high and mighty line with a mother who never spends a penny on herself. You're ready enough to laugh at my shabby furs and home-made dresses. This fortune for which you show so fine a scorn, but are only too ready to enjoy, was built up by your grandparents. They slaved and stinted all their lives in order that you might have an easier time than they had. . . . It should be sacred to you. . . ."

She felt that she had said enough, that she had driven her nail home. Robert stammeringly protested that it wasn't his fault if it took so long to become a doctor. His mother, the first heat of her anger past, replied that she wasn't blaming him, that he had all his life before him, and that the important thing was that he should make a success of it.

"But *this* little fool," she went on, raising her voice and turning to Pierrot, "is still young enough to be disciplined. I'm not going to have him going on as he's doing now."

Pierrot hung his head. The more his mother saw that her shafts were going home, the more recklessly did she shoot. It was all very nice, all very pleasant, spending his life just scribbling verses. . . . but there was no future in poetry. A man couldn't live on it, even when it was good. . . . But when, as in his case, it meant just nothing at all . . .

Pierrot jumped up and left the room without looking at her. Sobered now, she stopped talking, conscious of a faint sense of shame. Perhaps she had been wrong to say all that, but he did really put her beside herself.

"You *were* wrong," said Robert: "you ought to remember how young he is. . . ."

"What has his age got to do with it? He's no different from other boys."

"Yes, he is."

She protested. What he needed was a man in the house to keep him in order. Deep in her heart, Léonie knew that he was different, but she would not admit that he lived on a higher level than the rest of them. Herself the daughter, grand-daughter and daughter-in-law of great merchants who had been the boast and glory of the city, she had inherited a pretty clear idea of what a man should be. She thought she knew what people meant when they said—"so-and-so is *somebody*."

"Well," she concluded, "there's nothing left for me to do but apologize for bringing you the gift of a fortune. . . . I rather expected you to take this attitude . . . still . . ."

"How could you think that this money would mean anything to me? I have lost everything that makes life worth living. . . ."

It pleased her to hear him speak like that though her heart was touched with pity. For once she rejoiced that he was so weak-willed. He had put the whole question of this marriage out of his mind already, had given up the Revolou girl without a struggle. Careful now to avoid a frontal attack she began to commiserate Rose . . . a victim, and so charming that one might perhaps have overlooked the disgrace attaching to her name. But he must realize that he was in no position to set up a home of his own. Before this awful thing had happened, the Revolous had made it clear that they intended to provide for the young couple, but now. . . .

Robert weakly ventured a suggestion: "Couldn't we live here?"

"You must be mad!—Where?—in your room? And what's to happen when the babies start coming? Besides, you seem to forget that you would have the whole family round your neck . . . or rather, *I* should have them round *mine*. . . . Come, you've got to face facts like a man. I know it's hard on you"—she said in conclusion, and put her arm round the shoulder of the great over-grown boy who was now quite openly sobbing.

Robert knew that she was basing her hopes on his weakness, knew, too, that she would not be disappointed in her calculations. What answer could he make?—that with Rose beside him he felt a different man, full of hope and courage? If he put thoughts like that into words, his mother would riddle them in a moment. . . .

Before going to his room, he looked in on Pierrot to have a few last words with him.

He found his brother sitting up in bed. "Go to sleep, old man. It's past midnight."

Without a glance at him, the boy snarled out:

"Their filthy money! . . ."

"We're all at cross-purposes," groaned Robert. "Poor mamma thought she had acted for the best this evening. What she did, she did as head of the family. I'm not sure she wasn't right to think us ungrateful. . . ."

"That's not the point . . ." Pierrot shook his head and stared in front of him. "I resent her being in the right, or rather, what I resent is that I had no answer to give her. I hate our money because it makes me into a prisoner. There's just no way out at all. I've thought the whole thing over. No one ever escapes from money. We live in a world that's made of money. Mother's right there. To rebel against money is to set oneself at odds with the very nature of the world, of life itself. . . . There are only two courses open, either to change the face of the earth . . . there's always that . . ."

"How do you mean?"

"The revolution . . . or, there's God."

The grandiose words filled the stuffy little room with its litter of books, reproductions of pictures and casts of Greek sculpture. Robert, still standing, pressed the boy's head to his side.

"Don't say silly things like that. . . ."

Pierrot made no reply, but hid his face against his elder brother. The latter made no move, but let his eyes wander to the bedside table and the notebook still open at the page which, but a short while ago, their mother had deciphered. He read and reread the lines he saw there.

What formless thing am I whom Ocean frets,
Who cannot in the circle of my arms
Contain him?—A queen about whose forehead wide
Dark weeds and coloured ooze are left by each sad murmuring tide?

"Listen," said Pierrot suddenly, clinging to Robert's shoulders. "You mustn't let her down . . . you won't, will you? . . . you won't let Rose Revolou down?"

The young man sighed and loosed his brother's grasp.

"What can I do? You've said yourself that we're bound hand and foot."

III

AS soon as Léonie had left the house, clutching the deed like a trophy, Lucienne Revolou went into Rose's room. Not a hair of her head was out of place, and high on the piled chignon the emerald star still glittered. But she had taken off her diamond necklace and her rings. Denis could see them lying in the open bag from which she kept on taking out a handkerchief, and dabbing at her eyes. The children were beyond noticing anything but her tears. Tears on the cheeks of that all-powerful being—their mother! To have thrown themselves into her arms would have been to do something of which, in their timidity, they were incapable.

"I suppose you heard?" she said.

It was Denis who put into vivid words what he had been feeling for the last ten minutes, the sensation he had had of lying, crushed but still living, beneath a weight of ruins.

"We're buried alive!"

Rose, her face hidden in her pillow, was sobbing quietly. It was self-pity that her tears expressed, and grief for her love, for the happiness which would never now be hers.

Madame Revolou addressed herself to Denis as though he were a grown man. She asked him what they had better do next.

"Go to Léognan at once, and pick Julien up on the way, at the Fredy-Duponts'."

"Please . . ." she begged: "I can't go there—everyone'll know what's happened."

Denis said that he would slip into the house by the back door. As it happened, however, they were spared this ordeal. Just as the three of them were getting into the carriage, Julien turned up, still in evening clothes, but pale as a sheet. Several of his friends had advised him to go home. "This is no place for you," they had said. "Better go straight back."

In the carriage, Madame Revolou gave him an account of the whole hateful scene. She had to shout in order to make herself heard above the rattling of the wheels on the cobbles. He appeared to be completely stunned, stunned as only a young man can be for whom the values of this world are absolute, whose correct manners and elegant bearing are matters of general admiration. He sat there, polishing his monocle like a mechanical doll, and when he spoke in his sharp nasal tones it was only to quote figures.

He was trying to establish the scale on which Regina Lorati had been living:

"The horses and servants alone," he said, "must have represented, at the lowest reckoning . . ."

That phrase, "at the lowest reckoning," kept on cropping up in his talk. He seemed carried away by this passion for figures, seemed to be clinging to it as for safety. What had happened affected him more nearly than any of the others. It was as though, mortally wounded, he did not yet realize that he had been hit—he whose nod, whose handshake, was a prize to be fought for, he the eldest of the Revolou boys, the member of the Union Club, the biggest matrimonial catch in the place. . . .

"Whatever happens, we'll pay up," he said, not once, but many times.

He began again his juggling with figures. The practice was worth so much. . . . Then there was Léognan and the house on the Place de la Bourse. . . . His mother refrained from pointing out that in all probability both properties were mortgaged. In the absence of any response, his ardour began to cool. His flat head, with its thin hair, jerked to the bumping rhythm of their progress.

Suddenly, Madame Revolou exclaimed in a loud voice:

"No, he can't do that—it would be the last straw!"

The children, with the exception of Rose still penned in her prison of despair, realized that she was thinking of possible suicide. It had been unceasingly present to the minds of the two boys. Julien, as a man of the world, took the view that it might be

2

better, in certain circumstances, to disappear entirely, like a
gambler slipping unnoticed from a room where he has been
caught cheating. Denis saw the prospect in a different light. He
was still young enough to feel the thrill of any dramatic occurrence. He had a secret love of the catastrophic. So far from putting the idea from him, he gave it scope, convinced (contrary to
the daily evidence of fact) that a tragedy anticipated never happens. When we have a presentiment—he believed—it scarcely
ever coincides with the actual. He began to set the scene in imagination—the great gates wide open, the staff in a state of collapse,
the Persian carpets muddied by policemen's boots.

Their mother continued with her monologue. "If he does *that*
to me! . . ." she said, as though oblivious of the fact that the
wretched man would first have done it to himself. But she had
been his wife—not, perhaps, for very long, still . . . his *woman*,
however indifferent she had fancied herself to be to his caresses.
And now, curiously, it was in the frigidity of her flesh that she
felt the wound. The fear that he might be dead struck to her
heart. She called to the coachman through the speaking-tube,
bidding him go faster.

They were driving now along a road which had long been
associated in the children's minds with the idea of holidays. The
sound of hooves and rattling wheels was waking suburbs which,
till now, Denis had seen only in the July dusk of prize day.
Gusts of rainy wind were fluttering the torn remnants of a poster
announcing a bull-fight. He remembered having noticed it the
summer before. Here and there the window of a wine-shop
glowed through the darkness, revealing an interior with men
clustered about a bar. He had taken Rose's hand in his—the hand
which would never now be given to Robert in marriage. Just to
be on the safe side, he added a few final touches to the imagined
scene of suicide, convinced that in a few more minutes he would
find the house as usual plunged in sleep.

"Besides," he said out loud, "Landin must have got there by
this time. We can trust Landin. . . ."

"Oh, Landin!" his mother's voice expressed angry annoyance.

"He's the man who runs the show, don't make any mistake about that!" said Julien. "Father's been utterly dependent on him for years."

"I'm sure he's up to something. I only wish I knew what it was. . . ."

"A bad lot . . . I bet *he's* pretty well covered. . . ."

"And in more ways than one. . . . There are some people who are going to get more than ruin out of this business. . . ."

Both mother and son, though they had no proof of misdemeanour, were bitter against Landin. They were actuated by nothing more specific than violent dislike. Denis, on the other hand, though he felt nothing but disgust for the senior clerk, had, like many boys of his age, a passion for justice. But he did not, on this occasion, raise his voice in protest. Landin meant nothing to him. They were drawing near the end of their journey. The smells of the countryside in winter came to him with a little shock of surprise. Life was going to be different from what he had expected. Life . . . life would go on. Suddenly he felt Rose's head upon his shoulder. She had drained herself of tears, and was no longer crying.

The carriage turned into the lane which skirted the park and led to the stable entrance. It was inconceivable that the scene of tragedy, mounted with so much care by Denis, could possibly turn out to be real. He knew perfectly well that there was no such thing as the gift of prophecy. The sound of the wheels on the gravel brought nothing but happy holiday memories. Had he been a musician, had he ever composed that opera of which Pierrot Costadot was forever dreaming, it should have formed one of the leading themes of his overture. The carriage lamps shone on the park wall. Here and there the black limbs of trees protruded through tumbled gaps. A few dead leaves hung in tatters from branches spread in an attitude of threat or supplication. He pressed his nose to the window and greedily drank in the reassuring evidences of the night. Sleep and rest was the message of this blackness in a world where nothing happened.

But—oh, God! Already fact and fiction had joined hands. Already his fantasies were taking substance and stepping down to greet him. So bright did the house look with all its windows lit, that at first he thought it must be on fire. A great splash of radiance lay upon the rain-drenched steps.

"Something's happened . . ." said Julien uncertainly.

Lucienne Revolou was muttering over and over again what sounded like a prayer:

"Don't let it be that . . . don't let him have done that."

Denis believed that he was about to look on a dead man, that he would be forced to see something he never yet had seen, the very thought of which froze him with horror. The chance meeting with a hearse in the street, the sense of an invisible presence supine beneath a lid, a sheet, had always been enough to send him scuttling up a side turning. So violent was this sense of repulsion that, at Léognan, he would never go into the empty room where his grandfather had died while he himself was still in the cradle. He had, however, screwed his courage to the point of pushing the door ajar, of poking his head into the dim interior which smelt of furniture and cloves, of taking a long look at the empty bed in which the incredible mystery had once been accomplished. The curtain hanging from the tester had seen it happen, and every chair and table. The clock had stopped when the old man's heart had ceased to beat. The mere fact that they had shared in that agony of mortal passing, in that journey into nothingness, endowed the objects in the room with a sort of reality at second hand. They had welcomed the grim visitor. . . . No, oh, no. . . . Death was not a person. . . . With a devil one could talk, with the worst of monsters one could reach some sort of understanding, make some kind of bargain. . . . Death was horrible just because it was *nothing*, because it had no existence, because it smothered all it touched, turned everything to emptiness. The bed, the curtains, the furniture, the clock, the mirror, the table with its greenish cloth—all had been washed by the flood of timelessness which, ebbing, had left on them the standing pools and marks of— nothing.

Poor Denis. Once, to have gone into the room where someone had died when he was born would have meant adventure. He was quite convinced now that he would see his father in one of those attitudes which had been haunting his imagination all through the long drive thither—collapsed over a table with his face hidden, unless, of course, he had been laid out on a bed.

Already the substance of his anticipations was turning out to be fact indeed. Cavailhes, the bailiff, had been on the look-out for them, and now made a sign to the coachman to pull up at the main gate. He brought out, one by one, all the remarks that Denis had earlier put into his mouth: "The inspector from Léognan won't let us move the body yet. He would like to ask you a few ques- tions first, ma'am. . . . Would you believe it, no one so much as heard the shot. . . . Monsieur Landin is seeing to everything. . . ."

The four Revolous stood beside the drive. Mother and daughter were still in their evening frocks, over which they had thrown a couple of dark wraps. Their skirts hung trailing in the puddles. The carriage lamps, and the lantern which Cavailhes was carrying, illuminated the little group, revealing four faces and four hearts. Léonie was already immured within her grief. She hid behind it as behind a defensive wall. It was her privi- lege to take no count of practical details, to make complete sur- render to catastrophe. No one would blame her. Julien, stripped of everything on which he had leaned in this world for support, had become a mere rag of a man, an ageless creature with a re- ceding forehead, thinning hair and a weak chin: a short-sighted man who had lost his spectacles and could not bear to hear Cavailhes say—"You are the head of the family now, sir. . . . Monsieur Landin says that no one must decide anything without first consulting you. . . ." He protested. Let Landin arrange everything: whatever he did would be for the best.

"But, Julien," said Rose, in tones of reproach, "Landin ought not to take *our* place."

In a perfectly firm voice she comforted and sustained her mother. Now that she had lost all, nothing could touch her any more. It was she who led the way to the house, who told Cavailhes to take charge of Denis and ask his wife to look after him (she had been the boy's nurse). Did Denis, as he was carried away, really faint, or did he only pretend? Cavailhes showed no sign of weakening beneath the heavy weight of his sixteen-year-old load. With a firm step he crossed the garden and kicked open the door of his cottage. From behind closed eyes, the boy could hear his old nurse's cry of alarm. He was laid on the bed and undressed. The smell of vinegar made him sneeze. He felt a hot brick at his feet. It was lovely lying there. Maria Cavailhes kept putting fresh compresses on his forehead. The room was full of the smell of rancid butter and preserves. He leaned his head against Maria's bodice while she lulled him to sleep with a drone of words. The poor gentleman, she said, had had ten minutes in which to make his peace with God, and that was more than enough. Landin thought it would be possible to pay the creditors in full, and even, perhaps, to save Léognan—or at least the house. The land would have to be sold.

That, from their point of view, was what really mattered. For years now the Cavailhes had been hoping that their cottage, with the kitchen-garden, would be made over to them in perpetuity. They would live there as freeholders, but would still look after the family. . . . From time to time, her man put in a word. The house, he said, without the land would fetch next to nothing. Nobody wanted a great barrack of a place these days. The money he had saved was his own: it couldn't be touched. Monsieur Oscar had allowed him to use the outbuildings for storing his produce. He could show receipts for all the commission he had earned on sales properly signed and in order. . . . But Maria did not want to benefit from the Revolou tragedy to the extent of taking over the house. . . . And all the while, Denis was thinking

—"I shan't be able to go to college now. . . . We shall live here in a world of vegetables and chickens."

Maria Cavailhes had tiptoed from the room leaving the lighted candle behind her. Lying there beneath the swollen eiderdown Denis dreamed of an idyllic life. His job would be to frighten away the birds and tend the snares. They would eat rye bread. No question now of Rose marrying, or not for years. Later, perhaps, much later. For the moment at least the question would be shelved. . . . He breathed deeply and stretched his legs between the sheets. . . . But what about the dead man? . . . The next few days opened before him like a dreadful tunnel. He would be ill. People would say, "He's so sensitive. . . ." But once the dead are safely in the grave they are forgotten. Everything slips back into a natural order. . . .

Thus confusedly he dreamed. Not that he was a monster of perversity. It was just that he did not feel as yet in the substance of his body the sense of his father having gone from them for ever. He lay there in the great bed. The mattress stuffed with straw made a noise each time that he turned. The rough sheets were pleasant to the touch. The candle left by Maria had at first revealed only the red tiles of the floor, the blue and white striped chintz, and the faded figure of a lion on the strip of carpet. But now he saw a second bed in the corner opposite, and in it, humping the counterpane, a huddled body from which came sounds of calm, mysterious breathing.

It was the only other piece of furniture in the room. Sacks of grain stood piled in one corner, and some straw wrappings for bottles. Had he been alone, he would have felt frightened. But a breathing friendly warmth came from the recumbent body. He had no idea whether the comforting companion who lay so near to him was Irène, his foster-sister, the maid, or Isidore Cavailhes who was doing his military service at Tarbes but might well be home on leave. He turned over on to his right side and lay watching the distant island, the continent that rose above a sea of blankets, the vague smudge of hair that looked like a patch of tangled woodland. A cock crowed. Footsteps, murmurs of voices, a slammed door, bore witness to the fact that in the world outside the trivial human round was once again in motion.

Soon the dawn would break. In Denis, fresh from sleep, the blood began to flow strongly, and in the young, mysterious body whose slumber filled the room with a cosy assurance of animal warmth. He had a vague feeling that perhaps the drama in which he was involved had no real importance, that it would in no way affect the world's established order. He was conscious, suddenly, of feeling intensely bored. He needed someone else's awareness of his presence, and coughed in an attempt to wake the second sleeper. He raised his voice in audible complaint: "I feel so awfully *ill*!"—but the unknown, deep sunk in youth's well of sleep, made no response. At length he got up, and shaking with cold, crept across the chilly tiles to the second bed.

Even before he reached it he knew that its occupant was female. His nose told him that much. This was a woman, one of life's great mysteries, death being the other. He was afraid that she might see him, and felt ashamed of his narrow chest and skinny body. He dressed hurriedly without bothering to wash.

The kitchen door was open. The Cavailhes must have spent the night up at the house. Chrysanthemums looked ragged through the morning mist. The drive showed the recent marks of wheels. A dog fawned at him with muddy paws. He noticed a few nipped roses by the front steps. Should he go in? He must decide here and now. He took the plunge.

On the Empire table in the hall a lamp, overlooked the evening before, was still burning. The effect in the dawn light was sinister. From behind the door of his father's study came the murmur of voices, the sound of a drawer being closed. The great leather couch was half hidden under a pile of sodden, faded hats and cheap overcoats. Denis knew that "he" must already have been put in the room on the first floor which looked on to the garden. The shutters had been half closed over the windows.

He climbed the stairs, his thoughts playing aimlessly about the memory of his father, of that father who had seemed to notice him so little, to have been without interest in his work and his triumphs, that figure which seemed always to have wórn a mask. Polite questions had come from it which, somehow, seemed never to call for an answer. There had been moments, however, when the older man, coming suddenly on his son, had laid his hand upon his shoulder. The boy could remember clearly its brittle skin and nicotine-stained fingers, could see again the brown eyes with their puckered lids. They had shone with a gay and tender light as he leaned towards the small figure at his side. It had been to Rose, more frequently, that he had shown these brief moments of affection, bringing her flowers and scent with promises of a summer cruise, of a trip to Paris. . . .

He did not pause, but entered the room without giving himself time to think. Those seated about the doll-like object in evening dress which lay upon the bed did not know that dawn had come. The glass container of the lit lamp was almost empty. Two candles stood beside a crucifix in front of which a twig of boxwood had been laid. Denis looked first at the two feet sticking up beneath the sheet. The body had already assumed the shape of a coffin. The face was swathed in bandages from under which emerged the grizzled, fair moustache.

He began to tremble all over like a sapling. What did it matter whether this was his father or someone else? It was an emblem of death, of the death that lies deep down in all of us, ready to take charge, the one indubitable truth, the only certainty. How was it that the trams could run so heedlessly? Ought they not rather to have stopped, and the passengers been made to get out. "Don't you know that you have got to die?" What was the point of reading newspapers? How could anything in the world matter when death was the sentence under which it lay? *That* news emptied all other news of meaning. Why strive to learn, when tomorrow one would be cast forth as refuse, rotting and decayed? The only truth. . . . If there exists anything beyond, we do not know it. We can be sure only of death. Religion? Systems of philosophy?—so many columns raised to front the void, a seeming solidity in the mists that veil an utter emptiness.

He began to moan, not for a father lost, but because the sight of death was evidence of death's unalterable law. The sound was like the howl of an animal feeling its fate at hand. The calf rears with terror in the slaughter-house, the lamb smells the odour of spilled blood, and man, the eternal child, must gaze with open eyes upon the inevitable lot of human kind. How can people of flesh and blood act as they do, how busy themselves with trivial tasks, worrying of this and that, forming attachments for others less dedicated than themselves to nothingness, going through the movements that will give birth to future corpses and swell the ranks of death? . . . They may, perhaps, believe, have faith. . . . But death is not a matter of belief. We see it at each moment of the day, rub shoulders with it, salute it in the streets. . . .

He was conscious of Rose's arm about his shoulders and pressed his tear-stained face against her frail and tender breast. He clung to this living sister—living, yet but another destined victim of eventual death. Only stones are free from the necessity of dying.

Rose thought: 'I would never have believed that Denis was so fond of father. . . .' He felt that she was deceiving herself, that she was building up of him and of his grief an idea which he did not deserve. But he needed this illusion in her mind, that she might dedicate herself to him, serving him and no other. In her alone salvation lay. It was well that she should not see him as he was, but only as she flattered him in thought. For her he must have solidity, so that her love could find a hold, could twine and cling like ivy that shows green about a tree's dead trunk.

The tide of his despair began to ebb. He looked about him. Neither his mother nor Julien were there, but only Monsieur Landin. Rose put out the lamp and told him to sit by the window which she had just thrown open. Eagerly he drank in the milk of the early day.

From where he sat he watched Landin moving in the mingled gleam of waxing day and dwindling candlelight. Grief had brought nothing of nobility to the man's tearless face. He was gazing at the corpse upon the bed, and there was a kind of controlled eagerness in his concentration. He was, it might almost seem, learning the dead by heart. Never, perhaps, in life had he dared to look directly at those features. But now in death they were defenceless. At last he could assuage his curiosity. No longer did his master's eyes force him to avert his own. He could feast his fill upon a God stripped of his armour. He stored the details of that face for memory to feed upon, making provision for a future when memory would be his only sustenance. Perhaps, after the funeral, he would come back here and lie at the bed's foot like one of those faithful hounds of legend. He must have felt Denis watching him, for he turned on him his bright blue eyes. Getting up, he went round the bed, said something in Rose's ear, and then made for the door, signing to Denis to follow him.

"I shall need your help, Mr. Denis. Your brother Julien has shut himself in his room. He says that he won't come out, but will let himself starve to death. That mood will pass, but we need him. He is the eldest, the only one of all of you who is of age. I myself have no influence. . . . He doesn't much like me, as you know . . . but *you* can speak to him, *you* can remind him that it is his duty to take your father's place. . . ."

The smell in the room of the living was more oppressive than that in the room of the dead. Denis hurried across to the window and opened the shutters. Julien's head appeared above the sheets.

"For God's sake, leave the window alone! Who told you you might come in here?"

Denis, obedient to his instructions, told his brother that they were asking for him downstairs. The head disappeared once more beneath the blankets. Why couldn't they just let him fade out?—asked Julien. Nothing mattered any more.

"But you're the eldest, Julien: you're of age . . . you . . ."

"If I was mad or a half-wit, you could do without me . . . well,

I am. You can take your choice which it is to be. From now on I shall never leave my bed. I won't see anybody! If they don't send me up any food, I shall die, and the sooner the better. . . . You're too young to understand the extent of my fall. . . . You can't realize it"—he went on with a sort of gloomy exaltation. "You don't know what it meant socially to be a Revolou . . . the position to which that name entitled one. . . . I couldn't have climbed higher, as I realize only too well. When people said, "The Revolou boy," it meant something. . . . Do you begin to see how this terrible thing affects me? I have sometimes refused to shake hands with a man: no man has ever refused to shake hands with me. Those I once ignored will now be the first to pretend that they don't see me. . . ."

"You could go and live somewhere else," suggested Denis.

"Live somewhere else?—you must be mad! No, I shall behave with scrupulous dignity. I have already resigned from the Club. I have accepted my rôle as victim, and shall just disappear—disappear as utterly as a man can whose principles forbid him to take his own life. I shall just fade out. Let that filthy Landin—who's really responsible for all that has happened—scheme away to his heart's content. Let him squirm his way out as best he can. . . ."

"But you're forgetting mother and Rose. . . ."

"If I was a neurasthenic, you'd have to manage without me. Well, I am—I can't bear anybody to see me. I can't bear to meet people!"

He was like a bird making its nest. He settled down into his mania, building its protective sides higher and higher, hollowing out a little hole, padding it with feathers, snuggling down inside.

He turned his face to the wall and said no more.

IV

WHEN her sons had left the room, Léonie Costadot remained for a while seated on the bed, too tired to take off her clothes. The weariness that oppressed her was of the spirit rather than the body. She would never forget the look on Lucienne's face while she had been dragging the four hundred thousand francs out of her, the way in which the features seemed to have disintegrated. 'Was I too hard on her? No, I was only doing my duty. . . .' But she felt, not for the first time, that her sons' argument had touched a weak spot in her defences. Somehow, they always managed to disturb her, to set her scruples in action. She was angry with them for being in league with her conscience. Had they not sat in judgment on her she might have found oblivion now in sleep.

What she had said was, however, perfectly true. Fundamentally she took no interest in money, could be perfectly happy without it, and had never learned to spend it on herself. She was getting to be an old woman, and would die without ever having really known anything of the world. It had never occurred to her to travel—she had never wanted to. . . . When one becomes a landed proprietor. . . . The idea of possessing jewellery had, too, always left her cold—which was foolish, for precious stones are the soundest form of investment.

Her every thought was of money, yet she had never known either the spendthrift's or the miser's happiness. She had merely carried on the work begun by her parents, had shown herself faithful to the well-tested principles of order, thrift, economy. The central tenet of the creed she had inherited was that one spent half one's income and laid the rest out at interest. The essential thing was that investments should always maintain a proper balance based upon the theory of the distribution of risk. Never put all one's eggs in one basket, always keep enough liquid

41

capital available to meet taxation and death duties, an objective which it was becoming increasingly difficult to attain.

The two young fools did not understand that the decision not to take part in the game of money-grubbing had never been her's to make. She had followed in her parents' footsteps, had accepted without argument the rules laid down for her, as her sons, when the time came, would have to do as well. 'Money is our master and imposes its law on us,' she thought, 'whether, as in my case, one is only moderately well off or whether one is the possessor of a fortune so large as to set the imagination reeling. I *had* to do everything humanly possible to save those four hundred thousand francs: there was no other choice open to me. I would move heaven and earth for four hundred thousand francs. I can think of nothing I wouldn't do! . . .' When Robert and Pierrot came into their inheritance they too would conform to the exigencies of money. . . . Why not make over everything to them now? That was what she ought to do. It would compel them to see sense and convince them that her action had been wholly disinterested. 'It's all the same to me,' she sighed as she sank into bed: 'I am really beyond caring what happens.'

This was not the first time that she had played with the idea of sharing out the family fortune. The only thing that gave her pause was the knowledge that before she could do anything of the kind Pierrot would have to be declared legally of age. And why not? He would almost certainly leave the administration of his share in her hands or his brothers'. About Robert she felt no anxiety. Timid by nature, he would be desperately afraid of losing everything. The responsibilities of money would keep him in leading strings and compel his obedience. Even Gaston . . . who ran up small debts so long as he knew that his mother would pay them, but was not really a prodigal, and was far too fond of his pleasures to run the risk of seeing the source of them run dry. . . . Besides, she could always, if necessary, appoint legal trustees. . . .

What a magnificent way it would be of paying them out if

she could spring a surprise like that. "You thought I would do anything rather than give up this money," she would say: "well, here it is: you can have it. I shall keep just enough to save me from having to beg my bread. . . ." The mere imagination of that scene raised her spirits and so filled her with delight that she lost all sense of fatigue. She felt tempted to go straight to Robert's room, to knock at his door and tell him without more ado what she had decided. But she was temperamentally too prudent to yield to a sudden impulse. She must sleep on her plan, chew the cud of her resolution for several days, perhaps. The thought of dividing the family estate at once among the eventual heirs brought balm to her conscience, the thought that she might become as poor as Lucienne Revolou, not because of a scandalous financial collapse, but because she had voluntarily, nobly, decided to strip herself of all possessions.

She lay awake till dawn turning the matter over and over in her mind. She did not see that what she was really doing was to build a fortress in which she could take refuge from remorse, from something she had recently done in a house in the Place de la Bourse; to conjure into oblivion those gloomy Revolou faces that moved about her bed with fixed, inexorable eyes.

She slept for three hours, at the end of which time she was disturbed by the sound of somebody turning the pages of a newspaper. She opened her eyes. She heard Pierrot's voice. . . . "He killed himself last night. . . ." Robert, the tears running down his cheeks, was sitting on a chair at the foot of the bed.

"We mustn't lose our sense of proportion. It was about half-past-ten when I was at the Place de la Bourse. The tragedy occurred fifteen minutes later. There can't be any sort of connexion between Lucienne's signing of the deed and her husband's death. I can't see why you want to torture me. Actually, it would have been better if I hadn't spent all day making up my mind to do what I did. If I had taken the plunge in the afternoon, Oscar would be alive at this moment. What are you thinking about? Why are you looking at me like that?"

"But that's not all," said Robert. "While you were engaged in robbing his wife and children, our dear brother Gaston was eloping with his mistress. . . ."

"Well, I'm not to be blamed for that. You can't surely expect me to keep Gaston tied to my apron strings? Anyhow, the wretched man didn't know it was Gaston—at least, I don't think he did. . . . If *he* hadn't gone off with her, someone else would have done. . . . When women like that have sucked a man dry you know what to expect. . . . I just don't understand you. . . . I feel quite as badly as you do about what has happened, but we were powerless to prevent it. . . ."

If only they had been insolent, accusing! Why were they sitting there saying nothing, trying to keep her at a distance? Why were they being so unfair as to believe her incapable of sharing their distress? Robert's love. . . . Pierrot's friendship. . . . Hadn't she, too, got feelings? There had been a time, long ago, when those same feelings had thrilled to the charm of this Oscar Revolou about whom the morning's paper. . . . She appealed to their closed and silent faces. But hope died in her. She would never be able to break through that barrier of mistrust . . . unless. . . . . . . Suddenly she remembered what it was she had been planning as she lay awake in the darkness, her scheme for dividing the family fortune. She felt sorely tempted to throw her offer in their teeth. It was for their sakes only that she had clung to money. She certainly did not cling to it now, because now nothing any longer mattered. She had wasted her life, had sacrificed it on the altar of those sons who were utterly incapable of understanding her motives. All she wanted was to be left alone to die in a corner. If they really thought that she was governed by a craving for possessions, then the sooner they realized their mistake, the better! The laws are in league against the owners of property. . . . Nowadays their rights are only a myth. . . . She wanted nothing except to see the light of comprehension dawn on the faces of

these two young creatures who were presuming to sit in judgment on her. . . . She could resist the temptation no longer.

"My dear boys, the position is really very simple. While I lay
awake last night, long before I knew that Oscar Revolou was
dead, I came to a decision, and nothing will make me alter it. All
I can hope is that it will make you see how wrong you have been.
. . . I am quite determined to share what money there is between
the three of you. . . . Don't look so surprised: I mean precisely
what I say. It is merely a question of anticipating Pierrot's
majority by a few years. He is already eighteen, and I am prepared to take that risk, though on the understanding that he will
be sensible enough to let me go on administering what will
come to him."

The effect of these words came as a terrible disappointment to
her. The boys showed no surprise. Either they had not understood, or they did not believe her. She repeated her statement.
Didn't they grasp it? Couldn't they realize the importance of
what she was proposing?

"You mean that we are to have now what is due to us under
papa's will?"

"That, and everything as well that I hold in my own right.
Naturally, I shall retain a small life interest. After all, I must
live."

To Pierrot the offer meant nothing but a repetition of the
same hateful and everlasting words—title-deeds, income, real
property. The mere fact that he was to have his part in these
things did not lessen his loathing of them.

"No, mother dear, that's nonsense," said Robert. "You're
just overwrought. . . . If you did what you suggest, you'd never
forgive yourself. You must realize that the whole thing is impossible. . . ."

She protested. The strong wine of sacrifice had gone to her
head.

"As I said before, I spent the whole night thinking about it.
I knew nothing of what has happened at Léognan. You think I

am selfish and grasping, and nothing will make you change your minds. . . . But what if I give everything away, if I retain for myself no more than will keep me from starving?"

They did, at last, show signs of being shaken. Pierrot put a question:

"Then Robert can marry Rose after all?"

Not for a moment did she hesitate. "Certainly, if he wants to. But you must not go getting big ideas. You will be very far from rich. The value of the property is no more now than half what it originally was. Rents are falling. Our fortune is nothing like what it used to be, divided into three, and taking into account my own life-interest. . . . I want you to have no illusions. Robert certainly won't be able to afford to keep the whole Revolou family . . ."

"That's his concern," broke in Pierrot.

"Yes, it is his concern, and his only. But I have made up my mind and nothing will make me alter it . . . not even his decision to put a noose round his own neck."

Pierrot looked anxiously at his brother who had withdrawn slightly, and was smoking as though he was not personally concerned in what they were discussing.

"What are you thinking about, Robert?" There was a lack of firmness in the other's voice as he replied that he was wondering whether he oughtn't to go straight to Léognan.

"No," said Léonie with determination. "Your presence there would merely be an added source of pain. Write to the girl. Pierrot can break the news to Denis, and I will send a line to Lucienne. I rely on you, my boy, not to commit yourself until you know precisely how you will be placed. Wait at least until we've had time to get a proper valuation made, settled how much each share will be, and finished with the legal formalities."

"Oh, I quite realize that nothing's actually been *done* yet," interrupted Pierrot. "We'd certainly better wait until there's something tangible to go on."

Tears welled up in Léonie Costadot's eyes. The sight of them moved the boys to a show of affection. . . . Pierrot leaned forward to give her a kiss, but she avoided him.

"No, leave me alone. You are a pair of ungrateful children. Don't think I was influenced by the hope of getting justice from you. Even when I've stripped myself of everything, you'll still manage to find some excuse for regarding me as a worthless old woman! I have no illusions about either of you. You're both of you quite heartless. Gaston is merely irresponsible. He does wrong without meaning to. He follows his instincts. I may be foolish, but at least I realize *that*, and whatever else is wrong with him, at least he's got a heart. . . . No, no, go away . . . leave me in peace!"

"What makes it all so sad," said Pierrot, who had followed his brother to his room, "is that mother's tears leave me quite unmoved, though as a rule I can't bear to see people cry. Don't you think it's true that whether one behaves well or badly entirely depends on the people one happens to be dealing with?"

"All the same," said Robert, "we've shaken her up. She's not so confident as she used to be about her scale of values. I'm certain of one thing, though—she'll go through with this business of the family money. . . . I say, you're in luck's way, you know. What are you going to do with it all?" he added suddenly.

"I? D'you mean that *I'm* going to have money?"

"Of course—that's why you're to be declared of age."

The boy looked at his brother with shining eyes.

"I'll give it all to you, Robert—for your marriage!"

Robert laid a hand on his head.

"Dear old man, you really *must* be a bit mad!"

"You wouldn't want me at eighteen . . ."

It was as though, he felt, some illness of which he had thought as some far-distant possibility, as something that might be reserved for his latter days, had suddenly declared itself now in his first youth, and was about to lay him low. Poor Pierrot! What reason was there to expect that he would be stronger-minded than his fellows . . . unless, of course . . . there *was* one way. He might take to his heels and run, do nothing, just let things slide until everything was settled and Robert endowed with *his* share, as well as with what would come to him automatically. That done, all the documents duly signed, and the marriage an accomplished fact, he, Pierrot, could take himself off, no matter where so long as he could find work and live by his own unaided labours, dependent on nobody. . . .

V

MUCH later Denis remembered without bitterness the days that had followed his father's almost furtive burial. His mother, Rose and Landin started very early each morning for the city with the intention of beginning at once to clear up the tangle in which the family business had been left. They did not get back until evening. Only Julien, faithful to his self-imposed vow stayed behind, confined to his room. Denis continued to live with the Cavailhes. It was decided that he should leave college, and work at the local secondary school during the spring term for the second part of his "baccalauréat." The thought of this unexpected holiday excited him. He was still sleeping in the bed which stood within hailing distance of the one normally occupied by Irène, but the girl had now been moved into her parents' room. In the day-time she worked with a dressmaker in the village, not, said Madame Cavailhes, that she needed the money, but because people would have thought it odd if she had not been set to learn a trade. Besides, she had a talent for dressmaking, and her parents meant later to establish her in a business of her own. She returned after dark, just as Denis began to find time beginning to hang heavy on his hands.

While the light lasted he was far from bored. He had never

known what winter was like in the country, and was surprised that December could be so mild. He loved to sit by the wall at midday enjoying the diffused warmth of the sun as it hurried through its short course across the sky, and managed, with a final desperate effort, to pierce the mist, shedding about him, for a few brief hours, a sort of exhausted radiance. The landscape had more colour than he had expected, for the garden was full of ever-greens, and heath came almost to the fence. The dark green of its rolling distances could be seen from the first-floor windows. The streams at this time of the year had burst their banks and mirrored back the sun. The vines to the south had not yet been pruned, and their bare, wild shoots had about them the velvety softness of an animal's pelt. The reeds at the edges of the standing pools showed the colour of living flesh. The season's smell was less vegetable, more subtle, than that of summer, a mingling of stripped earth and the mineral tang of sodden clay.

He brooded on the thought of death. He knew it now at first hand. It took its place among the regular furniture of his mind. Death, that ultimate and only truth to which he knew that he had been converted, had room, he felt, only for primitive delights, for carnal intimacy with the earth which would finally absorb all flesh into itself. How short these brittle afternoons of menaced happiness! One tiny cloud sufficed to keep the sun from bringing comfort to the frozen earth.

When warmth had gone from the day, he went indoors to sit by the fire in Maria Cavailhes' kitchen. She did her best to make him talk. They shared the scraps of news that came to them— that the Bar Council, for instance, had assumed the duty of finding out the precise position of the Revolou practice. Then came a rumour that certain operations conducted by Monsieur Revolou had been distinctly shady. Maria was forever wondering how on earth the family managed to have everything they wanted. 'It's odd,' she thought, 'how rich people, even when they are ruined, never, somehow, change their way of living.'

About six o'clock Irène would come in and sit down to her

sewing, while Denis read to her from *Sans Famille* or *Andro-maque*, from *Phèdre* or *La Famille Fenouillard*. The girl's presence troubled his senses with a sweet delight, so that a sort of vague happiness spread through all his being. They ate slowly of the broth that had been simmering all day on a corner of the stove. Sometimes the smell of cooking would reach as far as the big house. . . . About nine the Cavailhes would take the logs off the fire, say good night and everyone would go to bed. A little later, Denis would be awakened from his first sleep by the sound of wheels on the gravel (for the first few days they had used the carriage, but soon had to resign themselves to going by tram)— and in a moment or two Rose would come in for a good-night kiss. She smelled of the city fog and gave vague answers to his questions. . . . "It's all too complicated. . . . I can't explain now . . . everything will come right in the end. . . . Now, go to sleep, dear." With assumed indifference she would ask whether there were any letters for her. He knew only too well what letter it was that she was expecting. "Nothing of any interest," he would reply.

It was a Thursday. Denis was sitting with his back propped against the wall of the kitchen-garden. Through the open door of the green-house came a smell of geranium and leaf-mould. A boy approached, pushing his bicycle. He recognized Pierre Costadot, whom he had not seen since the night of old mother Costadot's sinister visit to the house in the Place de la Bourse. He had no time to run away. At that moment he understood his brother Julien's state of mind. Like him he found himself suddenly wish-ing that he could be imprisoned within four walls, or that he could vanish into thin air. Pierrot stopped dead within a few yards of him, and Denis realized that his friend was in a state of considerable confusion. This was just another case, he thought, of someone who had painted a picture of him which had no con-nexion with reality, who had attributed to him all sorts of noble sentiments which had no part in the make-up of the flesh and

blood Denis. He had long given up trying to correct such
pictures of himself, had long ceased saying—"I'm not
what you think I am." It is not those who make us
worse than we are whom we should look on as our bitterest
enemies, but those who see us by the light of their own affections.
The thought of this meeting, which sooner or later was bound to
occur, had filled him with horror. It meant struggling through a
dense undergrowth of feelings which were entirely at odds with
the facts. It meant playing the rôle of a stranger, adapting himself
to the image of someone who was merely the product of young
Costadot's imagination.

"Aren't you going to shake hands with me?" asked Pierrot
shyly.

He leaned his bicycle against the green-house. Although he was
eighteen, he was very little taller than Denis, but in girth he was
already a man. The sun touched his ill-shaven face with a golden
haze. He was sweating in spite of the season, and a drop of per-
spiration hung from the tip of his small aquiline nose. Denis took
his outstretched hand and shook it. The visitor's embarrassment
melted in a sudden access of affection.

"I knew you'd be generous. . . . We've behaved appallingly to
you."

Denis gave a shrug.

"What's the use of talking about it?" he said wearily. "It
wasn't *your* fault."

"But I want you to know, Denis, that it'll weigh on my conscience as long as I live."

"You don't say so?" replied the other in a tone which implied
that nothing Pierrot was about to say could really matter much
to him one way or the other.

"I shall never forgive my mother for what she's done. I don't
suppose I have to tell you that everything's as it always was so far
as I'm concerned. . . . But look here, what I'm going to say now
you've jolly well got to keep to yourself. . . . I'm going away."

Denis showed no sign of emotion, not even of surprise.

"You've said that often enough before!"

Pierrot protested that this time he meant it. The only thing keeping him back was . . . well, surely Denis could guess?

The other shook his head.

". . . It's just the idea of leaving you, old man. Does that seem so very comic?"

"I shall wait till you're gone before I allow myself to be broken-hearted. . . ."

"Look here, Denis, I've got an idea. . . ." He went close to his friend, who seemed to be completely unmoved, and brought out suddenly:

"Why shouldn't we both of us go together?" He was prepared for abuse, for mockery, but not for this utter indifference, this apparent lack of interest. He began to wonder whether Denis had heard him.

"I was only joking," he went on: "I know perfectly well that you can't leave your family just now."

Denis kept himself from asking the question that was on the tip of his tongue—"Has your brother given up Rose?" The only thing that existed for him now was the dread that this engagement might not be broken. To such a degree was he obsessed by it that when, in order to break the silence, young Costadot said aimlessly, "Well, I suppose I'd better be going. . . ." he half-heartedly followed him down the garden.

They had almost reached the main road. Pierre was pushing his bicycle. It left marks on the muddy surface like the scaly track of a serpent. . . . Would they ever meet again? Was their friendship a thing of the past? At the very moment when Pierrot felt quite certain that everything was over between them, Denis suddenly spoke in the old familiar way:

"How's Atys getting on?" he asked.

It was so unexpected that at first young Costadot could say nothing. He had stopped by one of the elms which lined the road, and was busy turning up his coat-collar.

"Are you still interested?"

Denis replied: "You know I am. . . ."

It was perfectly true that for him, Pierre Costadot, author of *Atys and Cybele*, and "young Costadot" lived in two totally different worlds. What he felt for his friend was admiration rather than affection. No mist of fondness blurred his lucidity. He knew, at seventeen, that the master who had once confiscated the book in which Pierrot scribbled his verses, and had made the boy squirm with embarrassment by reading them out in front of the whole form, was a fool.

"I understand at last the nature of Cybele's martyrdom," said Pierrot. "She suffers in every fibre of her vast body. She is too big for the consummation of a merely human passion, if you see what I mean. . . . It's terribly difficult to explain. . . . Listen, this is what she says to Atys:

> Slowly my branches pierced the shredding haze.
> Like sparkling water did your laughter leap,
> And your face shone on Cybele's rapt gaze
> Brighter than all the blinded stars that keep
> Their ranks in Heaven. So did your image run
> On the cold ripples of my muddied stream.
> But of that tingling flesh, with my flesh one,
> Nothing I felt, but only the light run
> Of Atys's fingers playing with my hair: heard but the scream
> Of my torn heart so shrill upon the air
> It must have waked the folk of that sad place.
> Atys, with your small mouth you burned me there,
> That had no arms to bury, no hands to do you grace.

A stranger might, perhaps, have laughed at the nasal sing-song . . . but for Denis it was impossible to imagine the words spoken otherwise than as his friend recited them, or that their mystery could have found a fuller echo elsewhere than in this place of winter dusk, at the side of an empty road.

"Cybele is the earth, and she sees Atys as a world. . . . Just as the Greeks diminished the elements and the Heavenly bodies to the stature of human men and women, so, by a reverse process, she sees in her beloved shepherd all the secrets of an unknown land. . . . What I'm trying to do is to express something of that confused co-existence of a thinking being and a star, of a living body, a poor thing of flesh and blood, and a land filled with oceans, rolling valleys, peaks and gulfs and forests. . . ."

> A line of shore, a sand-dune's gentle swell,
> A fringe of spume and weed—and the great sea
> . . . . The faint trace of your lids that cannot quell
> Your dark and softened radiance. The thick-wooded scree
> That is your empty brow. The splendour of your bright
> And lovely eyes—twin planets of my night,
> Will, when you sleep, illumine endlessly
> Another world. Atys, a double truth about me lowers,
> The youth who tears my heart, the ocean that devours.

"Yes," said Denis, breaking the silence, "I see how it is for Cybele that Atys is a world. . . ."

"She realizes what it means to understand a person 'in the round'—as one says. . . ."

Pierre left the thought unfinished. Suddenly he exclaimed: "I never really believed that we should meet again. . . ."

He had straddled his bicycle, and sat there for a few moments motionless, his arm round Denis's neck.

"I'll bring you the manuscript of *Cybele* before I go. When you get it you'll know that my mind is made up."

He rode off, waving his hand in farewell, and disappeared into the gloom like any ordinary boy and not like one who carried a poem in his heart and in the very texture of his flesh. The electric tram came into view. Denis, still standing by the road, watched its headlight, like a Cyclop's eye, grow larger. He thought of some lines he had read in which a poet describes just such a tram, brushing the overhanging leaves, and letting fall upon him—

des harnais de sommeil en frôlant les feuillages.

He knew that the great yellow car held in its maw his mother, Rose and, almost certainly, Monsieur Landin, who was coming back to sleep one last night at Léognan—for the details of the winding-up were now all but finished. . . . Everything was to be sold, but Madame Revolou was still to enjoy the use of house and grounds.

He realized that they must have been deep in discussion all the way from town. But, when they appeared, Landin, for all he knew himself to be indispensable, brought up the rear, humble and timid as usual.

"It's all settled," said Madame Revolou to Denis. "At last we shall be able to get rid of this creature."

"Do be careful—he may overhear you. . . ."

"So much the better if he does."

Rose, who was walking with Landin, broke into a run in order to catch up with them.

"I've got a surprise for you," she whispered to Denis: "I've found a job. . . ."

"Don't jump to conclusions," said her mother. "We shall have to talk it over between ourselves. . . ."

"Oh, but, mummy, it's such a wonderful chance. . . ."

"That is scarcely the word I should have used. Humiliation would be more appropriate! I had resigned myself to the idea of your going out to work . . . as a governess, maybe. . . ."

"But what could I teach? I can't play the piano, and I know absolutely nothing about anything. . . ."

"You know quite enough to be able to take charge of young children. . . . But to think of my daughter—of Rose Revolou—serving in a shop!"

"Not just *a* shop, mummy: a *book-shop*—that makes all the difference. Chardon's offered to take me on, Denis."

"Chardon?—the man we get our books from?"

She was bubbling over with life and happiness. Denis had an uneasy feeling that she was too happy. He was shocked and irritated by such an exaggerated display of delight. As they passed through the gate, he said suddenly:

"Pierrot's been to see me. . . ."

"Ah!" she breathed.

It was too dark for him to see her face, but he noticed the change in her voice.

"Did he say anything about Robert?"

Denis said, no, he hadn't, and sniffed the fog with pleasure.

In the hall, Madame Revolou remarked:

"We won't come to any decision until we have heard what my eldest son has to say. . . ."

Rose gave way to an outburst of childish petulance:

"I don't need his advice about how I am to earn my living. . . ."

Her mother gave a start. "Rose!" she said, and then, in tones of parental severity:

"He is your elder brother, that should be enough for you. But remember, also, that he is ill, very ill."

"I'm sorry. Let's go and see him straight away. I've got to give Chardon an answer tomorrow."

The house was unheated.

"This staircase is like an ice-box," complained Madame Revolou.

She led the way up, holding a lamp. Rose followed, and Denis came last. Their three shadows danced before them, broken by the treads.

On the landing, Madame Revolou said:

"Wait for me here. I'll go and see whether he's asleep. . . ." and she handed the lamp to Rose.

Denis looked at his sister. He noticed how much she had changed in the last few weeks. It was as though what had happened had rained hammer-blows upon her face. Gone were the traces of her childhood. Deep shadows showed round her eyes, and in the hollows of cheeks and temples. Her long nose gave her an ugly look. Her shoulders now seemed not so much fragile as bony. . . . He felt a sudden flow of tenderness. He had only to say: "Pierrot came for the sole purpose of talking about you and Robert. . ." to bring happiness into the poor, worn face.

Their mother came back and indicated by signs that they could go into their brother's room.

A cloud of smoke, a smell of nicotine, drifted through the half-open door. Julien raised his head slightly above the green stuffed eiderdown . . . the fleshless head of a bird.

The illness to which he had fled for refuge now possessed him utterly. The walls of his protection had closed upon him. His sickness was no longer feigned, nor his powerlessness to achieve the slightest act of will. He had said that he would withdraw from life, but it was life that had withdrawn from him. One look was enough to make Rose repent of the hard things she had said about him just now. Filled with pity, she took, without repugnance, the hairy wrist which projected from his torn pyjama sleeve.

"It has been lovely today, Julien. There was a smell of spring in the air. Just when one thinks one has lost everything, one realizes that nothing is lost at all . . . nothing . . . sunlight, things, people are all there just as usual. . . ."

He turned his face to the wall.

"I do wish you wouldn't talk. . . . I don't want to be talked to," and then, as his mother insisted:

"Darling, we'll leave you to go to sleep in a few moments. . . . We just want to ask your advice about . . ."

"And especially not like that! . . . I don't want to know anything. . . . I have no advice to give . . . not now!"

"It has nothing to do with business. We only want to know what you think. You're the eldest, and it's for you to decide whether Rose ought to accept an offer which Chardon, the bookseller, has made her."

"She can do what she likes with her own life," he muttered brokenly. "Everything's gone . . . and when everything's gone . . ."

"Listen, Julien," said Rose. "What I'm going to say may give you rather a shock. You see, the idea of being one of the crowd of girls who fill the streets at closing-time, makes me very happy. . . . I'm going to begin a new life. . . . I shall have had two lives. . . . So could you, if you'd only . . ."

But he was not paying attention. In a tone of acute misery, he begged them to go away.

"Do have a little consideration, and leave me alone. Why do you want to torture me?"

He had pulled the sheet over his head. In a low voice, Madame Revolou said:

"It's no use, you're only exhausting him. Say no more, Rose. Can't you see he's made up his mind not to listen? Go down and start dinner without me," she added, "I shall stay up here with him. I am not hungry."

She settled down. Something warned her that she was to find, henceforward, in this room more than a refuge—an object in life. She would devote herself entirely to Julien, and it would be useless to expect anything else of her. To tend him would be her sole and special function, her only reason for living, her civic duty. Her universe would be limited by these walls of which her eldest son had made a prison. People would say of her—"She is really wonderful! Never so much as a word of complaint!"

VI

LANDIN was standing by his chair, waiting for them. He sat down only when the two young people had taken their places. He had a side-face view of Rose. She had thrown a shawl over her shoulders. Now and then she got up to fetch some bread. Landin suffered as much from his hosts' averted gaze as might others from being stared at. Occasionally, Denis would turn his head sharply away. Landin's hand, resting on the cloth, had come within his field of vision. It was short, a hirsute hand with bitten nails, one of those hands which seems to have been shaped by the acts it has accomplished, so that at last it looks like them.

Landin resigned himself to eating hungrily, thus sparing himself the necessity of lifting his eyes from his plate. His melancholy beard absorbed its share of every dish. His bald and knobbly head was a multiplicity of high-lights. He was in a hurry to be off, yet found a certain pleasure in the presence of brother and sister. He, too, was conscious of a small hand upon the cloth, of the outline of an ear, of the play of muscles. Here, in this room, two young and handsome creatures were breathing the same air as he was. It did not matter that he gave them the creeps. The great point was that they were there.

Rose heaved a deep sigh. He got up.

"Won't you have some cheese, Monsieur Landin?"

"No, thank you, Miss Rose. This is my last evening, and there are several documents that need classifying. One or two papers are still missing, but I have not given up hope of finding them in Monsieur Oscar's study. . ."

"I expect they've lit the fire. . . . I haven't asked after Mademoiselle Landin?"

"You are too kind. My sister has been suffering from an attack of shingles, as perhaps you know. But she is better now, and is leading her old life again."

His reply fell on deaf ears, Rose had "done her duty," and felt quit of all responsibility.

He carefully closed behind him the door of the study where he was to work for the last time, and sat down in an armchair before the desk, as he had done every evening for the last three weeks. With his head in his hands he gave himself up to enjoyment of the silence.

When a man is dead, there is no more to be feared from him—neither snubs nor contempt. He has no weapon left against the faithful heart, is utterly defenceless, can no longer oppose to the feelings he inspires the hostility of his living presence. Gone is the need to be tactful or evasive. Even when one's name is Landin, and the dead man was a creature as brilliant as was Oscar Revolou, one is free to surrender to the novel sentiment of pity. Landin was surprised to find that he felt pity for the one person in all the world for whom he had had a whole-hearted admiration. He set himself to realize in imagination the fears and torments to which, for the last few weeks of his life, Oscar Revolou had been a prey. They had been caused not so much by business worries as by Regina's treason. No doubt he had gambled and lost, but he would have recovered from *that*. A man of his calibre could have taken such troubles in his stride. If he had felt himself to be hamstrung, had let mere money matters send him hurtling to catastrophe, it was simply because his every faculty had been obsessed by one thing, and by one thing only, because all his thoughts had been centred on one single person. And what a person!—the Lorati woman! "From where you are now," said Landin in a low voice, "you can see the bitch as she really is!"

He felt perfectly certain that the dead can read the hearts of the living, and this conviction helped him to face the need for continued existence. Oscar Revolou could see the real Lorati now, as he could see the real Landin. The senior clerk believed sincerely in the power of death to bring lucidity of vision. The thought that this was so laid balm to his heart and showed him the path that he must follow. The dead man's affairs would no longer be a load upon his back. From now on, he would be at no one's beck and call. Whatever opportunities might come his way, he had quite decided to take a job that would give him plenty of leisure. For a while he had been tempted by an offer which had reached him from a business-man in Paris, a former lawyer, who, dazzled by Landin's capacities, had suggested that he join him on extremely favourable terms. But Landin felt that he was bound to Oscar Revolou. Dead or alive, the man's hold on him was complete.

His first duty was to put the estate in order, to protect his master's memory, should the need arise. But above all, and this thought filled him with a bitter joy, he must see that justice was done. So far as the Lorati woman was concerned, he knew the nature of his mission, though all, as yet, was vague in his mind, and he had had no time in which to think what precisely he should do. Put in the simplest terms, he had an account to settle, had got to extract, to the last penny, a debt of which he did not know, did not wish to know, the details. As with all his other passions, this hatred of which he was now conscious, took on for him the appearance of a duty. His taste for virtue compelled him to disguise his feelings in this way. It was only others who saw the terrible signs which might have put him on guard against himself—the furtive eyes, the way he moved, the way he talked. He, on the other hand, was lulled by a consciousness of virtue, so that he had become its dupe. He must, of course, have realized how people recoiled from his approaches, but he attributed their conduct to his odd appearance, and to the fact that his generous impulses were always a shade too obvious. The world, he told himself, is hard on the over-sensitive.

He was persuaded that he had a duty to perform in this matter of the Lorati woman. But he was in no hurry. It could wait. But he would never lose sight of the creature who had driven Oscar Revolou to his death. He would keep his nose to the scent.

Of such thoughts was the silence made which seemed to brood over the drowned house like an element, like a heavy weight of water. Monsieur Landin, secure from human enemies and a hostile world, was watching for the last time with the spirit of his adored master. He knew what the heirs thought about him, knew that once he had crossed the threshold of this house in farewell he would never return. If ever, he thought, the souls of the poor, lonely dead revisit their earthly haunts, tonight of all nights would have been the time for such a manifestation. Had the door of the study opened suddenly, had Oscar Revolou entered with that air of bustle which never left him; had he, without a glance, suddenly barked an order; had he gone to the window and leaned his forehead against the glass for a moment before seating himself at his desk, leaning back and jingling his keys in his pocket, opening a drawer and failing to find the papers he sought, pushing the documents aside with a weary sigh and taking from his case one of those cigars which cost so much and always gave Landin a sick headache—the senior clerk would have felt no surprise and asked no question. He would have sat there waiting, his dog-like eyes fixed not on the master's face, but only on the

3

hands that could not realize they were being watched and so did not try to avoid or flee from that fixed expression of loving servility.

Nothing of that kind could happen: nothing would ever happen again. Nevertheless, as Landin cut the string which held the last packet of papers, he was conscious of a vague emotion, as though all the repressed part of himself were suddenly alert and wakeful. What he held in his hand was a bundle of agendas and recent memoranda, annotated with scribbles which, for the most part, were illegible; business appointments, addresses, figures and algebraic formulæ. Here and there he came on some woman's name which meant nothing to him, some endearment with, as it were, the freshness of dew upon it, which woke in him no memory of a face, so that as he read it he felt that he was doing something shameful. For it was part of his private code that only those pleasures which his master had confided to him were to be regarded as legitimate.

And then, all of a sudden, in the middle of the minutes of a business meeting, or underneath a florist's address, he would come upon a jotted intimacy. It was as though Oscar Revolou were there in the room with him thinking out loud in that way he had, seemingly oblivious of his clerk's presence. What he had written down was made safe from prying eyes by sheer illegibility. Even Landin, who was familiar with each stroke, each eccentricity of that writing, had to take a magnifying glass in an effort to decipher the entry.

. . . The pleasure I experienced last night with my unknown was all the greater because there was no question of love between us, none of that mental distraction from which I suffer so abominably when I'm with Regina. The very fact that I love her makes me impotent, literally paralyses me. The presence of the beloved object is my complete undoing. I don't suppose I have ever possessed her save at second hand in some other woman's arms. I'd rather die than confess as much to *anyone* . . . and yet, only a short time ago, I did tell. . . .

Landin could not make out the next phrase, although he knew his master's handwriting so well that often, when Oscar Revolou could not read his own notes, he had appealed for help to his senior clerk. He could make out the first words two, but the third beat him. He managed to pick out a b, an a, a t—yes, it was "beastliness". . . . "I did tell that sack of beastliness. . . ."

Landin's face was impassive. He did not yet know who this sack of beastliness was. The bullet had pierced him, but the wound had closed upon it without bleeding. He read on calmly, occasionally using the magnifying glass to help him with the more difficult words.

His strong card is his ubiquity. He's always to hand like a waste-paper basket, an ash-tray, a doormat, a spittoon. What other men tell only to themselves in the street, or when dinner's over in a restaurant and they are surrounded by the hubbub of waiters clearing away, and the din of the orchestra— the kind of things that no human ear but their own ought ever to catch—*I* pour into that sack of beastliness. He has been part of my life ever since I was at school. He has never left me for a moment. He is a sort of open drain on the edge of which I have had to work and play, have had to love, have had to suffer. It wasn't I who chose him. He chose me. . . . Now that my life has reached its turning-point, I am filled with a feeling of horror to think that it has pursued its course under that sign, that it has been dominated and directed by a creature who marked me out to be his god. I suppose I'm the only person who knows that temperamentally he is a criminal. . . . I'm quite sure he does not know it himself. . . .

Landin raised his two hands to his throat, as though blood were about to jet forth and smother him. He went over to the mirror that hung above the mantelpiece, and stared at his own reflexion. His face was like the face of other men, a face made in the image and likeness of God. . . . Indeed, there was something in its expression purer than in that of other faces. The eyes were those of an overgrown child. Their light was that of dawn's freshness reflected in a puddle. He noticed the bald head, the boy's face with its inappropriate beard. The effect *ought* to have been just comic. How came it then that it should be terrible—a mask concealing a secret as yet unrevealed? What was this nameless tragedy, this play of which the action had not as yet begun?

The silence of the night was broken by the thud as of waves upon a shore. He could have sworn that evil spirits had lifted the house and set it down upon the ocean's brink. It was some seconds before he realized that the dull throbbing in his ears was the beating of his own blood. He passed his hands over his cheeks, his beard, his eyes—those eyes that were fine and striking and might have been loved. In a low voice he repeated the words with which his sister sometimes comforted him: "You poor dear...." He was filled with self-pity. If he had fallen dead at that moment and been summoned to the bar of the All-Highest, it would have been he, Landin, who would have called his Judge to account, demanding to know why he, Landin, existed at all. But the frail defences of his body stood firm against the thrust and batter of the sea within his ears. Humbly he went back to the desk, and sat down again before the sheet of paper covered with writing that no eyes but his could read.... But now he no longer needed a magnifying-glass.

... It is the talk of the place that Landin really runs my practice. The general belief is that he is my faithful slave—he is convinced of it himself, whereas actually it is I who am bound to the wheels of his beastliness. In me he has come to a point of concentration. I am, as it were, a sort of abscess, the centre of his fixation.... It seems that I have diverted his power of destruction to my own purposes, but the truth of the matter is that he owns me body and soul. He knows every single thing about me since my schooldays. I can see myself again as I was at twelve years old. Even what my confessor could not get out of me, *he* made me tell. He has made me aware, coldly, un-emotionally, but with utter ruthlessness, of all the things, I might have done. This witness whom I loathe, has given to each one of my actions its precise value, its exact weight in the scales of eternity. But loathing him has done me no good. His love has submerged my loathing and covered it. No matter which way I turn he is always there. The flaming circle moves as I move. It has always done so, expanding as I grew in size and strength. He has thriven on each service he has done me, on every secret I have confessed to him. He began by doing my verses for me at school, writing my essays, whispering answers across to me in form. All through my life I have gone on dis-charging on his devoted head everything that was not part of my pleasure and delight. Later, he saw me suffer, and I have shed tears in his presence which should have been concealed even from the eyes of God. The very groans torn from me by jealousy I let him hear, so much has he become a part of my-self, the incarnation of all the darker sides of my nature. I have smothered him with insults, trampled him underfoot—but my violent expressions of loathing served no other purpose than to prove the indestructible strength of the chain that bound us one to another. Perhaps I was born only to absorb his energies, to turn him from his true calling. Should he survive me, should he consent to survive me, what, I wonder, will happen when his powers are let loose in the world? Regina has often said to me, "Men have the friends they deserve . . . what corpse is the binding link between you? . . ." What corpse, indeed? . . . Of course he knows all my business secrets . . . but he would never make use of them against me. . . . He has never once sought to turn my admissions to his own advantage. . . . All the same, he will destroy me in the end. The mad rhythm of my life, the mass-production factory which my practice has become, is all his creation. I ask from him nothing except that it should pro-vide me with money. He has devoted himself to serving the passions which are eating me up—whereas, he should, by

rights, have hated them. What a mystery it all is! The obvious
explanation is that only thus can he keep himself in the centre
of the web that has caught and holds me. He will be the death
of me. But for him my instinct of self-preservation would
already have come into play. Increasing age would have begun
to deaden my desires. The horrible creature has put the whole
mechanism of my nature out of gear. It is *his* devotion that has
kept alive and nourished in me those relics of youthfulness that
others find so admirable. But *I* know that I have reached the
end, that my race is run. But he is all the time at my elbow,
ready with the plausible excuse, always managing at the last
moment to provide just the amount of money I need, watchful,
prepared, never at a loss. He forces leisure on me, and I am
killed by leisure. Passion is dragging me by the hair down the
road to destruction, and it is he who sweeps aside all the
obstacles which might otherwise have afforded me a breathing-
space. I see men about me who have found salvation in profes-
sional duties, in family affection. But the Revolou practice is no
longer me, it is this sack of beastliness. My family? He has
opened an impassable gulf between us. How? I can't explain
the fact, but I know that it is there . . . perhaps by creating
about us a shadowy zone into which those nearest to me can
never penetrate. He has built up a closed and haunted world
which keeps me from those who care for me. Worse than that,
he has mined the very ground beneath that domestic refuge
where, in spite of his mole-like burrowings, I can still at times
make contact with them. . . .

Landin pushed back his chair a few inches. He shook his head:
he cried "No! No!" to somebody who was not there. "Is all
that true?" he asked aloud. "Is there some grain of truth in what
he says?" He covered his eyes with his hand and spoke again. "I
must keep my head. . . . I must think back. . . . How was it when
we were at school? . . ." But he could not concentrate his
thoughts. The page of notes lying open on the table drew his

eyes like a magnet, demanding his attention, calling to him. He was on his feet now, nor did he again sit down, but merely leaned forward to read what still remained.

... When I am gone will this loathsome creature leave my children alone, or will he still haunt the places where they are, though I shall be there no longer? Will his power pass with my passing? shall I drag him with me into nothingness? ...

Landin, standing there motionless, leaned forward with both hands on the spread sheet. For a long time he remained like that. No one had thought to close the shutters, and Orion blazed behind the blackness of the panes. At last he picked up the scribbled pages, squatted in front of the embers, and watched while a flickering and uncertain flame attacked the paper, with difficulty caught its edges, went out, and once more leaped into life. From time to time he lifted the half consumed book in the tongs and moved it about until the fire once more took hold. He waited for a long time, till all that remained was a wisp of burnt-out ash.

Rose awoke with a start. She thought that she had heard a door open and the sound of footsteps on the stone flags of the hall. The great house, ramshackle and ill-secured, standing where town and country met, had never been lived in during the winter months. According to Madame Revolou it was the ideal setting for a crime. Rose, upright in bed, could hear nothing but the wind in the trees. 'I must have been dreaming,' she thought. It was four o'clock. She had still two more hours of sleep before her alarm-clock would ring. When that happened she would scramble into her clothes so as not to miss the first tram. Then her new life would begin, the life of a girl who goes out to earn a livelihood for her family. She would sit in the car looking at the faces opposite, waiting for some sign of friendly greeting. One day, she felt sure, Robert would push the shop-door open—or, no, he wouldn't do that, he would wander up and down the street waiting for her to come out. A flood of happiness welled up in her. . . No, life had not yet begun. Except for poor papa, this awfulness had killed no one except those who, like Julien, had already been dead, had never really been alive. She would go forward, never turning her head, drawing after her her little brother Denis. What she earned she would give to others. There was nothing she could do for them now but find them in food and lodging. . . . But Denis was different: she must see to it that he kept his place with Robert in her heart. . . . She was obsessed by the thought of her future happiness. It kept her awake, and when at last she did fall asleep it was only to be jerked into wakefulness a few seconds later by the sudden whirr of the alarm clock sounding as though for the Day of Judgment.

She dressed hurriedly in the bitter cold, her only light a candle. In the kitchen, the coffee-pot was standing in the embers where it had been put to keep warm. On the way back upstairs she noticed a line of light under the door of her father's study. Had Monsieur Landin really spent the whole night going through papers? She knocked, pushed the door open, and stood hesitating on the threshold. The room was empty, but the overturned chair, the cushions scattered about the floor, the remains of burnt paper in the grate, all seemed to tell of something that she did not understand. She remembered suddenly how she had woken with a start in the middle of the night. Perhaps Landin had been murdered? She was too frightened to move, too frightened even to look whether anyone were lurking in the shadowed corners. . . . Maybe, a body was lying somewhere, hidden . . . unless, of course Landin had merely gone to bed and forgotten to put the lights out. . . .

She left the lamp burning, crossed the great courtyard, and noticing a light in the Cavailhes' kitchen, tapped at the window. Madame Cavailhes half opened the door, and at once reassured her visitor. Monsieur Landin had asked her to open the front gates during the night. He had taken it into his head to walk back to Bordeaux—"so as not to waste any time. . . . From the way he acted you might have thought his house was on fire."

What—who—Rose wondered, had driven him to flight? She stood shivering at the point where the lane from the stables met the main road. Whom was he fighting now? Poor Landin! How frightful to be Landin! She watched the single headlight of the first tram grow bigger in the mist.

She sat among a crowd of workmen. Already she felt tired, and dreamed of those almost fabulous times when the sun had wakened her in her bed, and the maid had brought a steaming tray. She caught again the smell of toast mingled with the sweet, resinous scent of twigs crackling in the hearth. But now she was sharing the lot of the majority of the human herd. No longer would the sound of factory sirens, heard in the half-light of dawn, send her burrowing into her blankets with a passing thought for "those poor workmen." That summons had now a meaning for her, too. No, she was not now, as once she had been, cut off from the rest of the world, and this thought, far from appalling her, woke her from her mood of lethargy, and drove her onwards.

VII

"WE have been here longer than any of the other tenants," said Mademoiselle Félicia Landin to the concierge who had emerged pasty-faced from the basement, clutching her latest baby to her breast. "I regard you more as a friend than a concierge. I am not in the least put out by the thought that you may repeat to others what I am going to tell you; in fact, I hope you will. The people on the second floor are going round saying it's because of the Revolou crash that my brother has gone away, and that he's afraid he may be arrested. But don't please, Madame Joseph, *don't* think that I in any way hold it against *you*. It would be outrageous if you were to be held responsible for all the disgusting gossip that goes on in this house! But one thing's beyond question—as anyone can find out for himself by taking a little trouble—and that is that all the lawyers in the place have been trying to get hold of Landin. No one's reputation could stand higher. Only the other day, Boste's senior clerk was saying to me that nothing but Landin's genius for business could possibly have staved off the crash, with Revolou throwing his money away as he was doing. Don't make any mistake about it—lawyers and stockbrokers know an honest man when they see one! It was practically settled that Malbourget should take him on. All he asked was that he should be given enough time in which to wind up Monsieur Revolou's affairs. He has worked himself to a shadow, Madame Joseph. He has spent sleepless nights trying to straighten things out. But it no more occurred to the family to thank him than it occurs to them to say 'good-day' when we meet in the street. The trouble with Monsieur Landin is that he's as faithful as a dog—and pray don't think I mean that as flattery. Devoted sister though I am, I can't forgive him for ignoring the interests of his own flesh and blood, and sacrificing them in favour of people who treat us like so much dirt, though in matters of honour, religion, morality and all *that*, they can't hold a candle to *you*, Madame Joseph, as this wretched scandal has shown only too clearly.

"What they did to him the last night he spent at Léognan going through the papers, I'm sure I *don't* know. All I can tell you is that he got home in the early hours, long before the first tram was running, having made the journey entirely on foot! If he were anyone else one would hardly credit it! But you know what he's like. We all have our little manias, and his is for walking till he drops, even at night, *especially* at night, as a matter of fact, and through the least frequented districts, too, quite often down by the docks. It's a wonder to me he's never been set upon. I suppose it's because he looks so down-at-heel and so innocent. . . . If it comes to that, I've a very shrewd suspicion that he *was* knocked down once, though he never dared admit as much. . . . I assure you that if I did nothing else, I *still* couldn't keep his trousers clean of mud or prevent him from treading down his shoes. You've no idea the distances that man can cover without feeling tired. And then, all of a sudden, over he'll go as if he'd been pole-axed. Usually at week-ends, that is, and then he sleeps the clock round without even bothering to take his clothes off. So you see, it didn't surprise me to find him dripping with sweat, in spite of the cold, muddy to the waist, and looking almost as though he'd been drugged—as he usually does after such outings. . . . But what did make me sit up and take notice was the fact that he didn't go to bed as I should have expected him to do. . . . I don't mind admitting that usually when he comes in like that, I'm very careful not to say anything to him. As a rule, he's the gentlest of creatures, but after those mad walks of his he's no better than a wild animal, and it's no use pretending to you that he isn't, because you've seen him in those states more than once in the last fifteen years. . . . It doesn't often happen, but there's no knowing when one of the fits'll come on him. . . . Well, on this occasion, instead of going to bed, he told me to heat some coffee, and, while I was doing it, he said 'Félicia, give me a good brush.' 'Aren't you going to bed, Louis?' I asked him. 'No,' he said: 'I've got too much to do today.'

"He seemed gloomy, but not angry, and he kept on blowing his nose. When he'd eaten and drunk—luckily I had some bread and butter in the house—he wrote a telegram on a piece of paper and told me to send it from the branch office in the Place Saint-Projet, reply paid. 'I'll go when I've finished what I'm doing,' I said. 'No, I want you to go now, at once, Félicia, and I forbid you to read what I've written.'

"He spoke so gently that I felt frightened. I was trembling so violently, Madame Joseph, that I *couldn't* read. But at last I managed to control my agitation, and then I noticed that the telegram was addressed to Monsieur Edgar Salem, Rue Saint-Lazare, Paris. It ran as follows: 'Offer accepted. Wire if terms agreed. Arriving soon as possible.' I must tell you that this Salem is in a very big way of business, and had made Louis a really splendid offer. You know how he hates change. He would never dream of moving, though, if you'll excuse my saying so, your house is one of the few remaining in the city that hasn't got water laid on.

"'What does it all mean, Louis?' 'You can ask me questions when you've sent the telegram'. He didn't speak ill-temperedly, but in that serious way of his. I didn't try to wheedle anything out of him then, though I don't pretend I didn't make the most of my chance. I was mad with joy at the chance of seeing Paris at last. 'I'm absolutely staggered, Louis,' I said: 'but with joy!' 'Why?' he replied: 'it's not going to make any difference to you. You'll be staying on here.' 'All alone, Louis?'—I pulled a pretty long face, as you may imagine. I told him such a thing would be quite impossible, that we had never been parted, that it was all just another of the Revolous' underhand tricks. 'Don't think *they* are driving me away, Félicia: it's *he*.' 'Who do you mean?' 'Oscar.'

"He's a remarkable man, Madame Joseph, but you and I know that there is something odd about him. I think I've told you that our mother was neurasthenic. She had a perfect horror of our father. I remember the poor dear once saying to me—'I sometimes wonder how you and Louis ever came to be born at all. . . .' What was I saying? Oh, yes . . . you can imagine the effect his words had on me. 'But this Oscar of yours is dead, Louis: you know that!' 'People don't realize the power of the dead,' he answered. 'When they want to warn you off something they've got more than one way of doing it—they're cunning!' and he laughed—you know that way he has of laughing sometimes—until I could stand it no longer. 'Don't laugh like that, Louis!' I said: 'you'll make me have a breakdown. . . . Dearest, I really do think you must be going mad!' At that he became serious again. He stared at me with those lovely childlike eyes of his. My heart was torn, seeing him like that, his face all drawn with fatigue and looking so sad. 'It's *because* I'm mad that, from now on, I'm going to live like a madman. There's no point in living sensibly, Félicia, when one is mad. . . . ' "

At that moment, Madame Joseph's baby started to wail. She gave it a shaking, and asked a question. Didn't it ever occur to Mademoiselle Landin, that her brother sometimes drank a little too much?

"There's not a soberer man in the world! I've often known him *look* as though he were drunk when he hasn't touched a drop. It's something inside him that goes to his head, if you know what I mean . . . something to do with his nerves, I think. . . . But to go back to what I was saying about all the wicked talk that's going round. It's just as well that you should know he's still in close touch with the people who are winding up the Revolou estate, and will go on with his part of the business even though he *is* to live in Paris. He has made over the furniture and securities to me, and will send me three hundred francs a month—which is more than I shall need. But I shall feel worried about him. Not that I see much of him here—away all day at work, as he is, and running round the streets after dark, but sooner or later he always comes home, and looking after him gives me something to do. And there are days when he suddenly becomes quite calm, when he seems satisfied, relaxed, almost happy. Still, I shall go now and again to Paris to see him: he's promised that. . . . But how am I going to fill my days now that I've nothing to look forward to?"

"Perhaps Mr. Right'll come along, Miss. You're quite an heiress now—with your regular income, your securities, and a houseful of furniture!"

"How abominable! What do you take me for, Madame Joseph?"

"*I* don't see what's so abominable about it!" protested the concierge, thoroughly put out by this attack. "Life's not over at forty-five, you know."

Félicia Landin looked at the other's coarse and stringy figure:

"The very idea! . . ."

"All very well to turn your nose up, miss: but you don't know what you're turning it up *at*!"

VIII

THE life of the Revolou family gradually took on a definite shape and fell into a regular rhythm. Denis now companioned Rose on her early morning journeys, and stood with her waiting for the first tram. Almost always the car's cyclopean eye emerged from thick mist. Once inside, Denis would resume his interrupted sleep, leaning against his sister, and she, too, would doze until they reached the boulevards. From there on they went their different ways, he to school, she to her bookshop which was situated in an alley off the Rue Sainte-Catherine. It was a spot which had been familiar to both of them in the days when they had never wanted for pocket-money, and spent long hours every Thursday rummaging among the shelves.

It was a source of great comfort to Denis through those long and gloomy days that he could follow his sister in imagination as she moved about behind the counters, or climbed up and down ladders. They met at the half-past-six tram. Denis would always open the conversation by asking the same question: "Any of the customers ask your advice?" It had become a ritual phrase ever since, in the enthusiasm of her early days at the shop, Rose claimed to direct the reading of her fellow citizens and to guide their steps along the road to the masterpieces. But the first gentleman who had asked her help had wanted something "amusing." "Is it amusing? Are you sure that *La Négresse Blonde* is amusing? . . . And what about '*J'aurai un bel enterrement*'? D'you think it'll make me laugh?"

"Some find it amusing, and some don't," she had answered. "It is all a matter of temperament."

"How about this? Is it rather—you know what I mean? Not that I'm particularly keen on smutty books. . . . If one wants to imagine things, one doesn't need any help from books. . . ."

"He actually dared to say a thing like that to you?" Denis had been furious. "How many books of verse have you sold since you went there?"

"One *Jardin de l'Infante*, apart from what your friend Pierrot orders from the *Mercure*. . . ."

"You didn't tell me you had seen Pierrot. . . ."

In the daytime, the house, relieved of their presence, belonged to Julien. He had reached the point of condescending to leave his room while his mother gave it an airing and re-made his bed. One fine morning he ventured to take a turn round the garden, after first assuring himself that all the members of the Cavailhes family were out of sight. He would not run the risk of meeting any human creature. At five in the afternoon he went back to bed. His mother brought him his evening meal. He was forever deep in some detective story. Madame Revolou never saw her two younger children except at dinner. She descended as from some inaccessible star, bringing news of what was happening in that remote bedroom, as though the incidents enacted within its four walls could compete for interest with the occurrences of the great world. On the rare occasions when Julien consented to open his lips, she told them what he had said, adding her own marginal comments. She also reported on the state of his appetite and on his digestive whims.

One day there was terrific excitement. Julien had asked for a newspaper! Unfortunately, his eye had been caught by the account of a wedding, the guests at which were all personally known to him, and this had brought on a relapse. She blamed herself for being so careless. She ought to have gone through the paper before letting him see it. Now he would have to make up for all the ground he had lost.

What made her especially sad was to see the way in which her eldest son, who had once been so proud of his appearance, now refused to wash. "Don't you remember how he always used to take two baths a day, and regularly had his nails manicured? . . . I can keep his face and hands and feet reasonably clean . . . but otherwise! . . ."

Denis had devised a system by which, without listening to what she was saying, he could simulate the appearance of deep interest and concentrated attention. He would keep his eyes fixed on Rose, whose thoughts, like his own, were elsewhere. She was dropping with fatigue, she said, and it was true that her face had lost most of its colour since she had been at the shop and that her, eyes were ringed with shadow, even though old man Chardon, out of consideration for a former customer, did let her sit down when she was not actually serving. But she did not, in any way, excite pity. The glow of an inner happiness burned through her face to such an extent that Denis could almost feel a sensation of physical warmth. She laughed at his slightest word, as though there were in her an overplus of contentment and joy for which she had got to find an outlet. She had never been gentler with him. But she rarely asked him questions, and of this he complained bitterly.

"You're no longer interested in me."

"Do you want me to talk to you about your work? That, thank Heavens, has never been a cause of anxiety . . . and, after all, you *are* seventeen. . . ."

"It's not a question of my work, but of me, Rose, of me, your seventeen-year-old brother."

"But you know perfectly well that I listen to you. I do nothing else *but* listen to you. You're the one, really, who won't do the talking."

"What can one say to a great girl when she's one's sister?"

"Then what are you complaining of, silly?"

"I've explained it all once—of the fact that you're not interested in me, that you don't find me an interesting person."

"Oh, come now!"

"You think I'm much less intelligent than Pierrot Costadot."

"You've not got his peculiar gifts . . . which reminds me, I saw him yesterday. He's coming out here on Thursday. He wants to show you some bits of his *Cybele*."

"So you've seen him? What did you talk about?"

She said that they had talked about his poetry, but that he had not stayed long. . . . *He'd* pay a trip one Thursday too, thought Denis, just to see what was going on. . . . One part of the day, in particular, was a source of worry to him—the lunch interval, those two hours which she spent away from the shop. At six, after closing time, she ran for her tram. . . . It was not tact that made Denis hesitate to put his plan into execution, but fear of what he might discover, and a sort of apathy about Pierrot Costadot.

Sure enough, Thursday came bringing with it young Costadot on his bicycle, though a cold rain was falling. He arrived just as Denis was beginning to hope that he would not turn up at all. He took him into the small drawing-room, and at once turned the conversation on to *Cybele*, while all around them the country-side lay sodden under melting snow. He felt strongly that Pierrot had something he wanted to say to him, that he was with difficulty keeping back some piece of important news of which he was full. But he had no desire to know what it was, and kept the talk on the subject of his friend's poem, of which he was im-mensely fond.

"I haven't got much further with it," said Costadot. "My mind's been full of something quite different. . . . D'you really want me to talk about *Cybele*" (he was touched, indeed, quite overcome by his friend's enthusiasm). . . . "I've just got to the part where Atys is false to her, and where she surprises him with the nymph Sangaris. I've been grinding away for the last week at about twenty lines or so."

"Can you repeat them by heart?"

"Would you like to hear them—honestly?"

He threw away the cigarette which he had just lit.

"I needn't explain that here, as formerly, it's Cybele talking to herself. . . ."

He started, with that curious nasal drawl which, for the moment, had lost its power to charm his friend.

> In the high wood the tearing of the gale
> Mimicked the sea. Between the trunks a pale
> Flicker of light, for one brief moment toss'd
> About the darkness, showed, now wholly lost
> Each in the other, two pale worlds of flesh,
> Atys and Sangaris caught in the hot mesh
> Of love. And in that livid instant all my hate
> Stood suddenly at gaze. A bitter paradise
> Held them immune within my myriad arms
> That thresh'd above them. Safe from the alarms
> Of Heaven they lay in ecstasy. Powerless my eyes
> To start them from delight. Gleaming with rain and sweat
> Their bodies lay, nor could the fiery threat
> Of thunder touch them. On their joined langours fell
> Drop by slow drop, made harmless by the spell
> Of their linked slumbers, all the slow
> Seepage of my branches. To and fro
> I waved tormented arms. Body to body cleaves.
> The air is odorous with scent of wet and trodden leaves.

Denis took his two hands from his face. After a short pause, he said:

"Loneliness confronted by the love of others . . . that is what, fundamentally, your Cybele symbolizes: the mortal creature gazing into the unplumbed depths of a delight in which she can have no part, whose awareness of love is confined to a sense of that solitary flame burning within her, yet without the power to bring light or warmth to any human being. . . ."

"But, Denis, we have nothing to do with such things. Are you mad? We have not begun to love, you and I . . . not 'seriously,' as you used to say."

His friend made no reply, and Costadot, leaning over the fire, went on.

"And, until we do, we can find pleasure only in the love of

others. I wanted to be quite sure about that before I told you. . . .
I wouldn't say anything before it was all settled."

Denis had looked up now, and was staring at him. He was
filled with hatred for the face to which the effort of bicycling and
the warmth of the fire had imparted so high a colour; for the
downy fluff on the glowing cheeks.

"What has happened was so utterly unexpected! Robert and I
have been terribly wrong about poor mamma. She really is upset
by all the awful things that have happened to you . . . and now
she's made up her mind to do the very last thing we should ever
have expected of her. For a long time I just couldn't believe it,
but the evidence is too strong. I've been legally declared of age,
old man, and the family fortune is to be shared out between the
three of us—not only papa's money, but mamma's as well. . . ."

Denis broke in impatiently:

"What's that got to do with me?"

"But don't you understand, Denis? It means that Robert will
be independent, that he'll be able to manage now until he's
through with his medical studies—even with a wife. What d'you
say to that?"

Denis had got up. He stood facing the fireplace, his back to
Pierre. When he spoke it was without any sign of emotion.

"You forget that Rose has other things to bother about now.
She's turned the page, she's no longer interested in all *that*. Why
are you laughing like a little idiot?"

"Nonsense! she's not turned any page. . . . If she's said nothing
to you, it's because she didn't believe, any more than we did, that
my mother would be as good as her word . . . didn't want to
rouse hopes in you that might be disappointed."

"So, they've been seeing one another, is that it?" Denis's tone
was quite detached.

"For the last three weeks they've been lunching together at a
dairy not far from the Faculty of Medicine. I go there, too, on
Thursdays. I've been longing to tell you. It was Rose who didn't
want me to. Well, how about it, old man?"

Denis shook his head. He didn't see how Pierrot came into the picture at all.

"But I *do*—I'm terribly important. Between ourselves, mamma is frightfully keen about this sharing business, but she keeps on saying that landed property brings in less and less, that the cost of repairs is soaring, that taxes are increasing and dividends falling, and that Robert can't possibly take on the responsibility of keeping a whole family. . . . *Now* do you see?"

"You can reassure her on that point. We don't want a penny piece from her son."

He had turned round, and the face which he showed to Pierrot was drained of colour. His friend was struck with consternation.

"I've been a brute, Denis. Please forgive me. It's all so horribly sordid, and it doesn't matter two hoots. Robert'll be earning his living in a few years. . . besides, he'll have my all share, as well as his own. . . . The only thing that matters is that Rose's happiness should not be compromised . . . apart from that. . . ."

"So *you've* decided, have you, that Rose's happiness depends on your brother? Are you so sure of that?"

Costadot, touched on the raw, flared up. "That's a thing neither you nor I can decide. It concerns no one but them. My own view is. . . . Look here, Denis, I lunch with them every Thursday, and I keep my eyes skinned. Robert has to stay late at the hospital, and is always the last to turn up. If only you could see Rose's face when he comes in! 'Powerless my eyes to start them from delight'—d'you remember? . . . My Cybele cannot distinguish pleasure from happiness, but love can be wholly present even before a man and a woman have so much as exchanged a kiss."

Denis asked:

"Do they kiss?"

Pierrot's laugh was a shade too loud.

"What a question, old man!"

"It's time you started back, Pierrot," said Denis, who had walked over to the window. "It's snowing in earnest, and it'll soon be quite dark. The road will be impossible. . . . But I was forgetting: that doesn't matter to you now, does it? . . . you can afford a car."

"Please don't talk like that, Denis: I hate it."

They went down the back stairs in order to fetch Pierrot's bicycle from the kitchen where he had left it.

"Why should you hate it? Is it so awful to have a bank account and to be able to draw cheques? Not ashamed of that, are you? You've got your duty to think of, your duty as a respectable member of society. You'll end by being just like your mother. You're rather like her as it is. . . . You've got her voice, and if you go on putting on weight. . . ."

They were in the scullery which lay between the staircase and the kitchen. It was badly lit by a paraffin lamp. Denis could not see the effect of his mockery, but when Costadot spoke again he could barely recognize his voice.

"What have I done to you, Denis?"

There was no answer. He could hear Denis's loud breathing. Pots and pans gleamed on the shelves over their heads. Jars of jam stood ranged in rows. There was a pervasive smell of spices and washing. Denis panted as though he had been running. Suddenly, leaning against the wall, with his face in his hands, he burst into tears.

"Denis!" said Costadot again: "what have I done to you?"

He took his friend by the shoulders, but the latter shook himself free. Pierrot would not be silenced.

"Why won't you tell me that I've done to you?"

"I don't know . . . I'd tell you if I did . . . I don't know why I'm so miserable. . . ."

That night he complained of a headache and went to bed without eating any dinner. Rose sat by him for a while He wanted nothing but to be left in peace. His sister said that she would stay with him, reading and not saying a word. To this he agreed. She looked at him when she thought he could not see what she was doing. She knew that Pierrot had been there that afternoon.

'He's hurt because I haven't trusted him, because I've been deceitful,' she thought. He, for his part, interpreted her presence at his bedside as meaning 'I'm asking you to forgive me.' It seemed simpler to both of them to say nothing.

IX

IN the evenings it was always Robert Costadot who arrived first at the statue of "Youth and the Chimæra" in the broad walk of the Public Gardens. He knew that at that very moment Rose would be leaving Chardon's bookshop, and that in ten minutes' time he would see her coming towards him through the glittering lace-work of the sprinklers and the mingled smell of dust, wet grass and painted iron chairs. He waited for her, impatient to be confirmed in his belief that she really was like the image which he carried in his heart, like the Rose Revolou with whom he had danced all last season . . . and this year, too, with the same rapt and radiant face, always wearing dresses that matched so well the graceful slimness of her body. . . . It was seldom in those days that some little detail of negligence did not give evidence of her angelic indifference to trifles—a shoulder-strap showing, a hook unfastened, a rebellious lock of hair which had escaped the eagle eye of Monsieur Tardy. . . . "She is so untidy," said her mother. But Robert had loved her untidiness. In a girl who could command every refinement of luxury he had found it not unattractive.

Meanwhile, Rose would be hurriedly washing her hands in the back-shop, saying good-night to Chardon, and delightedly breathing in the fresh air as she walked along the Cours de l'Intendance. The setting sun would put an aureole about the dusty little figure, with its pale face and lustreless hair, which soon Robert would greet with that same sinking of the heart,

that same feeling of irritation, which came on him each evening
when he realized, with disappointment, how different she was
now from the adored image which he stored up in his memory.
But her eyes were lovelier than they had ever been, less focussed
even now than then upon this weary world where all, save love,
is care and torment.

She was blissfully unaware that her cheap little dress of mourning black had not been brushed, that the heels of her shoes were
trodden over. She flew on her way, crossing the Place de
Quinconces, seeing nobody, until, at the end of the Cours de
Gourgues, the great black and gold railings of the Public Gardens
came into view.

Then it was that Robert caught sight of her coming towards
him. He had had plenty of time during the past twenty-four
hours to forget what she really looked like. He took her hands,
bent towards her, caught the faint, sour odour of her body. Then
she broke free, the better to devour him with her eyes. She drank
in the sight of him, assuaging in long, deep draughts the thirst
that had been with her all through the weary day. But her eager
gaze was blind. She saw no disappointment in his face, nor how
his love changed suddenly to pity—pity for the girl whom
humble tasks had worn and fretted, pity for himself and for the
life which henceforth he must live within the narrow limits of
her poverty. And simultaneously, he was assailed by a sense of
shame that he should feel such things. He had to force himself to
make the gestures, to say the words, which might reassure her
should the slightest hint of doubt awake. But she judged his
tenderness by the standards of her own. Sometimes she said to
him:

"You look tired and depressed: you are working too hard."

It would never have occurred to her that he might be suffering
from disappointment. He had sought her hand in spite of the
disaster which had ruined and all but dishonoured the Revolous.
He had stood out against his terrifying mother. . . . Why, then,
should she have any doubts of him?

She led him always to their favourite bench which was on the island, behind the bandstand. If it was already occupied, they took two chairs. She said little, relaxing happily in the joy of his presence. Ducks and fat goldfish were busy quarrelling over scraps of bread thrown to them by some child. Rose had sailed into sheltered waters. She made vague answers when Robert talked about looking for a flat, about choosing furniture. Whatever he did would be right. Already, in anticipation, she loved the place where they would live together, the room in which he would hold her all night in his arms. Her thoughts would go no further than that shared repose. She was already building the nest, in imagination, which promised sleep beside him. She would be going out to work no longer. He had suggested that she should leave Chardon's at once, but this she had refused to do, saying that she would not be an expense to him before she bore his name.

Had he really insisted she would, no doubt, have yielded. Perhaps, he thought, he had admitted the soundness of her arguments a little too quickly, as though he were anxious that she should not abandon her means of livelihood. Could it be that some unadmitted thought lurked at the back of his mind? Did he believe that there was still time to go back on the decision already made? The small, confiding head lay heavy on his shoulder. The lustreless, dusty hair tickled his cheek. . . . Such an idea was unimaginable, unthinkable.

"We've got only an hour before the last tram leaves," he said.

They went to a dairy and had two eggs each and a cup of chocolate. Rose paid no attention to what she was eating. Things that shocked Robert had no effect on her—a badly washed cup, grease stains, and the dirty marks left by glasses on the table. She saw only her love. The squalid world about it, inhabited by those who have no money, she banished from her consciousness.

On this particular evening he said:

"No one would ever believe that you used to live in one of the finest houses in this city. It has taken only two months for you to get quite out of the habit of luxury."

"Luxury?"

She raised her tired eyes to his. He noticed a few blackheads on the side of her nose. Her neck, he saw, was thin.

"There is only *one* luxury."

He understood. She meant their love.

His large hand closed on her little one with its worn nails. She must never know, never guess! All his life must be one long deceit. It would be so easy to pull the wool over eyes so wholly blind.

He walked with her to the boulevard where the Léognan tram was waiting.

"Don't forget about Saturday," she said: "the day after to-morrow. You're coming to Léognan, you know, for the night. We shall have the whole evening together: we shall have until the next morning. We can stay out late: the evenings are so still."

He was, he reflected, about to rivet yet another link to the chain which held him. On Saturday he would enter her home in the guise of one officially betrothed.

She was already on the platform of the tram. A street lamp picked out the posters on the walls of the terminus. He waved his hand. Rose kept her eyes fixed on her future husband until the tram turned the corner. Then she went inside and sat down absorbed in her happiness.

She knew when they were approaching the open country without having to open her eyes. Into the city stench there drifted a smell of fig-trees and cattle-sheds.

While she was driving deeper into the peace of the rural world, Robert, moving in the opposite direction, plunged into the heart of the stifling city, padding softly past walls that were burning hot to the touch. Here and there the heady smell of limes spilled into the street from near-by gardens. He could see through open windows into unlit rooms, and make out against the dark interiors the vague white smudges of human faces.

It was impossible for him to go to his room without first looking in on his mother. It had become an established rule that she could never go to sleep until her sons were all back, and had come to give her a good-night kiss. Besides, it was only nine o'clock, and he knew that she would be sitting in the darkness by her open window. He dreaded the coming interview, yet longed for it as for something that might bring him help, though what kind of help he did not know. What had seemed, a moment back, utterly inconceivable, took its place, on a sudden, among a host of possibilities. Hadn't he so often heardhis mot her, calm and unperturbed in many a crisis, say—"We'll find a way out, never fear"?

And she always did find a way out. He had never lost the habit of seeing his mother through the eyes of a child. Nothing irreparable could ever happen so long as she was there.

Still, she seemed resigned now to the idea of his marriage, and no longer raised objections, though he noticed that she had so far refrained from mentioning any specific date. Like Rose, she wouldn't hurry him, because of the examination hanging over his head. . . .

As he mounted the stairs he was seized by a spasm of self-disgust. . . . He wouldn't let himself even think such things. . . . Rose was to be his wife. Already an older picture was before his eyes, the picture of his partner at last winter's balls. And it ousted from his vision a shabby little work-girl who no longer had a mother's watchful eye upon her.

X

MADAME COSTADOT was seated, not by the open window, but at her desk which was lit by a reading-lamp. The room was hermetically sealed against the intrusion of mosquitoes. A bunch of lavender always used to be kept in the night table, and this piece of furniture still retained a dubious odour.

The old lady presented her forehead to Robert. But she did not look at him.

"I was just going through the estimate for the Cours de Gourgues."

She always referred to her house-property by the names of the streets in which the various houses were situated. She would say: "We shall soon have to think about a new roof for the Cours de Martinique," or "There's a gutter needed in the Quai de Paludate."

"I'm afraid we've chosen a bad year for handing over your inheritance. I'm beginning to wonder whether I oughtn't to advance you something . . . yes," she went on, her mind busy with its own thoughts, "but where am I to find the money?"

He made no answer. She could hear her words echoing in the emptiness of the poor weak-willed creature at her side. She could feel that he was in some way cut off from her, but did not know what to do for the best. With every day that passed he would become a little more deeply involved. But she had made up her mind that until the date of the marriage was actually fixed, she would make no frontal attack. But her least word, little though she consciously realized the fact, did, to some extent, take on the nature of an attack.

Robert gazed at the solid mass of his mother, the desk and the chair. In the harsh concentration of the light they looked as though they had been, all three, carved in a single piece from a solid block of wood. His vacillating heart went out suddenly to the child, who at that very moment was feeling on her closed eyes the first faint touch of country air less than three miles from the city limits, and smelling already the scent of heath and pine.

The tram stopped, and Rose got out. When, as usual, she said to the conductor—"See you in the morning," he replied:

"Not tomorrow, miss: Lavaud's on duty tomorrow morning."

He had had some skin disease when young, and there was still something about him of the ailing child, though he wore a thick wedding-ring on his finger. She wished him good-night and began to skirt the shadowy park. She had a feeling that she would like to stroke the branches which pushed beyond the low wall in which tufts of maiden-hair fern were growing. Better than any human beings they knew of her love. It would be truer to say that they formed part of it, that they played a rôle in the secret world of her delight, wrapping it round with the rustle of their leaves. It mattered nothing to them that she was shabbily dressed and as ill-cared-for as any other poor working-girl who gets up early by candle-light and has no hot water in which to wash. They spread above her now the same fronds under which she had wandered in the gay summer dresses that had looked like flowers.

There was a "snack" regularly left out for her in the dining-room. As always when she got home, Denis was standing at the far end. He did not come forward to kiss her. It was she who went and laid a hand upon his forehead.

"You ought to get your hair cut," she said.

His tousled head looked bigger than ever. He fixed her with an owl-like eye.

"How's Robert?" he asked.

"All right," she said. "You know, don't you, that he's coming on Saturday to dine and spend the night?"

Denis wanted to know in which room they were to put him.

"The Green Room."

"We can't, it's got a leaky gutter."

"That won't matter in this weather."

"A single storm would be enough to make it overflow. Why not the Carnation Room?"

"Yes, perhaps that *would* be better."

She had always imagined Robert in the Green Room. Hastily in her imagination she rearranged the fancied setting, and transported him to the narrower stage of the room he was to be given where the chintz had a pattern of carnations, red and pink.

Denis asked her whether she would like a stroll before going to bed. She would have dearly liked to walk down the avenue where the stunted trees gave glimpses of the spangled sky, but her legs would not support her a moment longer. She would scarcely be able to get through her prayers, and would fall at once into a sleep of sheer exhaustion.

As she passed Julien's door, she heard her mother's voice.

"Is that you, Rose? Don't come in: your brother is washing. Any news?"

"No; Robert's coming on Saturday."

"So he is. . . . I've got a surprise for you both. Yes, I have," she insisted, her voice taking on the intonation of a child. . . . "A real surprise, you'll see!"

Rose hated it when her mother spoke in that affected, roguish way. She said to herself as she undressed, "Poor mummy's not her old self."

Denis wandered alone down the tree-shadowed paths. The darkness was in tune with his own inner gloom. Among all the planets, the earth alone was alive with scraping crickets. 'In ten years,' he said to himself, 'in twenty, I shall remember this evening, and how miserable I felt!' He was alone, not in the middle of a stretching plain, not in a garden, but in the spaces of a universe peopled with innumerable worlds. In two days' time, at this same hour, Robert would be with them . . . and suddenly he was aware of the scent of lime as, on that evening still in the future, when the two lovers would be aware of it in their turn. He could feel in anticipation the way in which their love would bring disturbance to this scene of peace. On a sudden, the leaves above his head began to rustle, as though the trees were responding to a passion of which they soon would be the witnesses. Denis thought: 'Perhaps by Saturday the weather will have broken. We may have a storm. . . .' and at once, in imagination, he was breathing in the scent of sodden earth and branches weighed down with a load of moisture. He could feel upon his forehead, as Rose and Robert would feel it, a shower of warm drops. Only through the hearts of others did the night reach him. There was nothing direct and immediate in his contact with it.

He turned and went back to the house, dreaming what such a night would have meant to Pierrot Costadot, whose only relations with human kind came through the mediation of nature. He had never been able to free himself, or others, not even God, from the obsessive influence of the tangible world. . . . How did that odd poem go which Pierrot had written for Rose when he had had that dog-like adoration for her? He could remember only the two first verses, and began to murmur them.

> Still unawakened in the mesh
> Of sense I face the shadowed dawn:
> Nor yet can free myself forlorn
> From being captive to your flesh.
>
> I lay me down in the noon glare,
> Burned up by all your body's heat.
> All through the day till night shall greet
> My eyes, I feel that furnace there.

Was Pierrot still in love with Rose? Was he jealous of his brother? His passions lay silenced in an adoring contemplation of *things*. 'What do *I* care,' thought Denis, 'about the earth and the grass and things that are blind, deaf and without feeling?'

His candle was burning on the hall table. When he reached the second floor it occurred to him to pay a visit to the Carnation Room where Robert would be sleeping. Another name for it was "Uncle Devize's room," after that great uncle who had died during the Second Empire. It belonged to nobody in particular, and the children entered it only when they were playing hide and seek over the whole house.

He set his candle on the chest-of-drawers. The furniture dated from the Bourbon Restoration. He remembered that the vases which stood under glass bells on the mantelpiece had, on one side, an engraved design of a pair of shepherds, and, on the other, two angels adoring a chalice—so that they could be used indifferently in a living-room or on an altar. He remembered, too, that he had once amused himself by shaking the low railing outside the window which had worked loose in its sockets. He pushed open the shutters that gave upon the fresh and scented emptiness of night, just to make sure that the rail did, in fact, move beneath his hand. Exerting all his strength, he tried in vain to pull it from its fastenings. He saw, in imagination, Robert leaning against it with his great athletic frame which never gave the impression of power because the face above it was so devoid of energy, because its owner was so undecided in his movements. How was it that so manifest a contradiction did not move Rose with feelings of disgust and irritation? Denis could imagine the great chest leaning against this perilous support . . . pitching forward . . . falling . . . . He drove the image from his mind and shut the window.

XI

ON Saturday, Rose, Robert and Denis all travelled by the six o'clock tram. Denis stood on the front platform, but because Rose was tired, the engaged couple went inside and sat down. She did not look at Robert. His presence was enough for her. She could feel the material of his sleeve against her bare arm. For two whole days they would be together. Such happiness seemed to her almost unimaginable. . . . But what were those few hours when set against the intimacy of every day and every night? How marvellous life was! Robert said not a word. She knew how difficult it was to get inside his mind. . . . But she would have all the time she needed for learning the mystery of his thoughts.

The tram overtook the Saturday evening cyclists. There was much tinkling of bells, much young laughter. Cows in the burnt-up fields were nosing round in search of scattered tufts of grass. A strong smell came from the open cattle-sheds.

'This is a decisive step,' Robert was thinking. 'In the eyes of the world, of the servants, I am being welcomed as an affianced lover . . . and it is just as well. When something has been decided, one can't go back on it.' He was quite calm, and sensitive to the atmosphere of happiness of which he knew himself to be the cause.

Denis did not so much as glance at the seated pair within the tram. When the pace increased he closed his eyes, threw back his head, and felt the country freshness on his face. A series of confused pictures took shape within his mind. These he followed until they reached a certain point of shamelessness, and then abandoned. No one would ever know the things he thought about. Do others, he wondered, carry within themselves the same sort of hidden world, the existence of which they never betray in words? Is there, in all men, this gap between what they will admit and what conceal? Does God see the swarming confusion deep in the heart of every human creature? What does "getting rid" of evil thoughts mean?—just refusing to be aware of what is there, all the same. . . . He heard Rose's voice.

"Denis, take Robert's bag."

When the tram stopped at the point where a short lane led off to the stables, they were suddenly aware of scraping crickets and an immense humming of bees round a lime-tree. While Rose went to change her dress, Denis took Robert up to Uncle Devize's room.

"It looks north, so the heat won't bother you. When you undress to-night, you'd better go to bed in the dark because of the mosquitoes."

He left their guest but pushed open the door again to say:

"Be careful of that rail in front of the window . . . it's loose. . . . This is a frightful old barn of a place. . . ."

"I thought your father had done a good deal in the way of repairs. . . ."

"He did . . . the least important ones, but not the most expensive. . . ."

Denis had made the remark quite innocently, but he kept his eyes on Robert.

"Which do you call the most expensive?" asked the latter.

"In the first place, the roof. We've had to put you in this room facing north, because the one you ought to have had lets in the rain. When there's a storm we have to put buckets and bowls up in the attics. All the ceilings are more or less in holes. You can imagine what re-roofing a great barrack of a place like this would mean. . . . Even in his most prosperous days, my father kept putting off the evil moment when he'd really have to shell out . . . and now it won't wait any longer."

"What are you going to do about it?"

Denis hesitated for a moment, and then said:

"I think mother means to ask your advice. . . ."

"I've none to give" (a note of firmness had suddenly come into Robert's voice). "It's no business of mine. We've got too many houses on our hands as it is. . . ."

"Then we shall just have to sell," sighed Denis, "and for next to nothing. . . . Don't say anything about that to Rose or mamma. . . . It would be a terrible blow to them. . . . You see, they've been living in a bit of a dream world . . . imagining that you'd take all that off their shoulders. . . ."

"I most certainly shall say something about it," broke in Robert drily: " . . . I'm determined to get it all clear."

(His voice, the very way he stressed his words, was his mother's.)

"I don't want there to be any misunderstanding."

"Are you there, Robert?"

Rose came into the room. She was wearing a white dress trimmed with broderie anglaise. Her neck and arms were bare. She must have had a bath. A smell of freshness and Eau de Cologne hung about her. Despite the thinness of her features and

4

the way in which the sinews of her neck showed too promi-
nently, she did now resemble his cherished memories of her. He
drew her to him and gently sniffed the sweetness of her body.
She showed no surprise, was fearful only that he might crush the
beautiful trimming of her dress. She stepped back a pace and
passed her hand over the rough skin of his cheeks, over his reddish
moustache and handsome lips. He bit her finger. Suddenly they
heard something heavy crash into the rhododendron bush. Rose
uttered a faint cry.

"It's the rail in front of your window," said Denis. "I pitched
it down."

Rose clutched Robert's arm.

"Why, you might have leaned on it!"

Denis's face as he looked at them was pale.

"Here's the surprise I was telling you about!"

Julien was standing by his mother. In his short jacket and black
tie he looked fat, pale and almost dignified, as though conscious
of the solemn note struck by his presence at the evening's festi-
vities. There was a self-satisfied smile on the vapid face.

"You have achieved a miracle, Robert, a real miracle," went
on Madame Revolou in the rather mincing tones which she
assumed on social occasions.

"I am not forgetful of the fact that I am the head of the
Revolou family," said Julien. "It was my duty to welcome you
to Léognan. I have assumed the weight of my obligations. . . . I
shall pay dearly for such rashness . . . but no matter."

His mother was radiant. She listened with amazement to the
questions he was putting to Robert Costadot.

"Was the Horse-Show as brilliant as ever this year? Who won
the Cup? Castelbajec, I'll bet, and with Favori II, eh? That's
pretty comic, I must say! I suppose you know I almost bought
him last year?—what, you don't?—Saw his capabilities at the first
glance—a foal out of Stella. . . . Remember Stella?"

Robert looked at Rose. Yes, she really was like the girl he had

once danced with. She had drunk a glass of champagne, and her
cheeks were flushed. But that bright happiness in her eyes?—no,
it was he who was responsible for that!

He heard Denis's voice.

"D'you know what happened just now up in Uncle Devize's
room, mamma?—the rail in front of the window. . . ."

Madame Revolou sighed:

"This house is just falling to pieces. It's a never-ending source
of anxiety . . ." and she glanced at Robert.

He was bending above his plate, and made no reply. She took
the opportunity, therefore, of pressing her point:

"Sell, you'll say. . . . But what sort of a price should we get? It
does at least give us a roof over our heads, and provides us with
poultry, vegetables, milk and wood. . . . I sometimes wonder
what will become of us. . . ."

To this particular expression of wonder Robert was clearly
expected to respond, but he had put up a thick screen of indifference. He could hear, as distinctly as the whirr of an alarm-clock,
his mother's words of warning: "Pretend you're deaf: pretend
not to understand!"

A certain awkwardness hung over the rest of the meal, which
came to an end before the lamps were brought in. There was
something about the shadowy room, in which only the cloth and
Julien's shirt-front reflected the fading light, that Rose found
faintly menacing. She drew Robert into the front hall, and
slipped an old cape over her white dress.

"Let's get away while they're having coffee. Come on, hurry.
There's not a scrap of wind. It's just as I imagined it would be!"

He took her bare arm and gently squeezed it. He said to himself: 'I must concentrate my thoughts on this arm, this body
which is already mine. . . . I'll let them get rid of Léognan . . .
we'll have a tiny home of our own in Bordeaux. . . . But even so
I shall have to fork out so's her family can live somewhere. . . .
Perhaps it'll mean no more than making a 'contribution'. . . .
After all they're not absolutely on their beam-ends.'

Rose began to hurry. She was eager to reach the bench in the lime-grove which she had fixed on in her mind as the place that was to be the scene of their happiness. She felt as though she were lifted high above the earth, as though she were being carried forward, drawn on, by some power she could not name. It seemed to sweep across the plain with a noise that almost deafened her. Two hedgehogs moved across the path.

"Here we are," she said: "follow me."

Feeling him physically there beside her in the deeper darkness made by the lime-grove at the heart of the dark night, she grieved to think that her happiness was slipping, second by second, through her fingers and could not be halted. But there was comfort in the knowledge that the current was as yet but in its upper waters. So far she had but dipped a cup in the magic liquid and raised it to her lips. She could spend all the rest of her life bathing in it. Why worry? These moments were less precious than she had supposed them to be. She heard him breathing at her side, and it seemed as though she were afloat upon the rhythmically moving waves of the sea. To them she could trust herself, on them embark with no thought of turning back. Month by month and year by year she would be carried on into eternity by the flesh, the blood, the heart of this man who was her man, her's among the host of his fellows. She could feel his agitation. There was nothing to warn her that the being at her side was full of base and troubled thoughts, that his mind was muddied with suspicions and at grip with figures. His great body was all that, just then, responded to the young girl. He had loosed it from constraint and now it followed at a little distance like a hunter who, with mind elsewhere, traces, though without consciously seeing, the movements of his dog as it sniffs at the leaves and scratches at the damp earth.

In the billiard-room, with its window wide open to the terrace, Madame Revolou was saying to Julien:

"They won't be back yet awhile. You mustn't wait for them. You've been up long enough for the first time. When two young people are engaged, one must forgive them a lot, but I can't help feeling that they are offering a poor return for the effort you have made . . . slipping off like that without so much as a word of apology!"

"There is no reason for them to show gratitude. It was my duty to be here tonight. I was determined even if it killed me, to do the honours of the house to my sister's future husband. There are times when a man should forget his poor broken-down body. The price I shall have to pay will be a heavy one. . . . I know perfectly well that I shan't get a wink of sleep tonight."

"Won't you take some allonal?"

"What an extraordinary person you are! Don't you realize even yet that my liver can't stand it? . . . It's the same with any kind of narcotic. . . . Oh, Denis! if you *must* smoke do for goodness sake go outside!"

Denis got up, strolled for a while on the terrace, and then sank into a wicker chair. At regular intervals, from close at hand, a toad gave forth a note purer than that of any nightingale. Bats lumbered into sudden view and vanished. Toads, bats, nightingales, the star-pocked night, the limes, the misery at his heart, were not of this world. Nothing in it could slake his spirits' thirst. He sat there, a dry and bitter youth, listening with all his ears. The plain was alive with sounds, but no human footfall came to break them. . . . Why was he afraid of death? He imagined himself, as he so often did, lying on his bed, opening a tube of sleeping tablets, and heard within himself of the familiar cry of terror. . . . No! he was alive, he was seventeen! Leaning down, he touched the warm flagstones. His mother raised her voice.

"All the same, I can't help being a little bit anxious. He might have said *something* reassuring. It was so obvious that he meant us to realize that he had nothing whatever to do with Léognan. . . . It's possible, of course, that he is just being merely tactful . . . or wholly indifferent."

"We've *got* to face the problem," said Julien. "The ceiling in

my room is in a perfectly appalling condition. One of these fine
days it will come crashing down on my head."

"I think my original plan offers the best chance. . . ."

Julien yawned.

"Which plan do you mean?"

"That I should make Léognan over to Rose when she marries,
on condition that we are allowed to stay here as long as we live, he
to be responsible for the upkeep of the place, and we paying an
annual rent. He'll have to promise, of course, not to sell it. If he
does, this arrangement must be considered null and void. . . ."
She paused and then continued: "That would be far the best
thing, but Léonie would never agree to his accepting such
terms. . . ."

Denis called from the terrace:

"He's not so weak as you think. He did at least have the
courage to stick to his intention of marrying her."

"Put out your cigarette and come in here." He did as he was
told and took a seat beside his mother. He heard Julien slap himself and grumble something about mosquitoes.

"What do *you* think we ought to do, Denis?" she asked.

"I think we'd better get Rose to find out how the land lies."

"She'd never agree . . . besides, mightn't it be a bit dangerous?"

"Oh, he's pretty well hooked. . . . There are *ways* of doing
these things, you know."

"There's no reason why she shouldn't say 'My mother wants
to sell Léognan. But that would break my heart. I'd always
dreamed of living here with you.' . . ."

"He ought to be made to see," said Julien, "that money spent
on the place would be a good investment. He might take up
cattle-farming, for instance."

"No harm in making the suggestion. We could always dis-
suade him later, after they are married. If he really went in for
that sort of thing, he might easily lose every penny he's got. . . .
So long as that's understood, I don't think it's at all a bad idea to
put things in that light. It might get round Léonie's objections."

"Then you agree that I should mention the matter to Rose?" asked Denis.

At that very moment, in the lime-grove, the young girl was saying in a low voice:

"Take your hand away—*please*, and sit further off."

She pulled her skirt down over her knees, and proceeded to tidy her hair. Was he angry, she asked? "Of course not," he replied, and took out his cigarette-case. A slight breach had appeared in the walls of her dream-world. She tried to read the expression on his face as it sprang suddenly into view when he cupped the flame of the match with his two hands. He had done nothing, tried to do nothing, that any engaged young man of his age would not have thought perfectly natural. But she felt sad. He had startled her into wakefulness, had forced her to listen to tones in his voice which she had never heard before, to take notice of actions that were strange to her, to find a new meaning even in his silence. . . . It was as though she were there with someone who bore no resemblance to the man who never left her heart. She wanted to find that man again.

He half turned from her.

"You *are* angry?"

"Of course I'm not. . . . It's only that you . . . that you don't understand, that you're so terribly innocent. . . . It seems to you quite natural to snuggle up to me, and then to start away. . . ."

He sounded sullen. There was a hint of vulgarity in his voice. She felt lonelier than if he had not been there at all.

He mustn't see that she was crying. She dared not move for fear of betraying herself. Her tears turned cold upon her cheeks. She felt her unhappiness as an offence against him. He threw away his cigarette. She took his hand and raised it humbly to her lips. He did not withdraw it, and pretended not to have noticed that her cheeks were wet. He thought vaguely of those other women he had left, who had not died as a result. . . . But she . . . he might just as well take her thin little bird's neck in his two hands and strangle her on the spot. He drew her to him again in a mingled access of pity, shame and desire. She lay in his arms motionless and trembling. She did not know what he wanted. He was breathing quickly. She said:

"There's someone on the path!"

She recognized Denis's footstep, and called out:

"We're here—in the lime-grove!"

Her brother took a few steps towards them.

"You'd better come in," he said. "Julien's told them to shut the windows and lock the front door."

He looked at the two indistinct figures that were just discernible in the dark shadows of the grove. The path, by comparison, seemed light when they emerged upon it.

They walked, all three, in silence, and entered by the billiard-room, blinking their eyes. Denis gave them both a hasty glance that took in her dishevelled dress, her tear-stained face, and Robert's expression of bewilderment.

He said:

"The candlesticks are over there. You, as guest, have the right to a lamp."

As soon as she was in her room, Rose went over to the window and leaned out.

'We didn't do anything wrong,' she thought: 'It's only because he loves me. . . .' But the word had lost its power to intoxicate. The sound in her ears was not the pulsing of her blood, but came from somewhere deeper. Was it a voice? *What* was it? Later she was to wonder whether she had not had a presentiment that evening. Something had happened inside her, something that was like a touch, so light as to be barely noticeable.

'Tomorrow morning I shall be happy again. I don't know what has happened to me tonight. . . .' She was impatient to see Robert's face by daylight. With the sun on it, she would look at it with different eyes, and be comforted.

Robert forgot to shut his window. A mosquito, two mosquitoes, sounded a warning, but too late. Hurriedly he extinguished the lamp, but was tormented all night long. The window from which the rail was missing framed a square of sky cut in a thin black tracery of leaves. The yawning hole made him feel as though he were sleeping in a house that was already half in ruins. Perhaps they had put him in that room deliberately, in order that he should see how necessary it was to have the place patched up? He refused to let his mind dwell on so absurd a thought, and concentrated it upon the memory of Rose. Surely, tonight, he had loved and wanted her? Nothing else mattered. He would go off with her and not bother his head about the Revolou family. But it was essential to get things straightened out before the marriage actually took place. . . . When the mosquitoes, gorged with his blood, or paralysed, perhaps, by the chill of dawn, left him a little peace, he fell asleep.

When, next morning, he saw Rose again in the dining-room, he thought that he had overcome his more dishonourable thoughts. She was dressed for church. Her muslin frock had been bought in the time when she and her mother had always got their clothes from Habrias. In the estate 'bus, drawn by a cart-horse and driven by Cavailhes, he felt himself one of the family. He joined with Rose and Denis in laughing at the bailiff who, though he had condescended to perform the functions of a coachman, made a point of not wearing any livery, but sported, instead, an old greenish bowler hat which he wore cocked at an angle over one eye. But when they had taken their places in the pew, the intense stares and whisperings of the congregation, and the proud, excited look on Rose's face, revived his sense of irritation. Anything that marked him out publicly as an affianced lover, he found intolerable. But was not the die cast? Could it be that he was still conscious of a mental reservation? He hated to feel that the door was locked and bolted behind him, though he fully realized that there was not the remotest hope of escape.

When the time for the sermon came, the faithful took advantage of the scraping of chairs as they resumed their seats to turn their heads and devour him with their eyes. He felt ashamed, and longed to comfort Rose with some such words as "What I'm feeling at this moment proves nothing." Yet, at the same time, her presence there caused him acute irritation. He charged her silently with harbouring a sense of triumph. 'I've managed to grab a husband even though we *are* ruined'—he imagined her thinking. He was just a poor fool who had been caught in a snare, lured into a trap, he, who might have married anybody. All these people must be thinking: 'It isn't as though there weren't heaps of pretty girls and with money, too.'

The Square was burned up with sunlight. Several old folk approached Robert and peered at him. He took refuge in the 'bus, where he sat waiting until Madame Revolou and Rose should have finished their shopping. He began to grumble:

"Why must all those fools keep looking at me like that?"

"They're revelling in their first sight of Miss Rose's intended," said Denis, with a malicious smirk.

"I thought the engagement was to be kept secret."

"Such a thing's impossible. You don't imagine that the Cavailhes are going to remain mum, do you?"

"If it was so impossible, why that solemn undertaking that no announcement should be made for a year?"

"Are you really and truly annoyed?" Denis asked the question with an air of innocence.

"Nothing irritates me more, I must confess, than this mania people have for making promises which they know perfectly well they can't keep. . . . It would have been far better, as soon as we realized that we shouldn't be able to get married for some time. . . ."

"I don't mind betting you won't wait until you've finished your time at the hospital. . . . We all feel sure of that."

Robert flushed with anger.

"Do you, really? Well, we'll see about that. I haven't *started* at the hospital yet."

Denis winked, protesting with a knowing leer that everyone knew what lovers were like. . . . The arrival of Rose and her mother kept Robert from making any answer.

"Mind the fruit tart," said Madame Revolou, "and those cream buns for Julien."

The 'bus ambled along through the fierce heat. Robert, scarlet in the face, looked through the window, and pretended not to notice that Rose was trying to catch his eye.

He left, as arranged, about five o'clock so as not to be late for his class that evening. The heat had been sufficient excuse for not going a walk with Rose. They had spent the afternoon in the billiard-room looking at old bound volumes of *Le Monde Illustré*. Rose went with him as far as the tram-stop, and arranged to meet him next day in the public gardens. She felt some surprise at his attitude, though she interpreted it not as coldness but as evidence that he was feeling awkward after what had happened, last evening, in the lime-grove. There was no pain in her heart as she watched him climb into the car. Groups of cyclists passed them: motor-cars hurried by, raising clouds of dust and hooting. She felt almost glad to be alone again.

In order to avoid having to go back to the house, she turned off under the trees. It was still very hot. They had found it impossible to get anybody to help with the hay harvest, and the high grass had encroached upon the path. Suddenly she saw Denis emerge from the green tangle. She would have much preferred to be alone, but he came towards her and started walking at her side, saying nothing. There were grass stains on his linen coat and rope-soled sandals.

At last he burst out with:

"You're sorry it's me! You wish it was somebody else!"

She put her arm round his shoulders.

"What a silly you are!" she said, "no one will ever take my little brother's place with me."

He was walking with hanging head, breaking off stalks of grass and chewing them. She said:

"There are things private to our two selves which no one else will ever share."

He looked up.

"Honest, Rose? You're not pulling my leg? You do really believe that?"

"I do. No matter how fond a woman may be of the man she's going to marry, and God knows . . ." (instinctively she left the sentence unfinished) . . . "there are whole tracts of herself," she went on after the short silence, "into which, however great and lasting their love may be, he will succeed in penetrating only after many years, and perhaps never. . . ."

"While with me? . . ."

"We don't need words, you and I. There are certain things that we both feel at precisely the same moment."

"Our life here, you mean, our childhood. . . . When I think that for Robert Léognan is just a house he wants to be quit of. . . ."

He stopped, waiting for her to say something. But already she was conscious of feeling irritated.

"Oh, for Heaven's sake don't go plaguing him about Léognan!"

"It's important—for all of us, Rose, but specially for you. You don't realize. I know Robert mustn't be plagued, as you put it, but I've had a brain-wave. Mother's all for it, but I want to know what you think."

He listened to himself speaking as he embarked on the explanation which he had so carefully prepared. It must never be said that a daughter of the Revolous had gone to her husband empty-handed. Léognan would be her dowry. Standing, as it did, just outside the city bounds and at a point where four main roads met, it must be worth, at the very least, a million. Almost certainly, Robert would undertake not to sell, and could be persuaded to make himself responsible for keeping it up. That, of course, would be a liability. On the other hand, it would provide them with everything they needed. Once let them get rid of the Cavailhes, and they would be assured not only of a roof over their heads, but of food and fuel as well. She, Rose, would be in charge of the poultry, the rabbits, the kitchen-garden and the livestock. With Bordeaux so near, they would have a guaranteed market for milk, eggs, vegetables and fruit.

He spoke with all the more assurance because the subject was one that had been familiar to him as well as to his sister ever since their childhood. Not the least of their pleasures had been to look forward to the time when they would live on the estate playing at farmer and farmer's wife.

"It would be ever so much nicer for you than having to spend all your time in Chardon's shop. . . ."

"And we could all be together: nothing need be changed."

He could not hold back the words that rose to his lips:

"Needn't it? . . . *He'll* be here. . . ."

"You don't know him."

"Oh, yes, I do. I know why you like him much better than you do yourself." He spoke with a little burst of ill-temper. "Just you wait and see how much of him you're left with after. . . ."

She put her hand on his mouth, but he twisted free.

"You know as well as I do that all the intelligence available to the Costadot family has gone into Pierrot. There's nothing left over for the others. Now *he is* worthy of you. . . ."

Rose pressed her brother's arm.

"If Pierrot were not a child, if it had been Pierrot I was in love with, you'd have felt just as resentful about him—be honest, Denis."

"Of course I should," he replied in a low voice, "I do anyhow."

"What has the poor boy done to you?" Denis drew a deep breath and passed the back of his hand over his moist forehead.

"I'm talking nonsense—forgive me . . . I'm very fond of Pierrot, and I'd be very fond of Robert, too, of the whole lot, if only you and I could stay as we are. We *must* keep Léognan, darling. If Robert accepts my plan, well and good . . . but will it be asking too much of him to take such a gift?"

Rose promised to mention the subject, provided they let her choose her own time.

"This is where you were yesterday evening," Denis said suddenly.

He had come to a halt just where a narrow path led off into the lime-grove, and was staring at the empty bench.

"The night wasn't dark enough for you!" he said with bitterness, "you had to hide as well."

Rose flared up. Why didn't he mind his own business? She spoke in the voice she had always used in their childish quarrels. He replied that, since their father was dead, and Julien useless, it *was* his business to keep an eye on her. She shrugged her shoulders, turned off the path, and took a short cut across the paddock.

"You've said quite enough . . . I'm not going to have you following me round!"

But he ran after her. Blue butterflies fluttered up about their feet. The crickets were silent.

"I suppose you think you're different!" he shouted, all out of breath. "But girls are all the same. They can only resist the boys they don't care for, and even then . . ."

"Where have you read all these great thoughts, you little idiot?"

"I haven't read them anywhere. I know a good deal more about life than you think . . . perhaps my knowledge isn't quite so first-hand as yours—since last night, that's to say. . . ."

She was walking quickly, with him hard on her heels. She swung round, and asked what precisely he meant by that. He could see that she was white with anger.

"I mean that since last night certain things must seem rather less mysterious than they did."

A couple of slaps set his cheeks tingling. "That's going a bit too far!"

She ran off towards the house. He stayed where he was, his arms dangling, his face on fire.

Their presence in the paddock had interrupted the sounds of hidden life, but now these began again—sounds of summer evenings that rise in us from the depths of our unhappy childhood. He seemed in his misery to have taken root. For the insects he might have been a tree. A butterfly, of the kind known as "aiguillons" perched on his shoulder, opening and shutting its wings. Ants clung to this strange trunk of woven stuff. Beetles and cockchafers boomed in the lower leaves of the oaks which the sun had turned to flame. He stood quite still, hoping thus to blunt the edge of his unhappiness. This was how one ought to die—growing into death by sheer virtue of immobility, feeling the blood turn to sap, slipping without effort into the vegetable world, passing from one plane to another, from love and wretchedness to sleep, which is but another form of life.

The gong sounded for dinner. Rose appeared once more at the far end of the paddock, and came towards him. When she was quite close she put her arm round his neck and kissed his burning cheeks.

"I oughtn't to have done that, but you made me so angry."

He let her kiss him but did not kiss her back. He remained entirely passive. Rose laughed.

"Don't stare at me like that, you old owl!"

But he, partly in fun, partly to give her a fright, remained even more motionless than before, and gazed at her without blinking. Rose picked a piece of grass and began to tickle his nose and the corners of his mouth until he burst out laughing with all the fresh gaiety of childhood.

That same evening, as soon as dinner at the Costadots was ended, Pierre, as was his habit, went to his room. But Robert stayed on for a few moments in the small drawing-room before starting to work. His mother never asked him direct questions, though quite often, by means of an interjection or a glance, she would help him out with something he had to say. On this occasion Robert made it clear that, even against her better judgment, Rose would serve the interests of her family in the matter of Léognan.

"I'm sure you're wrong, my dear boy," his mother protested. "I can't believe that, knowing her as I do. Naturally, I don't share your illusions about her—you could hardly expect me to. I have never believed her to be resourceful, though I may be wrong. Courageous she most certainly is, but good tendencies don't make up for qualities that are absent. The poor child—and this is really serious—has no powers of resistance. When you brought her to see me the other day it was the first time I had set eyes on her since the tragedy, and really, I should hardly have recognized her. . . . She *must* give up working, I don't mean *before* your marriage, because you haven't any right, no matter what the excuse, to deprive her of her means of livelihood, but certainly afterwards. . . . I only hope she won't start having children too soon. . . . Men really are the oddest creatures. How you can possibly take pleasure in so lethargic a person is more than I shall ever be able to understand. But as to believing her capable of scheming, of trying to influence your actions. . . ."

Robert protested that he had never so much as suspected any such thing. All he had meant was that she might allow others to work on her.

"In that event, my dear, you have merely got to bring her up short the moment she embarks on the subject. There are two sorts of young girls: those who leave home without a backward glance and make their husbands' interests their own as soon as they get married, and those who remain at bottom their parents' children, and, in so doing, show themselves false to their new obligations. Were Rose to belong to the second category, I should pity you, and I should pity *us*. Your—our—future is quite black enough as it is. This marriage, coming at the very beginning of your career, is, anyhow, little short of a disaster. . . ."

He got up.

"Why must you try to work me up into a state?" he asked

querulously. "It is almost as though you found a kind of pleasure in irritating me."

She protested.

"I?—trying to work *you* into a state?"

He took a step in her direction.

"What's at the back of your mind? This marriage of mine is no longer in question. It's as good as completed. For Heaven's sake, do let us try to look on the bright side!"

She brushed his remark aside.

"There is no bright side."

"Be that as it may. I have given my word."

"You will give your word, when the time comes, before the Mayor and before the priest. At the moment, you have done no more than promise. . . . You'll hate me for what I'm going to say now, but that can't be helped. . . . Until the very last moment I shall continue to hope that something may happen to stop it— an illness, an earthquake, just as I should were my son lying under sentence of death. . . ."

She expected some sort of angry outburst, but for a few seconds he said nothing. At last, in a low voice:

"It would kill her," he muttered.

Léonie Costadot swallowed as though her mouth were full of saliva, struggled heavily up from her chair, put her two hands on his shoulders, and tried to make him look at her.

"My dear boy, you have no illusions about this marriage. You are putting your neck into a halter with your eyes wide open."

He assured her, but without much conviction, that he loved Rose, and that, in any case, it was too late now. He repeated that any turning back on his part would kill her.

"She would suffer—I don't deny that for a moment: but she would suffer a great deal more if she found herself tied to a man who could never forgive her for having ruined his life."

She felt that she ought to leave well alone, and not press her advantage. But she could not resist the temptation to take from her desk the file which contained the details of her sons' inheritance. To Robert this yellow folder was now a familiar object.

"I got an approximate estimate yesterday of what you will have after all legal and other charges have been paid. The most you can hope for in the way of income is ten thousand francs. . . ."

"What about all the house property?"

"The rents go almost entirely in maintenance costs."

There was a different note in his voice as he said:

"You're hypnotized by this problem of money. You can't see beyond it. Don't you realize that another human being is involved, that the life and happiness of a young girl hopelessly exposed to the harshness of the world, is at stake?"

She drew him to her:

"It's you I'm thinking of, darling. You mustn't be angry. After all, it *is* natural that my son should take first place in my thoughts. I don't want you to be unhappy."

"I shall be happy if she is happy," he said fervently. "If I thought that I had been instrumental in causing her pain, I couldn't bear it."

"I understand exactly how you feel," she answered. "You must do nothing which might make you feel ashamed later on."

"Well, then? If you can say that, it shows you can see as clearly as I do that there is no way out."

She detected a note of disappointment in his voice, and very cautiously ventured a step further:

"There is always a way out, though sometimes one doesn't see at once what it is. . . ."

As he was leaving the room, he turned and said:

"I don't want you to think that I am weakening. . . ."

"I don't think anything of the sort. Try to get some sleep, and don't work too late."

XII

FOR the last two days the threat of a storm had been hanging over Bordeaux.

"If it rains," she had said to him, "wait for me at the confectioner's opposite the park; Jaeger's, it's called. There's never anybody there at six."

A quarter to six had struck. Robert had already eaten three cakes, and was now feeling sick. The rain was beating against the shop window, 'If she's not here in five minutes, I shall go,' he told himself. . . . Storms always affected his nerves, and he knew it. He recognized only too well, and dreaded, the well-nigh uncontrollable state of irritability which thunder produced in him. He pressed his nose to the glass—as he used to do as a small boy—and watched the tiny jets of water which the drops made upon the pavement.

He told himself that Rose must have been delayed by the rain. She was so forgetful that she would almost certainly have left her umbrella at home, and would arrive soaked to the skin. . . . He glanced towards the two young women who had brought his tea and were now chattering in whispers behind the counter. He tried to imagine the effect that Rose would produce on them, and felt ashamed of feeling ashamed. Just as he had got up, leaving a coin on the table, he saw her. She had stopped in the doorway and was with difficulty trying to shut a ridiculous man's umbrella which Chardon must have lent her. The wind was blowing her damp skirt against her legs. She entered the shop looking round for somewhere to put her dripping umbrella. One of the young women cut short her hesitation by taking the object from her.

She sat down at Robert's side.

"I ran," she said.

He gave her an almost furtive glance.

"You're in a frightful state! You'll catch your death of cold!"

"I'm stronger than you think. My skirt is sodden and my feet are sopping. It'll be two hours before I can change . . . but what does that matter? . . . we are together."

"You don't take enough care of yourself, Rose, you're too casual . . ."

She broke in on him, thinking that he spoke in praise:

"No, no, you mustn't say that . . . I'm no braver than anyone else. . . . There is nothing meritorious in my self-neglect. . . . It's just that nothing matters except *us*. . . ." she answered in a low voice.

A glass of Malaga had been put before her. She raised it to her lips.

"But you ought to think about me too," he said, "and about the little Rose whom I loved in the old days."

She stared at him in amazement. He went on:

"*She* never had a soaking skirt, or drenched shoes, or rats'-tails sticking out under an old hat. . . . I'm not blaming you," he added hurriedly, "but if sometimes I have to make an effort, you must forgive me. . . ."

Her eyes had never left his face. He began to feel uncomfortable.

"I can't help wishing that you'd be a little more considerate to *yourself* . . . that you'd pay rather more attention, I mean, to your face, your hands, your general appearance. . . ."

Quickly she hid her hands under the table. The colour had drained from her cheeks.

"Don't you like my looks any more?"

"That's not the question, Rose . . . I want you to show some consideration for yourself. You are the only woman I know who never looks at herself in a mirror. The merest glance would show you what I mean."

The heavy curtain of the rain and the thick foliage of the elms in the Cours de Gourgues, made it dark in the shop. Her head was drooping above the baba on her plate. He realized that she was crying, but the knowledge did nothing to soften his mood. The irritation, the nervous tension, to which he was a prey, found expression in a few barely audible words:

"Oh, Lord, now we're going to have tears!" Still keeping her eyes lowered, she said:

"I deserve everything you say about me, darling—I know I do, but let me explain. I was brought up from childhood expecting to have things done for me. My bath was got ready, my dressing-gown was warmed, a maid gave me massage and did my hair. Do you realize that until quite recently I had never even buttoned my boots for myself? But now I get home late and rise at dawn, with the result that I reduce my dressing to its simplest elements. I know I don't do all I should. . . . It never occurred to me that all those little things could matter to *us*. . . . I thought that our love. . . ."

She could not go on. Her voice was broken by a sob. He did not help her by so much as a word, but waited, feeling vaguely that their feet were set on a road which might lead further than he had ever dared to hope.

Suddenly she seized his hand. He saw her damp, yellowish little face close to his own. He could smell her sour breath.

"All the same, last Saturday in the lime-grove, you found me attractive?"

In a voice of patient boredom he said: "Who ever said I didn't?"

She called him "Robert." She felt that he was withdrawn, that he was so far away that her voice could not reach him. But how could that be true? She saw him sitting there opposite: only a table stood between them. He was engaged to her. In October she would be his wife. The fact of her misery was born in on him at the same moment. He fought down a desire to strike at her.

"You'll catch cold," he said, "You'd better come home with me, and I'll light a fire."

She thanked him humbly. Together they plunged into the rain, and until they reached the house Costadot spoke not a word. He knew that this was the evening his mother gave to her Charity

meeting, and that she would not be back until late. He took
Rose, not into his own room, but into the small drawing-room.
He had some vine-twigs brought from the kitchen. He told her
to take off her shoes. She blushed.

"I'm afraid I've got a hole in my stocking. I'm sorry. . . ."

He turned away his head. A cloud of steam rose from her
clothes. Suddenly in the mirror above the mantelpiece, she
caught a glimpse of herself as he must be seeing her. She took off
her hat and tried to tidy her bedraggled hair. He had removed
her shoes, felt the soles with his hand, and put them by the fire.
She was standing, he sitting a short distance off. She leaned over
him and took his head in both her hands, trying to make him
look at her.

"What a good man you are!" she said in a sudden access of
affection.

He protested violently:

"No, Rose, you're wrong, I'm *not* good, at all."

On the spur of the moment words that he had not intended to
utter, a sentence which had taken form without his conscious
intention, slipped from him like a jet of saliva, of sap or of blood:

"Forgive me, Rose; I'm not in love with you any more."

She uttered no cry. She gave no sign either of pain or astonish-
ment. She thought: 'So that's that: he's said it: it's all over.'
And simultaneously another idea came to her: 'He's still there:
nothing is lost.'

She could have touched his hair again, his cheeks, the lovely
mouth which looked so much like that of a sulky child. If only he
didn't go she could still fight, still resist, still win him back. In a
lucid flash she saw all her past foolishness. Suddenly she heard
herself saying in the silent depths of her heart what all women say
when they have learned the ways of the world: "With men one
has got to. . . . The best way of holding a man. . . ." *He* was a
man, a poor creature of flesh and blood. There was still time to
pursue him in his flight, still time to catch up with him in that

melancholy world of tricks and endearments where women play out their age-long game. Her anxiety grew less. In a moment or two she would be comforted. She heard herself speaking in a voice that was almost gay:

"You only *think* that, darling. It won't last. I knew you didn't care for me this evening, and it's all my fault. I'm looking terrible! No wonder you're scared. But just wait until to-morrow. . . ."

There was a pitiable note of cajolery in her voice. "You didn't feel like that the other evening, did you?" Once more she took his head between her hands and strove to catch and hold his shifting glance. 'She'll get me again,' he thought, 'I mustn't let her do that.' He was trembling like a shipwrecked sailor who, when he sees above the waves two small and desperate hands clutching at the boat, hesitates to force them loose.

She kept on, hammering away at the same point:

"Remember Saturday night in the lime-grove. . . . I wasn't cold and dirty then as I am now, but your own little girl. I was wearing my Habrias dress. You behaved like a madman—remember?—all worked up and feverish. . . . It wasn't my imagination, it was *real*. . . . Say what you want to say, anything, everything."

He was frightened. She must be made to loosen her grip. He said:

"That proves nothing, you don't know what you're talking about. Any young man with a young girl beside him in the darkness. . . . It doesn't mean a thing. . . . Any woman would have had the same effect on me."

"But it wasn't just any woman: it was me, *Rose*, me, me!"

She should have stopped her ears so as not to catch the sense of the answer he had the effrontery to make that it had been dark under the limes, that he hadn't been able to see her, that if he had. . . .

"No!" she cried, "No! no!"

Her hand was at her throat: she leaned towards the fire. He who had spoken was the man who, when they were ruined, she had given up, but who had sought her again. She could not understand. She uttered no such words as Robert expected, words which should have expressed the outraged fury of a woman scorned. Had she done so he could have given blow for blow. The whole wretched affair would have worked itself out in a spate of embittered recrimination. He would not then have been forced into the position of a frightened murderer giving the *coup de grâce* to a helpless child. But Rose could only suffer and love on. How strong she was, thus stripped and vulnerable! If he yielded now to his sense of pity, all would be lost, and he once more in the toils. He had struck his blow: the hardest part of the business was behind him.

"You must think I'm behaving like a cad, but it's you I'm thinking of. . . . I'm not certain any longer that I could make you happy. If I have changed it's only because you have changed. It wouldn't do any good your just wearing the clothes you used to wear. You'll never again be the Rose I knew a year ago."

He argued, gave reasons for his decision. She began to hope again.

"But nothing's changed: I'm just as I always was. I'll give up Chardon's. From tomorrow on, you'll see the Rose you used to see. I'll stay at Léognan. . . . I can make more money by looking after the animals and the vegetables. You see . . ." she made the point on the spur of the moment, as though suddenly inspired . . . "I'm no portionless bride. . . . I've got a handsome dowry. Léognan's to be given to me—it's all settled . . . Léognan: do you realize what that means? I know, of course, that it will involve you in expense, but at least we shall be living on our own land. Life there won't cost us a penny. . . . We don't, as it is, go to the butcher more than once a week. . . ."

He let her run on. He could never have dared to hope that she would take this line. He felt anger surge within him. Now, at last, he would be able to give it rein. She thought that he was weakening, and drove ahead.

"It's impossible to say what an estate like Léognan is worth . . . perhaps a million. . . ."

He broke in on her. His voice was hard, incisive.

"You really think so? In that case wouldn't it be wiser to sell?"

"Oh, but we shouldn't have the right to sell. . . ."

"But if the property is to be ours?"

She replied with a sort of childlike innocence, as though it were all perfectly simple, that her family would give them Léognan only because that would be the best way of keeping it. He got up; he spoke harshly:

"Your family must think me a bigger fool than I am. What they're giving me is an estate that will cost a fortune to keep up, with the additional obligation of supporting all its inhabitants— isn't that it?"

Oh, Heavens! she had been on the wrong tack!

"What inhabitants?" she stammered.

"Your mother, Julien, Denis. . . . I don't suppose they're proposing to clear out?"

"But, Robert . . . it's such a big house. There's room in it for all of us. . . ."

He forced a laugh:

"For all of us! That's precisely what I meant!"

She realized then that he had found a pretext, that his grievances had now got solid foothold, that she was indeed lost.

"I didn't think of it like that, or, rather, I wouldn't let myself. . . ." she admitted humbly. "I knew there might be difficulties, but I told myself that you would find a way out of them. I believed in you so utterly that I put all the weight of the future on your shoulders. I thought you loved me," she went on, speaking now through tears, "and I judged of love by my own feelings. Love, as I know it, never looks at the troubles that may lie ahead, never feels the burden of obligations, or if it does, it accepts them in advance as something blest and beautiful. For your sake I would have accepted anything . . . so, naturally, I thought . . ."

He had moved to the open window. She realized that he was

waiting for her to go. At that moment, for the first time, she knew—physically knew—that the end of her happiness had come, that never again. . . . Yet, he was still there in the room with her. She could have touched the curling hair at the back of his head. Already she was moving towards the door. Robert was thinking, 'In a moment now it'll be all over.' He was aware of a feeling of great lightness in his chest. But she stopped, came back into the room, began to speak again.

"Listen, Robert. I accept your decision. I will not be your wife. All I ask is that you do not abandon me utterly, that you keep a tiny place in your heart for me. . . . Perhaps you may be able to feel a little love for me when it is no longer a question of our getting married. . . . Let me see you sometimes. . . ."

He kept his eyes averted. In a very low voice she added:

"You can do what you like with me. . . ."

He felt ashamed for her, and said:

"Why must you degrade yourself by saying a thing like that? You would never forgive yourself when you came to your senses. . . . You must believe that I've completely forgotten what you've just said, that I attach no importance to it whatever. . . ."

In a voice broken with misery she uttered her protest:

"But, Robert, I don't feel it as a degradation. I belong to you. That is a fact, and it remains a fact whether you want it or no. Nothing in the world can stop me from being yours. You may reject me, but I am your property just the same."

He was conscious of that ignoble irritation which is felt by every man who knows himself to be in the grip of a despairing and tenacious woman. That masculine ferocity which is roused by the obstinate clinging of the unwanted female, came out in bitter words!

"If you wanted to win me back, you could have hit on no worse way than to offer me your body. This really is the end. . . . You are befouling and trampling in the mud the memory of you that I might have treasured. . . ."

He knew perfectly well how flat and foolish the trivial words must sound. He knew that Rose was far above all baseness, but he knew also that the goal of freedom was almost within his reach. One more effort and the way would be clear before him, and then he would make a "snug little life" for himself. He scarcely heard her next words:

"Befoul? . . . Trample in the mud?"

She could not understand. She was a stranger to words which are used merely to gain advantage in an argument, which no longer express true feeling or living passion. Probably never in her life had it occurred to her to make use of an expression that was not in the likeness of her heart. But she was keenly sensitive to any inconsistency of word or thought in others—save in the single case of Robert. He was to her an unknown quantity. The very fact of her love had come between them. They had been separated by the ocean of her love. But this evening, the hatred felt for her by the man she loved had quite destroyed the mirage of her feelings. The two coast-lines had joined across the intervening sea. Suddenly he was there confronting her, an enemy and at point-blank range. She could see, quite close, the look in his face, could feel in the air about her the movement of his cowardly and lying words. At last, stripped of all disguises, his soul was set before her eyes such as it really was, such as he had deliberately ignored, such as she had refused to see it, for she had been dominated by that deliberate blindness which is always the mark, in every traffic between individuals, of the one whose greatness of heart is at odds with the base and ugly. She knew now that she could expect, while still she remained in this room with him, no cry torn from true depths of feeling, but only feigned and dishonest words. She realized clearly that even before her feet had crossed the threshold or touched the topmost stair, the road on which they were set led to the waste places, and she was eager now to start upon that journey. But her eyes were blinded with tears. She groped unavailingly for the way out. Robert, his face glued to the window, made no attempt to help her. She turned a handle and opened a door, only to find herself not on the landing but in

the larger drawing-room adjoining. She half stumbled against a
large, a motionless, body crowned by a hat on the summit of
which quivered a bunch of black grapes.

"I've just come back from my Charity Committee," Léonie
Costadot hastened to explain, "and I've only this moment been
told that you were here. . . ."

Rose, obedient to her early training, made the brief curtsey
becoming to her age. Then, in a calm, clear voice, she said:

"I am on my way out. I beg of you, Madame, not to disturb
yourself. My tram will be leaving in a few minutes. Robert is in
the small drawing-room."

"No doubt I shall be seeing you again soon, Rose. I trust that
all at Léognan are well. Don't forget to give my kindest regards
to my old friend."

She followed the girl downstairs to the hall. She had a feeling
that she ought to go with her to the tram, to follow her at a
discreet distance. . . . She was still hesitating, not knowing what
was the best course to pursue, when the slam of the front door
reached her ears. She felt a sudden need for support, and leaned
against the wall, not fully understanding the nature of her emotion. For the first time she had been brought face to face with the
result of one of her own actions. Not always can we thus recognize the very features of our deeds. It is but rarely that our
crimes are shown to us in the guise of a young creature mortally
wounded.

Standing there on the doorstep, she called up to Robert:

"Quick, bring her back!"

He shook his head, remarking that it was too late.

"Not if you run . . ."

He dared not look at her, but stood wiping his hands on
his handkerchief.

"You don't really mean that, mamma, do you? It was perfectly
frightful while it lasted, but it's all over now."

Léonie was amazed that he could be so calm. He couldn't have
seen the girl's face, not possibly; couldn't have looked at her.

Robert went close to his mother.

"I don't understand you," he said in a low voice, "aren't you pleased?"

No, pleased she certainly was not. Naturally, she did not want this marriage, but neither did she want him to behave like a brute. The last thing she desired was to have to blush for her son.

"Logic has never been your strong suit. It's you who got me into this state, and you can't deny it. You're always complaining that I've got no will of my own, and now that I've shown I have. . . ."

She broke in on his words. Didn't he realize, she asked, that lack of self-control was in itself a manifestation of weakness? Only a thoroughly weak person would strike blindly at a poor defenceless child, when, with a little patience, he could so easily have detached her gradually. . . . She turned away her head.

"Perhaps you are right," he admitted, in a different tone. "I hit out at random because I wanted to get it all over quickly. Did you hear what I was saying to her?"

"Only the last few words, but they were enough . . . I *saw* her."

After a brief silence, she asked whether the girl was going back to Léognan alone. Yes, he said, but that particular point had not occurred to him.

"I am afraid we shall neither of us get much sleep tonight," said Léonie Costadot in a very low voice.

Robert told her that he had decided not to go to bed until late. She mustn't ask what he was going to do. He was a free man now, and that was a lovely feeling, in spite of everything. Free . . .

Humbled he might be, but he was sly, and knew that he had found the weak spot in his mother's armour. He laughed. He had drunk nothing, but at times our actions can intoxicate. Suddenly a fixed look came into his eyes. He mentioned Pierrot's name.

"I didn't think of him: where is he?"

"He is dining with friends. You know I have no authority over him now. He has even given up asking my permission. . . ."

Robert's hangdog expression was getting on her nerves. He kept on saying:

"What am I to tell him?"

"Do remember, Robert, that you are the elder, and that you are not accountable to him for your actions."

He shook his head. She did not know Pierrot: did not realize the lengths to which he might go.

When he had left the room, Léonie quite forgot to take off her hat. The black grapes trembled above her head. The calculating machine which she carried within it had suddenly ceased to function. No longer was her mind a confused pattern of estimates: no longer did she see in imagination the oppressive vision of bricks and mortar crying aloud for repairs. For the time being she was not concerned with this or that insurance policy now overdue for renewal, nor with some mislaid account which she must at all costs find among her papers. This release from her customary obsession lasted only for a few moments. Already she was straining every nerve to fight down the emotional weakness to which she had yielded, to follow the natural instinct which prompted her to take up the reins with a firm hand.

'The sooner he gets married the better,' she thought. 'One Gaston in the family is quite enough. There must be no more playing fast and loose. There are as good fish in the sea as ever came out of it—better, in fact. I must see to it that next time he picks on somebody with money, and without a set of relations who might hang round his neck like a millstone. Eligible young women don't grow on every tree. What he needs is someone who is solid rather than showy. Why not look about in the country? There might be somebody in the Landes. . . . That's where the future lies. . . . Trees are going up in value. . . . Some good, sound match. . . . I've pulled the old suit to pieces, I'd better sit down now and get on with a bit of sewing at the new one.'

XIII

PIERROT was not dining with friends that evening, as he had led his mother to suppose. He had no friend, except Denis Revolou, with whom he could have dined at a restaurant. Seated alone at a table in a small pot-house near the docks, he was making a meal off mussels, eels, salad and some Roquefort cheese which he had crumbled and soaked with Armagnac. He was just about finishing "unaided" a bottle of Clos Fourtet, and was already drunk, but only to that stage of the light head and the lucid brain which manifested itself in a private buzz of odds and ends of poetry. Ideas of a dazzling brilliance flashed across his mind like shooting stars. A thousand enchanting vistas opened to his inward eye. He saw objects in a strange juxtaposition, and delivered himself of startling literary judgments. He jotted nothing down for he felt too rich to see the necessity of picking up the diamonds that fell from his pockets. There were more than enough of them, he decided, for his needs.

The really difficult thing was to count out his money, to get up from his chair, to walk without staggering to where his coat was hanging, to reach the door without falling down, and to recapture, in the open air, that sense of true solitude with which he spent his every day—that old companion of his who sat watching there behind the great glazed window.

Lost in the stream of people pouring on to the Quays from the slum district of Saint-Michel, he moved forward, burdened by the weight of all that wealth which he could share with no one in this crowd. If only Denis had been with him: dear old Denis with his owl-like eyes, who took but could never give. . . . There was no one else he wanted . . . though of course there was always Rose, who was soon to become his sister—in other words, an inaccessible being.

The swifts were crying in the tail-end of the storm which had drawn a veil across the sky. The empty river was churning its muddy waters to the ocean. A few black lighters lay against the wharves. The young grass showed dark on the distant hill-sides. The world, he thought, was justified by her beauty.

He walked up the Cours des Fosses. Humanity, this evening, was a confusion of men in shirt-sleeves and braces, lolling on chairs at their house-doors. But he did not notice them. His eyes were for the wider spaces above their heads. Like the dizzy criss-cross of swifts' wings, the verses which he had written down the night before and was now all eagerness to read on the margin of his natural history book, flickered about his mind. With many breaks and pauses he chanted to himself (heedless of the girl who had stopped in the middle of the pavement and was following his progress with a laughing eye) his Cybele's sad plaint:

> My body feels the pull of many streams
> Where pebbles break the tiny tides that sway
> The tresses of white nymphs at drownéd play
> Above the sleeping fishes' watery dreams.
> Sad comfort for the heart that thou hast slain,
> Cold lover with thy stained and muddied face!
> They weigh not in its scale with the light trace
> Of tears that seam thy cheeks' unheeding grace. . . .

The words swarmed like bees within his brain. Still moving to their music, he reached the Cathedral and the Square that lay close to his home. In the middle of it there stood a bronze statue erected to the memory of those who had been defeated in 1870. On a bench close to the tram terminus a woman was sitting. She looked like Rose. As he drew closer, he recognized her, or thought he did, for he was still uncertain whether it were really she. He spoke her name and she gave a start.

"I came over rather giddy," she said, "I expect it was the storm. I must look a perfect fright. . . . I've come straight here from your house. I'm feeling better, but the last tram has gone. . . . No, don't disturb Robert. . . . As a matter of fact, it wouldn't be any use, because he's gone out to work with some of his friends. . . . If you could find me a cab. . . ."

Pierrot remembered a livery-stable in the Rue des Trois-Conils. As soon as he had left her, she dipped her handkerchief in the Wallace fountain, dabbed at her eyes and cheeks, and washed her hands.

An open carriage drew up and Pierrot got out.

"*Of course* I'm coming with you. You don't think I'd let you go home alone at this time of night, and in your present state? . . . Besides, I should enjoy a drive in the dark. . . ."

She protested, but in vain, and did not feel up to arguing. He was already seated at her side, and the ancient Victoria was bumping over the cobbles. Rose prattled away to prevent him from noticing that anything was wrong, They wouldn't, she said, be in the least worried about her at Léognan. She had missed the last tram before now. Pierrot started to sing "O Star of Eve" in a tuneless voice.

"As a matter of fact, I've had rather a lot to drink . . . not too much," he added hastily, "but, well, rather a lot. . . . Couldn't have hoped for anything nicer than this, though . . . it's lovely . . . and quite unexpected. . . . Country'll be smelling delicious after the rain."

Rather shyly he felt for her hand where it lay beside her on the seat. Rose let him hold it. At first she had been terrified at having to endure his presence all the way to Léognan, but now she experienced a sense of comfort in his companionship, and in the grasp of his large, hot hand. It grew moist, but even so it never occurred to her to withdraw her own. This confiding gesture on her part did not surprise him. He sat there with his head thrown back, conscious that the sky was no longer hemmed in by buildings, but already spanned a cool suburban landscape. The moon rose behind the Rabat property. He felt an access of his old tenderness, but it brought peace to him now, and comfort. Sitting thus, with her tiny, trusting hand in his great paw, he was stealing nothing from his brother.

"Rose," he said suddenly, and as though he were thinking aloud, "do you believe that children can love—really love, I mean?"

"I don't know," she replied, and compressed her lips.

"You *can't* know how much I loved you . . . and always will. Don't laugh at me," there was a note of supplication in his voice. "Say anything you like, but don't *laugh*. I know I'm eighteen. You mustn't look at me, I want you to forget what my face is like. . . ."

"There is no need for me to do any such thing," she said, without turning towards him. "Your face is in my heart and always will be. In years to come when you are famous and the whole world knows your name, I shall see you just as you are now, this evening, sitting beside me. This evening in particular. . . . I shall never forget this evening. . . ."

She could not finish. A storm of misery shook her body. She could no more resist it than she could have resisted an epileptic fit. But they were passing over a stretch of cobbled road, and the jolting and the noise made it possible for her to control her feelings by degrees before Pierrot had a chance of noticing that anything was wrong. He was leaning back against the leather cushion.

"D'you remember the beach at Pontaillac . . . two years ago . . . doesn't seem that long? . . . We were drying ourselves in the sun. . . . I'd given you a poem, and it had offended you. . . . What you hadn't realized was that it wasn't only you the poem was about. You were its starting-point, but by the time it was finished you had become for me a sort of mythical being. . . . Even now it's almost always you I take as a starting-point."

The wave of misery flooded back, swelling her breast to bursting. "If," she thought, "he could recite that poem, it would give me time to calm down. . . ."

He laughed and said:

"Funny, isn't it, to think I was inspired by your sunburn . . . remember? . . ."

> I followed on your body's map strange ways.
> "That's where the sun has burned my skin," you said:
> And then again, "My upturned breast is spread
> A target for his arrows. See how he flays

My languid arms." But on the burned-up waste
I nothing saw but an entangled skein
Of footmarks by some unknown hunter traced,
Fanning from trodden camp-fires on the plain.

"And then," he said, laughing, "came the lines which so much
annoyed you. You thought they referred to you. . . ."

"They wouldn't annoy me this evening, Pierre." ('If only he'd
go on: if only he wouldn't stop!')

"And then? . . ." she said with the eager breathlessness of a
child to whom a grown-up is telling a story.

"And then? . . . Oh, I've forgotten. . . ."

He paused, trying to remember. He thought he heard something very much like a sniffle. He turned and looked at her, but
because her head was thrown back could see only the taut line of
her throat and the angle of her chin. But she seemed quite calm.

"I'm not asleep, if that's what you're thinking," she said, "I'm
listening."

There was a break in her voice which surprised him. Perhaps,
he thought, this drive through the darkness of the rain-soaked
countryside and the moonlight had worked her up emotionally,
or the poetry he had been declaiming. It was she now who took
his hand and pressed it.

"Do go on," she begged, "begin with the next bit you remember."

He had scarcely embarked on:

> Happy the man who found the secret way
> To where my hunger is for ever unappeased!
> I feel within my body the mysterious play
> Of your young blood—a river never eased
> Of its strong urgency. Oh, might it pour into my heart,
> And you come forth thorough my gaping side.

—when, and this time there could be no mistake, the hand he
held in his trembled. The motion spread to her arm, to her whole
body. At first he could not grasp her stammered words.

"It's ended. . . . It's all over!"

He drew her closer, and asked:

"What's all over?"

He did not realize at once that it was of Robert she was speaking when she said:

"He has left me; he doesn't love me any more: it's over."

His first reaction was to exclaim:

"Over?—Just you wait! Tomorrow I'll have him crawling back to you on his knees! D'you hear me?—on his knees!"

She shook her head. She moaned rather than spoke her next words:

"There's nothing you can do—nothing anyone can do. Even he is powerless to alter the fact that he has stopped loving me. One can't give life to a corpse. If you had seen his face—if you had heard his voice!"

Seldom is it given to a man to realize the precise day and hour, the exact spot on his journey through life, when one whole part of his being falls away, and his face, till then marked by the soft indefiniteness of childhood, suddenly takes on the rigid structure which it will carry with it to the grave. For as long as he lived, and maybe in the hour of death, Pierre Costadot would always see in memory the hill sloping up to the lane which led off to the stables, where the horse fell automatically into a walk: the shadow cast by the Victoria and its driver on the grassy margin of the road: would hear the murmur of the wet and stormy night, and Rose's voice pleading for his brother, and condemning him the more surely with every phrase of attempted defence.

Pierrot clenched his teeth. All his loathing and disgust fused into one solid block of contempt. Such was the strength of his feelings that for a brief space it was as though his heart had died. He felt no pity for the adored creature whose tears were wetting the fabric of his jacket. She belonged to the world which he had determined to vomit up. Impossible now to make distinction between the spider and the fly. He must tear the whole complex from his living flesh, victim and executioner together, must destroy it utterly. But first he must fight his way out of the world in which they lived, that he might have no part in it. The same spiritual excitement that wine had brought him was once more active in his consciousness. The physical sense of her torment there beside him did not prevent him from seeing clearly—as clearly as he saw the road beneath the moon—the alternatives between which, from now on, he must for ever oscillate—either to change himself or to change the world. Which should it be? Should he slash a trail through his own living flesh to God, or, mistrustful of his power to reach perfection, give himself utterly, fatally, to the cause of destruction, batter down the old walls, declare war to the death against all the Costadots of the earth, and send the whole system sky-high? . . .

"I did wrong to mention those repairs to him," said Rose in low, conversational tones, so as not to attract the driver's attention. "He got the idea that there was a plot against him. He may even have thought that I was trying to trick him. And then, you see, I wasn't a credit to him. Being a shop-girl oughtn't to have made me forget that I owed it to him to be even daintier and neater than before. . . ."

Pierre broke in on her:

"Please don't go on—it's all so *beastly*. . . ."

She thought that he was drained of pity, but he was thinking: 'Each one of the sentiments she is expressing deserves the death-sentence. Mankind needs a new scheme of justice. We must build a world in which such calculations will be inconceivable. . . .'

As they reached the top of the slope the horse once more broke into a trot. Pierre saw a little way off a shadowy figure standing by the lane leading to the stables. Good Lord! he had quite forgotten Denis!

"He's standing there by the roadside, waiting for us. How on earth are we going to tell him?"

Rose's miserable semblance of a laugh shocked him.

"Don't worry," she said: "He'll be rather pleased than distressed when he hears what has happened. . . . Perhaps he won't even be very much surprised. . . . I'm pretty clear-sighted about some things," she added in a low voice.

"No, Rose, dear—you mustn't say that. . . ."

Had he, then, realized too? She told the coachman to draw up on the main road so as not to wake the household. Denis ran up to the carriage:

"What's wrong?"

"Quite a lot's wrong," said Pierrot, helping Rose out. "We'll explain in a moment. . . ."

Denis recognized him and, without offering his hand, said irritably:

"Oh, so it's you, is it? Did you bring her back? Were you two alone?"

At that moment young Costadot saw and touched, as materially as though he had actually weighed it in his hand, the hard pebble against which his friendship for Denis, the feeling of tenderness which Denis inspired in him, had always struck and broken. That, too, must be torn out, burned, destroyed! for, like all the rest, it belonged to a world which it was his task to set tumbling about their ears.

They walked up the lane, the three of them abreast, Rose in the middle.

Denis repeated the question he had just asked.

"Why did you bring her back? Has Robert? . . ."

No sooner had the hated name passed his lips than he broke off. Even if he had not guessed everything after that first, brief glance at the scarcely recognizable face which his sister raised to him in greeting, her kiss would have told him, the salt taste of her tearworn cheek. . . . Without the slightest show of emotion, she said:

"I would very much rather that Robert's name should not be mentioned between us. It's all perfectly simple. He no longer loves me enough to be willing to face the difficulties of our marriage or the financial liabilities with which it would saddle him. . . . We have broken off our engagement by mutual consent, that's all."

"But only for the moment!" growled Denis. "As soon as you and I are alone, I shall ask a number of questions to which I have a right to demand an answer."

She sighed:

"Ask them now, then, and let us get it over."

"Not while there's a stranger here."

They had reached the front-door. Denis felt his arm held in a vice-like grip.

"Let me go, you brute!" he shouted.

But Pierrot only held him the tighter.

"Listen to me," he said. "From now on we *shall* be strangers. But here, on this spot, with you as witness, I wish to remind Rose that everything I am and everything I possess is her's absolutely. . . . Wherever I may hide myself, I shall see to it that she has my address, that she knows where I can be found."

Rose stood in the middle of the lane, motionless, detached, as one dead.

"The only thing you and your family can do for her is to get out of her life. You have always been a curse—her curse, and ours!"

"But of that curse, you too, Denis, are a part. If ever she wearies of your protection, if ever she needs me to defend her against you . . ."

Denis raised a nerveless fist, but Pierre caught and held it before it could strike. "Denis!" he cried, and his voice belied his action. He did not quail before the other's furious eye, which was that of a bird of prey foiled of its pounce. Perhaps at that moment he was saying goodbye to a face that had been very dear to him, to the many vague and ill-defined emotions for which men have never found a name. "Good-bye," he said, and turned and ran back to the main road where the lamps of the carriage were gleaming through the darkness.

"What a brute!" said Denis, rubbing his wrist. "The question I wanted to ask you . . ." he went on as he climbed the front steps in Rose's wake, "was . . . Oh, yes, I know . . . how did *he* come to be in the carriage?"

At the door of the billiard-room she turned:

"How I can manage to stand upright, Denis, I don't know. It is extraordinary to think that my heart can go on beating. All I ask is that you should leave me alone. Tomorrow I've got to get up at my usual time, and go to work. There's no question of my doing anything else. I am all you've got left now, and it is more than ever necessary that I should face the music. What I shall feel like tomorrow I haven't the faintest idea. All I know is that I have got to catch the early tram. . . ."

She could say no more, but walked across the room and out into the hall which was lit by a few candles. Denis followed, repeating over and over again:

"And what about me? You're reckoning without me, Rose."

"You?"

She shrugged her shoulders and grasped the handrail of the staircase. . . . As though relations can help us in the miseries of love! No aid of that kind can ever be forthcoming whether from a father, a brother or a son. We are shut within a circle of damnation which they cannot cross. Rose's affection for Denis was very great, but she would never get from him a single cooling drop of water. He realized in that instant of her going that this break with Robert, so far from forging a stronger bond between his sister and himself, had actually widened the gap that separated them. The agony of mind of which Robert was the cause had set the girl in a no-man's land into which he could never penetrate. The heart's despair is boundless as the sea. All he could do was to lie there on the shore and look on while she suffered.

As Pierre drove home he rehearsed in solitude the scene which he meant to have with his brother before the night was many hours older. . . . No, he wouldn't wait till morning, but would burst into the wretched creature's room, wrench him awake, and say . . . well, what *should* he say? Time enough to think of that.

Driving at night along an open road, beneath a sky in which the stars are all awash in the radiance of a waning moon, the traveller feels as though he will never reach his journey's end.

But already the sound of the wheels was starting echoes from sleeping suburban streets. The lamps, turned low, shone on rows of gloomy buildings packed tight with human slumber. Here and there an open window showed black. By every door the house-hold refuse stood waiting for the scavenger.

At last there came in sight the dour frontage of the house where he had been born, where, tonight, he would accomplish the plan that he had formed. . . . He pushed open the door of Robert's room without knocking, and, even before he had lit the candle, realized that it was empty. He saw the turned-down bed, the carefully arranged table. How well he knew that mingled scent of tobacco and ambergris—and that other smell redolent of the animal, which had been familiar to his nose since childhood. Sooner or later the prowling beast would sneak back to its lair.

Though he was dropping with sleep, he was determined to wait for his brother. Seated in the padded armchair into which he had so often snuggled, he kept himself awake by counting the invitation cards stuck in the frame of the mirror. Having done that, he tried to remember the diatribe he had prepared. But no, he decided, it would be much better to rely upon the inspiration of the moment. What agony it was to keep his eyes from closing! Now and again he heard from the street the sound of footsteps that seemed about to stop at the front-door but passed on. A carriage drew near, gave him the impression that it was slowing down, and then drove by at a dispirited trot. He forgot why he was trying to keep awake. Some lines from *Atys* rose to the surface of his memory. A horrible thought broke in his mind: why should not Cybele transform Atys into a pine, not to revenge herself upon him for his faithlessness, but so that she might possess him through eternity and be possessed, so that they might grow together as earth and tree for ever? . . . He fell into a dream that drew him far from Atys and from Robert, from Cybele and from Rose.

A footstep paused uncertainly outside the door. He ought to have recognized it, but heard nothing. Robert, standing in the doorway, saw his young brother, his right cheek pressed against the wing of the chair, and was momentarily tempted to take to his heels. But what good would that do? Whatever happened he had got, sooner or later, to face the boy's anger. From whom could he have heard the news? On the point of waking the sleeper, Robert paused. He had suddenly caught sight of his own face in the mirror of the wardrobe. It bore no tell-tale traces of the evening's traffic. He did not look more washed-out than usual. What do people mean when they talk of an "unsullied brow"? Certainly, the phrase was applicable to his own as it confronted him with its crown of auburn hair touched here and there with gold by the dawn-light filtering through the venetian blinds. On the chimney-stack a pigeon cooed. All the sparrows of the Square Pey-Berland awoke in concert. Pierre, his mouth half open, was breathing peacefully. Was Rose still sleeping at this hour? Had she had sufficient strength of mind to take off her clothes and lie down? Perhaps it was via Denis that Pierre had had news of her . . . perhaps something terrible. . . .

"Pierrot!" he suddenly cried aloud, "Pierrot, what has happened?"

The boy opened his eyes, fixed them absent-mindedly on his brother, smiled affectionately, and then, in a flash, remembered.

"You swine!" he shouted.

Robert seemed not to have heard him, but went on asking questions. Had he had news of Rose?

Pierre by this time was on his feet.

"I saw her: I went back with her to Léognan. Oh, don't worry yourself, she was quite alive and well when I left her, almost calm. I just wanted to let you know, before I leave for good, how contemptible I find you, how utterly I repudiate any connexion with you. . . ."

"Those are big words, old man."

Quite without intention, moved unconsciously by an instinct of self-preservation, Robert had let his voice fall into that warm and melancholy tone which people found irresistible. In the presence of his big brother Pierre felt his strength of mind slipping away . . . "I'll get my major to punch your head!"—the words came back to him from those far-off days when he was only five and the older boys were bullying him: "I'll get my major to punch your head!" He hadn't meant Gaston, the eldest, but this man whose beseeching eyes he could not bear to watch. There was not much change in him since their boyhood. Even at five years old, Pierre had adored him as someone incredibly strong, tall and handsome, and now there was still in Robert's face, in Robert's voice, something of the same weak charm, something of the old childishness.

"Why did you do it?" asked Pierre miserably.

The guilty man spread his arms slightly in a vague and helpless gesture. In response to the other's single query—"Money?" he shrugged.

"No, Pierrot. . . . You've *got* to understand."

But how was he to make this eighteen-year old judge realize the misery of a man of twenty-three, how make him see the weakness of character that lay behind such an air of adequacy and apparent strength? Robert had thought it all out during those night-hours from which he was just emerging. His mind was never clearer than when he was in places, and with people, of a certain type. Low company released him from his inhibitions. Dogged forever by his weakness, he felt genuinely free only when he was with the kind of woman who pays no heed to, cares not a straw for, the character of her casual customers. Through the long, dark hours, therefore, he had been thinking over what he had done. Could he have expressed his true mind he would have said: "Certainly it was money that finally weighed down the scales, money, and the horror of having all her family hanging like a millstone round my neck . . . but fundamentally it wasn't so much that as a craving for the gutter which goes in constant fear of being repressed and controlled by the presence in my life of someone really pure, like Rose. While I was in love with her, while I wanted her as a *woman*, it was possible for me to hold at bay that part of me which turned from her in terror. But once work and poverty had transformed her into a shabby little shop-girl who no longer roused my senses, I could not remain deaf to the inner voice which nothing had ever wholly silenced. . . . 'Once make this romantic creature your daily intimate,' it said, 'and it's good-bye to our delirious transports . . . or, if at times we do still indulge, it will have to be furtively and with a shame-faced feeling. We shall never be free of that atmosphere of *goodness* with which, because of her, you will be surrounded. You will live your life condemned to sacrifice, to poverty and to selflessness. . . . You know that I cannot be fobbed off with dribs and drabs. I cost a lot to satisfy, and you realize quite clearly that you haven't got enough money to meet with ease my exigent demands, and that you have never been sufficiently alone to catch my slightest whisper and, leaving all to follow me. . . .'"

"What are you thinking, Robert? What have you got to say to me?"

The other started and, for a moment, faced his questioner squarely. But no, such thoughts could not be put into words. It was impossible for him to speak his mind.

"My conduct has been unpardonable," he stammered. "I'm not going to try to excuse myself. I can only beg your forgiveness. And now, what have you got to say about it?"

"Just this—that whether I pass my exam or fail, I am going away. That is not altogether news to you, I imagine?"

Robert hung his head. It had been bound to come to this: "And no bad thing, either," murmured that inner voice, "to get this other embarrassing witness out of the way, this oversensitive, this insistent commentator and incorruptible judge. For this younger brother of yours has always made even me feel a bit awkward. More, perhaps, than Rose, he would have sentenced you to a life of moral grandeur, or, at least to its outward trappings. Now that *she* is out of your life for good, it is much better that he should go with her, and no longer be there to see our fall, our flight, our escape into the subterranean tunnel. All's for the best. He would have been perfectly capable of begging you to go back to the girl. And you're so weak! He might well have hoped to win you over. But, as it is, he has tried nothing of the sort. It's almost as though he had a presentiment that deep in yourself there lies a determination to refuse; almost as though he had smelt out my presence. Shed a few tears if you like: *I* don't mind. After all, you *are* losing this beloved brother of yours for ever. But rejoice, too, at the thought that there'll never be anyone again, not as long as you live, to look with accusing eyes at your —at our—delights."

He had been leaning on the back of another chair. He took his hands from his face. Only then did he see that Pierrot had left the room. The thin light of dawn dribbled through the blinds, and lit up every corner of the hideous room and the dead heart.

XIV

"WHY, of course I'll take your bag, Mademoiselle Landin," said the concierge, "I'm stronger than you are, and more used to that sort of thing."

"You mustn't talk while you're going upstairs, Madame Joseph, especially with a load like that. I've always done everything for myself, and I'm not ashamed to admit it, though it's true that all the time I was staying with my brother he wouldn't so much as hear of me lifting a finger. Would you believe it—he's got a butler and a cook—although there's no one there but himself. You've no idea the position he's made for himself in four

months. He's in charge of Monsieur Edgar Salem's claims de-
partment—though it's all too complicated for poor women
like you and me to understand. Monsieur Salem owns a number
of *very* respectable newspapers. Monsieur Landin says that their
policy is to *lash* the manners of the age—and they need some
lashing, believe me! These papers all profess different opinions,
because Monsieur Salem does not wish to be accused of taking
sides. He's afraid of nobody and attacks all the most powerful
men of the day, even if they *have* got the law on their side—
which is only natural seeing that they *made* it, didn't they?—so
you'd hardly expect it to be otherwise. That's where Louis comes
in with his genius for legal procedure. Monsieur Salem's a *very*
different sort of man from Oscar Revolou. *He* knows the meaning of gratitude. He's never sick of saying, 'Really, Landin, I
don't know what I should do without you'. . . ."

"He's sly, that brother of yours," broke in Madame Joseph.
"I don't mind betting that by this time he's got a proper hold on
his old man. . . ."

Félicia gave a start.

"That shows how little you know him! Sly? poor dear Louis
sly? Why, anyone, anyone at all, could twist him round his little
finger. You've no idea how easily he's taken in. I'm terrified that
he'll end up in the workhouse. Do you know what he does with
all the money he can't spend? You'd expect him to invest it,
wouldn't you, to take advantage of all the inside information
that comes his way? Not a bit of it! He's started a sort of charitable institution, a hostel for young foreigners in Paris, men of
under twenty-five, because, you see, he had to make an age-
limit of some sort. Most of them, as you can well imagine, have
got no money. Nobody realizes how truly Monsieur Landin
loves the common people. . . ."

"But why foreigners, Mademoiselle Landin? As though *we*
didn't have a hard enough time of it! Why shouldn't he give
French people a bit of a helping hand?"

"I must say, I rather agree with you, and I did speak to Louis about it once. But he's got his own ideas on that subject. He thinks that young Frenchmen are slovenly and immoral and ill-mannered. Not, mind you, that he doesn't take an interest in them too, but then who *doesn't* he take an interest in? You should hear his concierge talk! 'He's not one of your stuck-up ones,' she said to me. 'He just loves to listen to all my little troubles: always asking about my eldest, who's doing his military service, and about his little brother who's going to make his first Com-munion. It doesn't matter how many cares and troubles of his own he's got, he's always ready to listen to mine—sits up all night listening, so that it's a pleasure to talk to him, he's so interested. And he gives such good advice, too. Preaches to my husband—who's a bit too fond of the bottle. Your brother's more an angel than a man, Mademoiselle Landin,' she said, 'you can see it in his eyes.' Louis has changed a good deal in appearance, you know. He has shaved off his beard and really looks quite hand-some. . . . 'When I first got to know him,' the concierge told me, 'it was just when my youngest was being carried off with the meningitis . . . and he'd come in quite often and sit with me by the cradle. Never took his eyes off me, or off the poor little mite. Not that everyone wasn't very kind, but with them it was just come and go and a word of sympathy maybe, but he was there all the time and saw what we were going through'. . . ."

Mademoiselle Landin had taken off her hat. She leaned out of the window above the street filled with the noises of a July morning. A storm had burst during the night, and a few belated puddles were drying on the pavement.

"What *I* can't understand," said Madame Joseph, with her hand on the latch, "is how a kind and charitable gentleman like him can bring himself to do the work he's chosen—always having to be so hard on people. . . ."

Mademoiselle was about to reply, but changed her mind. Madame Joseph's bright and birdlike eye had given her timely warning. She was always being caught out like this! If only she wasn't so weak, wasn't forever angling for the admiration of her inferiors! She ought to know how to keep her distance. It wasn't, thank Heavens, that her brother had anything to hide, but he *had* told her not to talk about what she had seen in Paris, and now here she was, barely out of the train, almost before she'd taken off her hat, already breaking her word. She ought to have a greater sense of responsibility.

"Going so soon, Madame Joseph?"

She brought her back into the room, hoping that by indulging in a few more confidences she might undo the mischief of which she had been guilty by putting ideas into the head of one of the lower classes. Not that the woman wasn't always very pleasant spoken, but she might, all the same, be spiteful and dangerous.

"I could talk all day and all night about my brother, Madame Joseph. When he was poor he was always thinking of other people, so much so that he let himself be positively *skinned* by the Revolous. You can imagine, can't you, what it means for a man like that to have all the money he wants?"

"All the money he wants!" (here Madame Joseph clasped her hands). "How happy he must be! It's hard to believe that things like that can really happen!"

"He's too sensitive to be happy. There's scarcely a thing that doesn't cause him pain. He can't bear evil in any form. It's as though he were being flayed alive! The truth is he's too high-souled to bear with equanimity the ugliness of life. There's always something to make him suffer. 'You've got everything you can possibly want, Louis,' I said to him, 'so why are you so sad?' And do you know what he answered? 'One is always alone.' And that's true enough for the chosen few of this world."

"Well, I don't think it does anyone any good to be too perfect," said Madame Joseph. "What Monsieur Landin needs is to go on the bust-like, say once a month. It's as good as taking a dose of medicine!"

"You mustn't mind my saying, Madame Joseph, that there are certain refinements which you do not understand."

"I suppose this brother of yours is a proper saint. . . ."

Mademoiselle Landin protested that he was far from being any such thing, that he had a number of little weaknesses (she thought she caught a gleam in the birdlike eye), but the concierge who had now given up all idea of going away, said she could not imagine what the weaknesses of a man like that could possibly be.

"Tell me one of them," she urged, "just one, Mademoiselle Landin. You see, now—you can't!"

"Don't hurry me. Perhaps if I think very hard. . . . Well, it does sometimes happen (oh, very, very rarely) that he persuades himself he's doing something from a sense of duty when really he's only acting out of spite. . . . For instance, you probably know whom I mean by Regina Lorati?—she was a dancer at the Grand Theatre, the woman for whose sake Oscar Revolou ruined himself . . . after the crash she went off to Paris with that young Costadot. . . . Well, you've no idea the dance Louis has led her! Every one of Monsieur Salem's papers has been at her heels. She had to leave the Opéra Comique, and then the Olympia. . . . 'No, Louis,' I said to him, 'don't tell me that you're doing all this from a sense of justice. Your old master being dead doesn't make an atom of difference. You still belong to him body and soul, and it's he who is driving you on to commit this act of vengeance!' But he wouldn't listen to me, and of course, in a way, he *was* actuated by good feelings, if loyalty to the memory of the man who exploited him can be called a good feeling. . . . I'm telling you all this just to show you that Monsieur Landin has his faults like anyone else. . . . But that does not alter the fact that he's a very remarkable man! . . ."

"I don't doubt it, not for a moment. He wouldn't make all that money if he wasn't a remarkable man!"

With these words Madame Joseph took her leave, after receiving in her right hand which she managed at once both to proffer and withdraw, a franc piece.

Forgetting all about unpacking, Félicia Landin wandered about the flat in a state of considerable agitation, trying hard to remember what she had said. It wasn't her fault if she had never, in the whole course of her life, had anybody to talk to, so that she just "poured herself out" to the first person who showed a readiness to listen. Nothing had been further from her mind than to harm Louis. In fact, everything she had said had redounded to his greater glory. If the truth must be told, the picture she had drawn of him was to no small extent touched up. She hoped to goodness that there was nothing reprehensible in her brother's Paris life. But that, for the moment, was not what was bothering her. All that mattered was that she should not unwittingly have revealed something of his possible delinquencies in the course of the confidences with which (how foolishly!) she had honoured her concierge, who was certainly unworthy of the compliment thus paid her, and might, for all Félicia knew, be a dangerous woman. . . . How like Louis she felt herself to be! Far too lacking in self-respect, far too apt to get on over-familiar terms with the lower classes. Not that she loved them as he did. In fact, nothing would have pleased her better than that her brother should have given her an opportunity to get to know really *nice* people. But he had never made any effort to raise himself socially. . . .

Why had he paid so little attention to her during her stay in Paris? So marked had his lack of interest been that, after the first week, she had thought it better to clear out, lock, stock and barrel, and go to an hotel. She had worried herself sick over the whole business, and there wasn't a soul she could talk to. There were things she had stumbled on by accident, others at which she had guessed, and they made her terribly anxious. Somehow or other she had got to get this business off her chest. She had done parish work too long not to know most of what was to be known about charitable enterprises, and, frankly, she was deeply concerned about her brother's missionary activities. He was so terribly imprudent! What she had not told Madame Joseph was that Louis had packed her off to the hotel after a scene in the course of which she had not minced her words. "You think that everyone else is the same as you, and that if you're only kind enough to the poor, they'll be like lambs and eat out of your hand! Well, one of these days you'll discover your mistake! You'll be robbed and murdered in your bed—just you mark my words!"

It was after she'd said that that he had put his fingers in his ears and rushed out of the room. She had heard him shouting to Adolphe, the butler, "See that she packs her bags and gets out of here!" That was how he had treated her in front of a servant. But not for the world would she have breathed a word about it to anyone—not even to Madame Joseph.

XV

"PLOUGHED!" exclaimed Denis to his sister who was trying to make her way through the crowd of candidates surging round the notice-board.

"Are you sure?—I can't believe it! . . ."

He dragged her away. She had great difficulty in keeping up with him.

"Denis, dear, what do you say to us going home in a cab? I'll pay."

He protested irritably that that was the last thing in the world he wanted, and she made no attempt to over-persuade him. They stood at the corner of the Rue de Cursol, waiting for the tram. Thunderclouds hid the sun, but the city was sweltering. A strong smell came from the near-by hospital. It was as though the whole of the Sainte-Eulalie district had been drenched in phenol. Rose struggled to the surface of her unhappiness and, like a good swimmer, struck out in an effort to get close to her brother. 'It's the first time for three weeks that she has taken the slightest notice of me,' thought Denis. She struggled desperately to find something to say, and was foolish enough to ask whether Pierrot had got through.

"Yes, I think so," he answered.

He was amazed at the effect this set-back had had upon him, at the extent of his humiliation. He wondered what the masters at his college would think when they learned about this, and those at the Lycée where he had read for the second part of his baccalauréat. Not that, actually, it mattered much, because in any case his education would have had to be cut short. Léognan was to be sold in the autumn, and he would have to look about for a job. . . .

"It must have been that science paper . . ." Rose hazarded the suggestion, and he made no attempt to contradict it. But it wasn't the science paper that had been the trouble, but that wretched philosophy question . . . which he had treated too unconventionally. . . . They changed trams on the Boulevard. Already Denis had ceased to occupy the foreground of Rose's attention. Her eyes were fixed on something beyond him, on that moment of time which would forever be in her mind's centre. 'She's already forgotten that I am miserable.' . . . Being ploughed in an examination matters neither here nor there, but when one is seventeen, the feeling that for the first time one has suffered defeat matters a great deal. It sows the seed of self-doubt. Suddenly, with a sense of terror, one realizes that perhaps one isn't cleverer than, perhaps not even as clever as, one's neighbour. It comes to one as a shock that one is not of those who are masters of their destiny.

If only Rose had taken his hand, had turned on him that long, brooding gaze which he had so loved in the old days. If only she had made his sadness her own. If only they could have mingled their tears . . . then this evening would have held more joy than bitterness. . . . Was Rose to be for ever confined within the prison, the narrow cell, of her misery? Could a poor fish like Robert, a man who in any real sense hardly existed at all, so cut her off from life?

His mother seemed to be more deeply concerned at his failure than he had expected. It was of a piece with all her other anxieties of the moment. . . . Léognan would have to be sold before the winter, because they could not afford to have the roof seen to. . . . If only Denis had got through his examination it would have been easier to find him a job. If he failed again in October, hadn't he better give up all idea of going on with his education? Like the tributaries of a mighty river, every disaster that had fallen on Lucienne Revolou, beginning with Rose's broken engagement, flowed together into the one terrible current of anxieties that had its origin in Léognan. So long as it remained their home, she did not realize their ruin as something actual. But the thought of having to settle down in some horrible little flat in Bordeaux, indistinguishable from two thousand others, stood in her mind for destitution complete and irreparable. She was worried, too, about her health. Certain symptoms had recently sounded a warning note, though she had mentioned them to nobody. When she had gone, what would happen to Julien? He had had a relapse, and was now entirely confined to his room. His mother worked herself to the bone for him without getting so much as a "thank you." The silence which he had maintained in the first stage of his illness was a thing of the past. He spent most of his time now inveighing against Rose in a ceaseless monologue. It was she who was responsible for what had happened to them. What an unheard of piece of luck it had been, after everything had crashed about their ears, that she should have been sought in marriage by a Costadot! And then she must needs let him slip between her fingers! So much for intellectual ambitions!—their only effect was to bore a fellow so hopelessly that he just took to his heels! . . . That sort of chance didn't come more than once . . . so unimaginable, so unlooked-for a solution of all their difficulties! . . . And we're left to pay the bill!'

Didn't she want any fruit? Rose asked.

"I don't know *what* Julien is going to say about this news of yours, Denis, I had better go up and prepare him for it," said Madame Revolou, folding her napkin.

Denis got up too. He could not swallow another mouthful. Rose followed, and walked for a while beside him.

"The worst of it is that your holidays will be cut short."

He made no reply, hoping for a greater show of tenderness, for some sign that she had thrown in her lot with him and was prepared to enter the wretched and quite unimportant little world of unhappiness that closes round a young man who has been "ploughed." She thought that he was sulking, as he had been doing ever since her engagement had been broken off.

"You'll get through all right in October."

"What's the point now, even if I do? The most I can hope for is to spend the rest of my life scribbling away in some basement office. . . ."

She knew that she ought to have drawn closer to him, that what he needed was a sense of "inner" consolation . . . but her mind was otherwise occupied. She longed to be alone in her room so that she might read the letter which had come the previous evening. . . .

Suddenly she said:

"Perhaps you'd rather be left to yourself?"

"No, Rose, no: please don't go."

But he had spoken in too low a voice, and the girl had already moved away. She hastened to her room, hungry for the comfort and the joy which her letter would bring. She had refrained so far from even glancing at it, fearful lest she exhaust its possibilities of healing. Not that she expected to find in it the slightest excuse for hoping that he might return to her, but it might, at least, take the sting from those horrible words with which he had left her.

"All I thought of was something to say that would part us for ever. I had to get out of your life. . . ."

The whole letter was nothing but a prolonged commentary on this passage. At first, Rose had found it difficult to grasp, but by dint of dwelling on it she managed to associate the words with certain recollections which, for all her blindness, she could not fail to understand. So obsessed had she been, in the days of her happiness, with her picture of him as the perfect lover, that she had scarcely ever seen him as he was. Yet, in spite of herself, some inkling of the truth had come; certain aspects of him as a being of flesh and blood were deeply etched into her consciousness. The man from who Robert claimed that he had wanted to free her was no other than the frightening stranger, unrecognizable and unknown, whom she had pushed away that evening in the lime-grove. But she knew now that he was the real Robert, and she loved him.

In those first terrible days, whenever her mother set herself to repeat the rumours about "young Costadot" which she had got from Julien, Rose had left the table hurriedly so as not to hear more. But she knew well enough that the man of whom her mother said such terrible things did, in very fact, exist. This stranger was the Robert whom she loved. When one is in love one cannot pick and choose. One must needs take a man as he is —all of him, she thought. He is as God has made him, and one must square one's shoulders to carry the weight of his weaknesses. She believed with all her heart in those deep and secret bonds that hold more surely than the tie of blood.

"If," wrote Robert, "you are strong and brave enough, I beg of you not to reject me utterly. I should like to think that I was still part of your life, but without the horrible feeling that you were bound hand and foot to my miserable self."

So there was, even now, something she could do for him. Reading and re-reading his letter, she succeeded, as day followed day, in persuading herself ever more convincingly that she had never really been pious, that the formalities of her mother's religion—which was the only one she knew—meant nothing to her. Nevertheless, she had begun again the practice of saying her prayers. She had developed a new technique of praying, which was to think of Robert in Somebody else's presence, to call in as witness to her thoughts an invisible Being.

She would gladly have remained indefinitely on her knees, her face buried in the coverlet of her bed. This man, merely by abandoning her, had pointed the way, if not to a life of devotion, at least to the familiar presence of a Person who had now taken on for her a genuine existence, and who actually minded what happened to her, to Rose Revolou whom Robert Costadot had betrayed. But the mingled ecstasies and tears that came to her as she knelt there in her room, were shot through by feelings of anxiety for Denis. She ought never, this evening of all evenings, to have left her young brother to himself. His was a terribly sensitive nature, and the wound to his pride had gone deep. Pierre Costadot was fond of saying that Denis had a vocation for suffering. To make of prayer a pretext for neglecting her brother, she thought, was to be guilty of treachery to God. . . . Filled with remorse, she hurried downstairs and ran into the garden.

'She chooses this, of all evenings, when I have failed in my exam., to leave me alone!' said Denis to himself, not once but many times. 'There is no one in the whole world lonelier than I am.' The memory of Rose filled him with a sense of infinite bitterness. She had abandoned him. It was inexcusable. Never could she expiate such a crime, nor had she ever carried indifference to such lengths. He spoke aloud those two lines of Corneille for which he would gladly give all Pierre's adored Racine:

> Je l'envisage entier mais je n'en frémis point
> Notre malheur est grand, il est au plus haut point.

stressing the rhythm, making a pause at the cæsura, merging into a single powerful tide of bitterness the humiliating sense of his defeat, Rose's abandonment of him, and the certain knowledge that he was henceforth to be condemned to a life of dreary, grinding toil. He drank of his own unhappiness of as some heady wine. In a species of morbid exaltation he walked through the darkness towards the stable entrance.

The glowing end of a cigarette moved and went out. He heard

MINISTRY OF SOCIAL SECURITY

YS	55	48	83	B

Miss L M Thompson
Grove House
Newsham Hall Lane
Woodplumpton PRESTON

My course of full-time education/training **at**

.... *(name and address of*
School, University,
.... *College, Training*
.... *Centre, etc.)*

* is continuing. The course is expected to end on

....

Day   Month   Year

*has ended. The course lasted from
                              (If before fifteenth
.... *birthday insert "Before 15")*

Day   Month   Year

to..*(Any vacation period after*
attendance must not be included)

Permanent address (*if different from the address above*)

....

....

Signature...Date................................
* Please complete whichever alternative applies

Form CF 56 (Tear off)

Irène Cavailhes's laugh, and caught a brief glimpse of her face in the green glow of a Chinese lantern. The butcher's son jumped on to his bicycle and rode off.

"Caught in the act, Irène!" said Denis.

"What a fright you gave me! How d'you mean, caught in the act? It was only the Parage boy come for orders . . . what's wrong in that?"

"I thought the butcher wasn't bothering about us these days. . . ."

"Not about you, he isn't, but us."

Denis uttered a short laugh. Irène felt her cheeks flame. "I'm sorry," she said in sudden confusion.

He replied that there was nothing to be sorry about.

"Oh, yes, there is," she said, "I know perfectly well that what I said hurt your feelings," and embarked straightway on a flood of apologies.

He assured her that she was mistaken. It wasn't *that* he was worried about. He had failed in his written examination, and it had come as a horrible surprise.

"Failed? a clever boy like you? . . . Somebody must have had a down on you . . . perhaps because of your mother . . . people are so spiteful!" And then, as he started to protest: "Why, you know more than the lot of them put together!"

He felt ashamed that he should have to fall back for comfort on the ignorant admiration of a little idiot like this. He went close to her.

"I'm feeling miserable—console me a little."

"No," she said in a low voice. "I'm a good girl."

"Oh, come now. If I was young Parage . . ."

She protested. She had never done anything like that with the Parage boy, nor with anyone else. Besides, he was only a kid. . . . She'd never thought of him as anything but a child. She drew the back of her finger down his cheek.

"It's as smooth as a peach! You don't even have to shave!"

He replied heatedly that he shaved at least twice a week.

A beam of light fell on the privet hedge as Maria Cavailhes opened the kitchen door.

"Where are you, Irène?" she cried from the threshold.

"Here I am, mother, with Monsieur Denis."

"Come in, I'm going to lock up."

"Let her be," said Cavailhes, who was sitting on a bench in the porch. "I want a bit of air. Wait till I've finished my pipe."

"I don't like them being alone together in the dark."

"He's her foster-brother."

"Foster-brother my foot!" she muttered.

"You do as I say, and let her be."

What had got into him? she wondered. He sucked noisily at his pipe which had gone out. In the light of the match she could see the peak of his cap, his big nose, his enormous moustache worn à la Kaiser, and his hairy forearm. In spite of the heat he was wearing a knitted waistcoat, the lower buttons of which were unfastened. Though he was not fat, he had the beginnings of a paunch. He had never asked his wife's opinion about anything, and cared little for what she might think. She had always been his chattel, and still was—except in bed. He had made no bones about taking his pleasure with every woman who had worked on the estate. Irène was the only member of the family who had any influence over him. They were always confiding in one another, and would stop talking when Maria came into the room. . . .

"No," Irène was saying, "not in the lime-grove, Monsieur Denis. Why are you so keen to go there especially? It'll be stifling: the heat of the day hangs about so under the trees. Besides, we can't see each other there. This bench is much better for a chat. Let's sit down here."

He didn't, he said, want a chat, but to be consoled.

"Why do you let it get you down? That's just silly."

There was a short silence.

"What a big girl you're getting," he whispered.

"How d'you mean big?" She sounded annoyed.

"It's a compliment, I like big girls."

She drew back.

"As though it mattered, failing in an exam!" she was still harping on that. "What good is an exam. anyway?"

Not much good, he admitted, since he wouldn't be able to go on with his studies, but would have to look for work once Léognan was sold.

"Why shouldn't you stay here and help my father?"

She must know, he said, that his family wouldn't hear of such a thing.

"I can't see why they're so suspicious of him. If he took out a mortgage on the estate and worked the land, it wouldn't make the slightest difference to them. They could all go on living there just as they've always done. Your share of the profits would cover the interest. Doesn't your mother realize that we're devoted, heart and soul, to the family?"

"It's not my mother. I don't expect she'd mind. . . . But what about Julien and Rose?"

"Mademoiselle Rose is ever so proud," said Irène. "But she has to go out to work all the same, like everybody else."

Denis removed his arm from Irène's waist.

"So you think she's like everybody else, do you? Don't make me laugh! I know she's working for her living, but that doesn't make any difference. She could beg in the street, but it would still be obvious that she belonged to a different species, a different race!"

"You're proud, too."

He sighed.

"Oh, God, proud of what?"

He leaned his head on the "big girl's" shoulder, and she made no attempt to repulse him. She felt flattered and faintly moved. She stroked his hair and his forehead with a respectful hand. Little did she know what heavy load of bitterness and despair lay, at that moment, against her body. To himself he said: 'And this is the best I can find to bring me comfort for humiliation and defeat. . . .'

But why, since he lacked the instinct of the fighter, and more resembled those insects who find security in a mimic death . . . why not snuggle into this easy retreat and come to terms with the Cavailhes? He had always hated the idea of any such arrangement, because Rose had hated it. But that was because he had been a little fool. Why should he bother about what Rose minded? . . . 'Why deceive myself? I hate her.'

He did not realize that he had been speaking aloud.

"What was that you said?" asked Irène. He pressed close to her, shut his eyes, but said no more. He loved the dense darkness of these airless, starless nights. What was that distant rumble? Perhaps a storm, perhaps the noise of practice gun-fire from Saint-Médard . . . not as late as this, it must be a storm. But nothing would come of it. All that the earth could hope for was a little dew at dawn. There would be no comfort for roots or leaves or grass. And for him there would not even be dew. The path on which his feet were set led nowhere. No hope of love awaited him, no living creature with a word of welcome for the wanderer.

Suddenly he heard his sister's voice. She was calling his name.

"Hush! don't move," he whispered to Irène.

"Where are you, Denis?"

"She'll pass quite close to us," said Irène in a low voice. "You'd better tell her we're here. It would be awful if she found us. . . ."

"No! keep quiet!"

He guessed at, rather than saw, the shadowy figure moving uncertainly towards them. When she was quite close, he laughed softly. Rose uttered a cry.

"How you frightened me! Where are you?"

"Here, on the bench, with Irène."

The daughter of the Cavailhes had got up to say "good

evening, Mademoiselle." Rose's reply was far from cordial.
She spoke to Denis as though no one else were there.

"You know that mamma likes to bolt the front-door at ten.
You'd better come in."

"She can jolly well leave the door open to-night: I'll lock up."
She asked him at what time he meant to come in.
When he felt like it, he said.

"There's no reason for you to be out of doors. You ought to
go to bed after the trying day you've had."

"I don't want to go to bed; I want to be amused. Irène," he
said on the spur of the moment, "run along and ask your mother
for some brandy-plums. . . . We'll have a little feast, if your
parents are still up."

"Well, you must make your peace with mamma," said Rose in
a thin little voice. "Don't be surprised if you find the door
locked."

"If I do, I'll sleep at the Cavailhes', as I used to do when we first
came back here. D'you remember that first night, Irène? I was
put to bed in your room, though I didn't know it was you in the
other bed. . . . Something terrible had happened that night, but I
shall always associate it with strange and happy thoughts—
because of you, Irène. . . ."

For all the sign that she gave of her presence, Rose might have
been no longer there, but through the rustling of the leaves and
the subdued sound of many insects, he caught the light, almost
inaudible, whisper of her uneasy breathing.

"I'll see that the door is left open," she said at last.

She vanished into the darkness. Her mind was far from easy,
and she was conscious of a vague feeling of irritation not unmixed
with jealousy. She blamed herself for having left Denis alone
while he was still smarting under the sense of his failure, but what
chiefly worried her was what was known in the family as "The
Cavailhes' Plan." Better destitution complete and irremediable
than a life dependent on *them*, than a continual feeling of being
under an obligation. Let them buy the house and settle down

there if they had saved enough to pay the price. But all inter-
course between the two families must cease. 'God knows what
ideas they're putting into his head!'

Profoundly upset by these reflections, she knocked at Julien's
door and called her mother's name in a low voice. Madame
Revolou appeared wearing a dressing-gown, her grey hair
twisted into a heavy knot. 'How fat she looks in that wrap,'
thought Rose, 'she's getting really huge!' The bloodless face
should have moved her to feelings of compassion and uneasy
wondering. . . . But when a girl has sufferings of her own to
contend with, she is not likely to spare much attention for her
mother, though long before death comes he marks us with a sign
as clearly visible as the brand on a sheep's back.

"I'm worried. Denis is with the Cavailhes. Heaven knows
what they are trying to do with him!"

"Not so loud! . . . Why bother about it? I'm the one who will
have to take decisions."

"I know. But he's thinking of helping Cavailhes on the estate.
You know how utterly dependent we all are on that man."

Madame Revolou replied that, after all, he was a thoroughly
decent sort . . . and it was no use blinking facts. Julien was a permanent invalid, and she herself was beginning to feel her age.

"I shan't be here always. The Cavailhes have a great affection
for the family: they are devoted to us."

"So they say . . ."

"You're quite wrong. When I've gone, they will still regard
Julien as the head of the family. So far as they are concerned,
there will always be a Revolou."

The sound of a sleeper's confused muttering came from the
room.

"Go away now, Julien's getting restless. If he wakes up, I shall
have to read to him until it's light."

Instead of going to her room, Rose went down again into the
garden. The Cavailhes' door showed as a rectangle of light behind
the privet hedge. The father, the daughter and Denis were seated

round a table set with glasses and uncorked bottles. Cavailhes was saying something, but in tones so low that Rose could not hear. They touched glasses. Denis made a short speech broken by the laughter of his audience. He kissed Maria, and then Irène, who gurgled and put up a show of struggling.

When, at last, he left them, Maria accompanied him to the door and held the lamp high. He called back that he knew the way, and said good-night for the last time. The door was shut and bolted. He could not see the path in the darkness. A few heavy drops fell on his hair. He threw back his head so as to catch them on his face. The thin white wine had not made him drunk, but he no longer felt miserable. He heard the sound of rain upon the leaves. In a moment or two it would break through and reach him. Someone was moving on the path.

"Who's there?" he called.

"Me, Rose."

"So, you've taken to spying on me?"

They were so close that each could feel the warmth of the other's breath, though the darkness made both invisible. Such a thought had never occurred to her, she said. It was only that she was worried about what the Cavailhes might be plotting. Even allowing that they did not mean any harm, she did not want to be in their debt. Denis replied without the least show of excitement:

"People in our position can't stand on their dignity."

They had got to see reason, he said. If the Cavailhes raised a mortgage on the property, it meant that the most urgent of the repairs could be put in hand. Cavailhes would invest every penny of capital he had in the place, and would get everything possible out of the land: cattle, market-gardening. . . .

"He says that if it wasn't for him we should be ruined, but that if we stand in with him, we shall be amazed to find how much the estate will bring in. . . . He says that even when we have paid him the interest on his money, we shall still have enough left to live well and keep up appearances. . . . That keeping up appearances is a sort of mania with him. You've no idea what the family means to the Cavailhes."

"And what does Irène say to all these fine schemes?"

He was struck by the aggressive note in Rose's voice. The knowledge that she was both worried and hurt filled him with a mingled sense of anger and delight. He asked what Irène had to do with it. Rose said she couldn't believe there was nothing going on in the girl's head.

"And suppose there is something? . . . I don't have to account for my actions to anyone. If I take help where I can find it, I don't see what right you have to start meddling. . . ."

She was on the point of saying the one thing that might have brought her brother weeping into her arms. . . . "Am *I* not your help and your refuge?" but she did not say it. The fear of expressing our feelings is far more effective than any vice in the conduct of our lives. All that stood between them at that moment was a superficial anger and irritation. The pressure of a hand, a single word of tenderness and forgiveness, could have made all right. But Rose was held a prisoner in her silence. Denis believed that it denoted hostility, whereas really it was no more than a silly shyness, a childish dislike of taking the first step. Those few moments were enough to set a great gulf between them.

Nevertheless, Rose was realizing, as never before, that she must not take lightly the troubles of this poor, spikey child, that what had happened to him was indeed serious, that not only was his life involved, but all of his destiny that lay behind and beyond the visible accidents of mortality. What for the last week she had been feeling about Robert, she felt now about her brother. "Am I my brother's keeper?" The eternal question struck straight through all the accumulation of doubt and darkness which have gathered about it since man's first act of murder, and now found a target in the heart of a young girl standing at night in the suburban countryside somewhere near Bordeaux.

She tried to find the word that would open the door behind which Denis stood solitary in his suffering. But even while she hesitated, he began again to build his defensive wall of mockery and veiled threats. He could arrange his life without advice from anyone. He was not going to sacrifice his future on the altar of a ridiculous family pride.

She followed him, not daring to reply. In the hall, where their two candles were burning, she did, too late, what a while back he had hoped she might do—made as though to take him in her arms and kiss him. But he stiffened and, with a quick little motion of the head, avoided her lips.

Although she had already said her prayers, Rose knelt down again. It did not occur to her to repeat a second time the usual formulæ of her devotions. Instead, there rose from her defence-less heart a supplication which seemed to have its origin else-where than in her consciousness. She was speaking now, at last, to that Love of the shrouded countenance as though its name were not God, but, quite simply Love. She had crossed the last ditch, the last trench, the last strand of barbed wire. The agonies of slighted love had made her own particular cross. Her anxieties for her family were with her still, but she heard them only as one hears the confused murmur of daily cares. She was no longer at their centre but had moved beyond. "I know now that I am not walking aimlessly through trackless woods: that though my feet are wounded by the roots and briars, they are set on a path that stretches sure and clear before me. I follow it, but I am utterly alone. How that can be I do not understand, because at every moment You make it clear to me that I must tread that path with those whose fate You have given into my hands. I do not understand how it is that I have failed with those entrusted to my care by You. I *must* believe, I *do* believe, with all my heart, that all this only *seems*, and that some day I shall hear Denis running after me as he used to run when he was small, and shall hear his voice calling my name: that some day, at a turning in my path, I shall see someone sitting in the ditch, and shall recognize in him the man to whom You gave me, but who had no use for the gift. Instructed by You, and in spite of those who have no confidence in sinners, he will have taken a short cut, and there he will be, waiting for me. Perhaps he will have been there for years, and we shall mingle our sorrow and our kisses. Quite possibly that moment will come to me at the very gates of death. . . ."

The tears trickled down her cheeks, nor did she know whether her heart was on fire for the human creatures who were dearer to her than life itself, or for Him to whom she was speaking, that Being whose name might quite well not be the name of God.

But it was true that He had, too, another, a human, name. Why had she not thought of that? She had so often found herself using it by force of habit, but it had meant nothing to her mind or heart. It had been overlaid by empty formulæ and dead ceremonies, had been nothing but a mumbled sound with no message for her but boredom. And now, suddenly, it was a living reality, lighting her darkness with a tender glow. He was there.

The hiss of rain took to the countryside this new freshness, this sudden easing of constriction, of which she was conscious in herself. Her whole being shared in a sensation that was a strange mixture of suffering and delight. She ought to have gone to sleep, but sleep, she felt, would steal from her hours that might never come again, and prevent her from hearing the word that might never again be spoken. She felt for some object to touch, something on which her hand could close. A plaster crucifix hung on the wall. She had never really looked at it. It awoke no feeling in her. The fancy took her to rummage in the drawer of her wardrobe among a litter of boxes which had once held the presents given her at the time of her first Communion. Her hand lit on the case which held a rosary of lapis which she had never used—a "little jewel of a thing which would make a perfectly sweet bracelet. . . ." She looked now at the little heap of blue and golden beads lying in the hollow of her hand. She held them tight, once more a little girl of flesh and blood who needed a tangible sign of that mystery which now, at last, was to be revealed to her eyes.

XVI

"THE great thing, Madame, is that no time should be lost," said the young surgeon, looking at the lady in black. Her face seemed to "ring a bell" though he could attach no name to it. True to the method which he had learned from his master, he kept his verdict sufficiently vague to decide her in favour of an operation, while, at the same time, taking care to let it be seen that he did not consider her case as in any way hopeless. Lucienne Revolou never took her eyes from his face. She was trying to decide just how much she should believe, how much reject, of what this very young practitioner who was such a bad hand at lying, had said. Her body told her that sentence had been passed and pitted against the reasoning of her mind a peculiar anguish, a feeling of weariness that was quite different from her normal lassitude.

She coughed into her gloved hand and asked a question.

"We are in rather straitened circumstances at the moment, and I should like to know what it is all going to cost."

The doctor assured her that he always took his patients' financial position into account. She broke in on his words:

"Yes, yes . . . but what about the nursing-home? Their fees are very high. . . . The X-ray had already involved me in a lot of expense. . . . I do not want my children . . ."

"For those who are genuinely unable to pay there are a number of very comfortable rooms available at the hospital . . ." said the young man, reddening. "They open out of the general ward, but you would be quite private. . . ."

"No," she interrupted him incisively. "The hospital is out of the question. I am Madame Oscar Revolou," she added, as though to put an end to any further discussion.

The surgeon bowed and murmured: "An honour indeed, Madame. . . ."

"As I said before, doctor, I must know the whole truth. The question for me resolves itself into this: is the game worth the candle. What are my chances of recovery?"

She noticed his hesitation, and got up. She would not incur this expense. If she had got to die she did not wish to saddle her children with a heavy bill. The young surgeon realized that he had been lacking in diplomacy. He knew that her case was a very serious one, but could not believe that she would reject even a one in a thousand chance simply in order to save money.

As she buttoned her glove, she thought: 'I have made my decision. I will not be carved up.' That was the form she gave to her thought, and not—'I am certain to die, I am going to die.' Her imagination stopped on the hither side of the valley of shadows, and rested satisfied with the double certainty that she would avoid both the terrors and the expense of a useless operation. 'Even when they quote you a price, you can never be sure what you may not be let in for.'

First of all she must put her affairs in order. She went to the Jesuit Chapel in the Rue Margaux where any casual visitor could enter one or other of the numerous confessionals. Always the same old priest, the same smell of snuff, the same way of saying "my daughter," and sometimes an unexpected question which touched a hidden sore with its fine point, and made one tremble.

The priest who listened to her that day assured her that no one was obliged in conscience to undergo an operation the outcome of which was doubtful. All that God demanded was a childlike confidence and a complete acceptance of the Divine Will. He asked whether there was anything in her life that had caused her particular disquiet, anything that she would like to confess afresh. She thought. . . . She had not, she said, been always careful to see that her servants fulfilled their religious duties. Had she never been lacking in justice towards her fellow men? The full significance of the question escaped her, and she answered. "No, father."

She felt faintly humiliated that there was nothing at all in her life calling for reconsideration. It resembled a blank page across which an unknown master had scribbled, rather irritably, "Nothing." She made her penitence, chose in her missal the prayers and invocations which carried the largest number of indulgences, and went out. When she was in the street, breathless and fatigued as a result of the malignant thing she carried about with her (she could feel its weight in exactly the same spot as that in which she had felt the weight of her children, so that it was as though she were pregnant with her own death), she decided that she would run to the expense of a cab. *That* luxury, at least, she would give herself.

She hired a Victoria from a livery-stable in the Rue des Trois-Conils, the very same one in which her daughter's despair had been carried home. As she drove through the outer suburbs, where the signs of Autumn were already plain, her thoughts returned once again to that page of her life at which she had glanced in the intimacy of the confessional in the Chapel of the Rue Margaux. Nothing to report . . . and yet, and yet . . . there had been three children, relations, servants, household cares, the constant need to live up to her social position—in fact, the record of a whole life. Then, what about the anguish of these latter years? Léonie Costadot's visit, Oscar's suicide, Julien's illness, Rose's broken engagement, Denis' failure, and now? . . .

The cab trundled through the sweltering countryside where the first mists of the season were rising from the fields. Vats were being opened for airing before the grape harvest. Tubs, stained with the must of former years, stood piled at kitchen doors. Women were stripping the leaves from the vine plants, calling to one another the while from row to row. Lucienne Revolou, feeling the onset of her pain, sought a more comfortable position. For how much longer would she be able to look after herself? Whom ought she to tell? She must make things as easy as possible for the children. . . . What caused her most anxiety was wondering how Julien would get on, but she had an idea about that.

And Denis? little Denis, who had always made her feel so nervous? What a darling he had been up to fourteen! She thought of things he had said, and of how she had always so proudly repeated them. Now he was almost a man. Rose was sure that there was something between him and the Cavailhes girl—something more serious than a mere flirtation, as "serious" as it well could be, according to Rose. But Lucienne did not feel strong enough to let her mind grapple with the problem. In giving herself entirely, as she had done, to Julien, in confining all her efforts within the four walls of his room, she had probably been obeying, all unconsciously, the instinct which leads the mortally wounded animal to narrow the field of its activities, to make itself as small as possible. And even that was now becoming too much for her. Death does not leave us in peace merely because we accept his coming. Simple non-resistance to pain is of no avail in the blind world of the flesh, in that universe of cells and globules which obey the law of their being and take no account of ours, since, in truth, they are not us at all.

Irène and Denis, riding bicycles, passed the carriage in the narrow lane leading to the stables. They dismounted at the gate and stood waiting.

"Please ask your father to come up and see me after dinner," said Madame Revolou to Irène, "I shall be in the master's study."

The carriage drove on and the two young people exchanged glances. They walked, side by side, pushing their bicycles. It was rapidly getting dark. Thrushes in coveys were homing for the night, and migrant birds which Denis recognized by their song, though he called them by names quite different from the ones they bore in books of natural history. "That's a *site*," he would say, "that's a *tit*."

"It'll be too cold tonight to stay out of doors," murmured Irène.

He broke into verse:

We cannot sit down, the damp benches are cold;
The damp benches are cold, and the leaves turned to gold.

"What *are* you talking about?"

> The beginning of term and the dormitory wheezing:
> The poor devils out in the city streets freezing.

"What a silly you are!" she said, but she admired the way in which he came out with whatever happened to be in his mind—anything, no matter how idiotic, the sort of things that ordinary folk wouldn't understand. Denis was hugging himself at the thought of his sister's face when she saw their mother closeted with Cavailhes after dinner.

"I think it's all settled," he said, keeping his voice low.

Irène asked where they should meet.

"In my room. . . . Come in by the scullery entrance and up the back stairs. No, don't. . . . Come in openly by the billiard-room window."

"Your sister will see me. She's always spying."

There was a note of spite in the girl's voice.

"So much the better . . . she's got to get used to it," said Denis, and was seized with sudden disgust at the sound of Irène's shriek of laughter. She did not understand that by speaking thus of Rose, he was tearing at his own heart-strings.

Madame Revolou started to tidy Julien's room, seemingly deaf to the angry complaints that came from the alcove, to the effect that it was intolerable for a sick man to be left alone all day in a room without a bell! He'd had a perfectly frightful time! One of these days she'd find him at his last gasp, as she had found his father. . . .

He noticed that she had sat down to take off her hat.

"What's the matter with you?" he asked. Then, as she made no answer:

"I believe you're frightening me on purpose!"

She got up without a word, went to wash her hands, told Julien, as she came back through his room, that his meal would be sent up to him, and proceeded to the dining-room where Rose and Denis were standing behind their chairs, waiting for her. It was a family custom that she should always be the first to take her seat, and the rule was never broken. Denis swallowed his soup with the greediness of a famished dog. His body had filled out, and there was a healthy colour in his cheeks. Only by dint of a liberal application of grease could he keep his hair parted. When the little maid brought in the cheese she told Madame that Cavailhes was waiting in the study. Lucienne drank a glass of water and got up, pressing heavily with her hands on the table.

"Go on with your fruit and don't wait for me. I've finished."

The only sound to be heard was the clatter made by Denis with his spoon against the plate. Rose asked him whether he knew what Cavailhes wanted.

"It was mamma who told him to come up to the house," he replied in a rather furtive manner.

Rose got up, made her way to the door of her father's study from behind which she could hear the muffled sound of Cavailhes' voice, threw a cape round her shoulders, and plunged into the dampness of the night air. She had not sold a single book that day, only stationery. Old Chardon had deducted twenty francs from her month's money because she had forgotten that one particular line of envelopes had gone up in price. Her legs ached, but she could not stay still. Try as she might she could not help despising the girl Irène, and shrinking in horror from the animal look in Denis's face. She walked aimlessly, bowed down by her burden, cut adrift from the shore where, on a night of tears and ecstasies, she had once hoped to land. Again, as of old, prayer had become for her merely a matter of words, phrases, formulæ. God?—three letters signifying she knew not what. Robert?—a young man whom once she had attracted, only to be rejected with disgust. People were just people, and no more. Words conveyed nothing but their literal meaning. Rose Revolou, a shop-assistant at Chardon's, would go on vegetating in a corner of this old house put to rights with Cavailhes' money. Sooner or later the Cavailhes family would invade it.

The path led her back to the house. She saw Denis come out through the lit window of the billiard-room. He stood for a moment in the illuminated frame, and gave a signal. Irène Cavailhes followed him in. The light moved, vanished.

She felt the onset of mean and spiteful thoughts. She drove away the pictures that rose before her mind's eye, turned, went back along the little path that led to the lime-grove, sat down on the bench, rested her arms on its back, and buried her face in them. Her tears began to flow. The thick and withered branches heard the sound of sobs and strangled breathing. But her brain remained alert and lucid. 'It's all very well,' she told herself, 'for you to despise them. Don't you see that you're just like them, that you belong to the same species, that you're no whit better?'

She got up and hurried back to the house. As she drew near the front steps, her mother appeared, carrying a lamp, showing the bailiff out.

"Mind the step, Cavailhes."

"I hope you'll follow my advice, ma'am, and go and see the wise woman over at Gazinet. She'll put you to rights, mark my words, and it'll only cost five francs. Not that I believe in witchcraft, but I do believe in herbs."

"I'll think about it, Cavailhes. Then, it's agreed, isn't it, that your wife shall come in and look after Monsieur Julien, starting from tomorrow?"

She could rest easy on that score. The young gentleman would be thoroughly spoiled.

Rose heard her mother call after him:

"I did give you the estimate for the roof, didn't I?"

The girl remained standing in the shadow of the house until Cavailhes had gone. Then she hurried into the billiard-room, convinced that her mother had gone upstairs. But she was wrong. The old lady was sitting quite still, with the lamp on a table beside her.

"I do hope you've done nothing definite without asking me," said Rose. "After all, I've got a voice in all this, and it really would be too bad of you. . . ."

"You can be quite sure, dear, that nothing will be settled without your consent."

It was a long time since her mother had addressed her as "dear."

"True, I've got Cavailhes to agree that Maria shall look after Julien from now on. . . . I get very tired these days, though I may not show it. . . ."

"That's how they'll get a hold over us," said the girl, intent on her own train of thought. "They'll make themselves indispensable, and so gradually get what they're after. . . ."

"You're unfair on them. What they're 'after,' as you put it, is perfectly natural and sensible. Cavailhes is the best bailiff for miles round. He knows about market-gardening, and he's bound to succeed. He has even gone so far as to promise that he won't expect us to pay interest on his money until the place begins to show a profit. He says it is absolutely essential that you should be here all the time. He wants you to have complete control. Once the legal formalities are through, you are to leave Chardon's. . . ."

"Why didn't you confess at once that everything has been settled? What was the point of all this silly pretence?" Rose was furious. "If that's how things are to be, it's one reason the more why I should stay on at Chardon's. I want to be independent. If needs be, I'll live in Bordeaux alone. . . ."

"Oh, please, Rose, be a little kind to me."

The girl gave her mother a long look. Never before had she said a thing like that, or spoken precisely in that tone.

"One has got to take the Cavailhes as they are, darling. It's quite likely that they may make us all unhappy—especially you. But at least you will be able to rely on them. You are young and impulsive. It is natural that you should be. But it is also natural that I should look at things differently. In my condition. . . ."

Rose was conscious of a shock. She studied the shadowy figure sitting there within the narrow circle of lamplight, talking. Her mind was often, in the future, to go back to this September evening, to the picture of her mother as she had seen her then, the veins standing out, and the swollen hands lying flat on the little table at her side. She had not thrown herself into her arms, had not drawn down on to her shoulder the old head that was full of those anxieties about money which the approach of death, so far from dissipating, merely strengthens and exacerbates. She had not done any of these things, but had asked in anger:

"D'you know whom Denis had up in his room all the time you were letting Cavailhes get the better of you? D'you know whom we should find up in his room now, if we went and looked?"

"Spare me! spare me!" She raised her two hands as though to ward off a blow. "Don't tell me! I don't want to know!"

The old lady had assumed that childish, plaintive tone which Rose so hated because it confirmed her suspicion that "poor mamma is not her old self." She leaned down for what she meant to be a perfunctory kiss. But her mother flung both arms round her neck, and clung to her as she had never done before.

XVII

POOR Lucienne, it seemed, was very, very tired. Whenever Léonie Costadot said of any of her friends that they were very, very tired, it meant that one had better think about getting one's mourning ready. She was obsessed by the need to have a talk with poor Lucienne before it should be too late. More than once, in the course of the winter, she had put out feelers to this end, but it was not until early in April that she felt certain that her friend would see her. Her vast Delaunay-Belleville did the journey in less than an hour. The sound of the car roused Lucienne from her state of drugged stupor. Rose went to the window.

"Here she is. I'll show her up and then leave you together. . . . I can't bear . . ."

"But not for more than ten minutes!" begged the sick woman.

Léonie gave a quick peck at the cheeks that were the colour of rye-bread. "You're looking *much* better," she said.

Lucienne, in a low voice, expressed a fear that she might linger for a long while yet.

"You must *believe* that you'll get well, dear. You must make up your mind that you *will* get well. While there's life. . . . But should it be God's will to take you to Himself, I can't bear the thought of your going without first forgiving me."

Lucienne's voice was very weak.

"You did your duty: you did what you had to do."

"I'm so glad you see it like that. One's first thoughts *must* be for one's children. After all, one is responsible for their financial future. If I had it to do all over again, I should act in precisely the same way, but I have always lacked *unction*—as Mother de Langalerie used to say when we were at the Convent—do you remember?"

Without looking at her, the sick woman said:

"What you did to me doesn't matter. But my poor Rose. . . . *She* had never harmed you!" Suddenly the voice became loud and challenging. "It was *your* son who came, after we were ruined, to seek her out, and it was he who cast her away."

She raised her head from the pillow. Her face looked ghastly. Death had already set two dark hollows above the toothless mouth.

"Go away, Léonie!"

But no more now than on the evening of the Fredy-Duponts' ball would Léonie take her departure without first getting what she had come for.

"You must forgive me," she urged with harsh obstinacy. "A great unhappiness has come on us. I am not referring to Gaston, who is fast ruining himself with that Lorati woman and will end by marrying her, nor yet to Robert. . . . Those things don't matter . . . but have you heard what mad thing my youngest has done? . . . yes, Pierrot. . . ."

"He wrote to Rose that he had enlisted in the Chasseurs d'Afrique. . . ."

"But why *should* he do a thing like that? And he left without even giving me a kiss. . . . I was wicked enough to have him declared of age, and this is how he has used his freedom! But can you tell me why?" she cried, without a thought for the sick woman who could not bear loud voices. "A young anarchist, incapable of submitting to any authority. . . . Does Rose know why he did it?"

"No. Pierrot merely sent her his new address. That was all." Rose came in.

"I am afraid you must go now, Madame. She gets tired very easily."

Léonie leaned over the bed and embraced her friend. In a low voice she said:

"But you do forgive me, you do, don't you? Say you do!"

For the sake of peace and quiet Lucienne nodded her head, lay back and closed her eyes. "If only she would go!" she thought, "If only she would go!"

"Dear Rose doesn't come into Bordeaux these days, does she?"

The sick woman answered in something like her old clear tones:

"No, she is working here. She looks after the accounts. The estate's become a large concern—a very large concern. . . . We've managed to raise capital."

Léonie turned back to the bed. There was a hungry look in her eyes as she put the next question.

"They say in Bordeaux that Denis is up every day with the lark, and goes to market. Is that true?"

"Only twice a week. . . . Cavailhes concentrates on the cows and the vegetables . . . he leaves the fruit to Denis. We're too near town to make the vines pay. . . . Yes, it's a very large concern," she kept harping on that, "My children will be very comfortably off. Fifty hectares lying at the junction of four main roads, only a few miles out of Bordeaux, and in full yield . . . that's not to be sneezed at! . . . I can't tell you what we owe to the Cavailhes. . . . In the hands of a ne'er-do-weel the place would have gone to rack and ruin."

Léonie had already reached the door when this parting shot struck her.

"Well, I've given *her* something to think about," the sick woman reflected with profound satisfaction.

She closed her eyes.

The cockchafers were bumbling round the pink and white chestnuts. It would be a good wine year, said Léonie Costadot. Would Rose promise to write to her whenever she got a letter from Pierrot? His first leave would fall due about the time of the grape-harvest. She hoisted herself with difficulty into the Delaunay. For a moment the exhaust drowned the scent of the lilac.

It was on the day following this visit that she had her first stroke. As things turned out her own death preceded by a month that of her friend Lucienne whom she had found looking "so tired." Robert was the only one of her sons who was with her in her last moments. Up to the very end she spoke to him only of Gaston and of Pierrot.

XVIII

'I'VE got to think this thing out,' said Pierre Costadot to himself, as he always did when he had been dining alone and drinking too much. On these occasions, though his brain had become sharpened to a fine point of lucidity, he was inclined to go careering off down every proffered side-track of thought, instead of keeping to the main-road. The idea of enlisting in the Chasseurs d'Afrique had not yet occurred to him. He was already well on the road to that mad enterprise, though he did not realize it. He had been settled in Paris now for two months, and every time he came into this restaurant in the Rue Royale, where the orchestra was always playing the most recent tunes from Vienna, he felt that his presence there was something far worse than a sign that his determination had grown weak. It stood, in fact, for a clear confession of defeat. His conscience told him clearly enough what he ought to have done. He *ought* to have learned a manual trade and become an apprentice. It was not open to him to regard such a step as utopian and impracticable. An American friend of his had turned his back on an excessively rich family, and was now working in a factory. 'I've no right,' thought Pierrot, 'even if I were rationally justified in doing so, to fall back on such arguments as—a man's first duty is to make the best use of his natural gifts: or, the best way of helping the working class is to remain true to oneself. It is not permissible for me to invoke arguments like that, however sound they may be, because it is not *they* that are determining my actions, but my ingrained habits of mind, my love of comfort (provided it doesn't prevent me from using my brain), my spirit of independence. . . . I just can't submit to the orders and bullying of a boss or a foreman while I've got the material means at hand which make it possible for me to tell them to go to hell. In two years' time I shall be re-signed to letting myself be bullied by a sergeant, because I shan't be able to help myself. . . . But the fact remains that I get a cheque every month, and don't in the least know where the money comes from, whether from house-rents, bonds or industrial shares. . . . I just cash it, and live on the proceeds. . . .'

Yes, but hadn't he a spark of genius? There was nothing ridiculous in using such a word in these silent colloquies with himself. It had been enough for the young American to read *Atys* and to talk about it to his friends, for a sort of intellectual eddy to start forming about the poem. He had, he kept on saying to himself, only one real duty, one supreme obligation, and that was to open up a channel in himself down which the waters of this subterranean sea of song, this crude lava of poetry, might flow. But that didn't stand in the way of his being on the side of the poor. . . . What an idiotic way of putting it! There was no such thing as a "side of the poor." It was merely a question of choosing between two ways of exploiting the poor—the right way and the left way. Was it really incumbent upon him to become one of the exploited in order to avoid becoming one of the exploiters? That was more than he could face. . . . There was, for those who had faith, one other course open—to assume the soutane, or a monkish habit, white or brown. . . . Was there any religious order that could truly be called mendicant? Of what avail was the individual vow of poverty if one belonged to a rich and powerful corporation? . . . And what about chastity? How did he stand on that score? There were times when he felt himself to be a criminal, others when, on the contrary, he was tempted to minimize the importance of the itch in the blood. He could not keep his mind from brooding on even the most trivial things that happened to him in this connexion, and one whole day would stand out in his thoughts as darkened and fouled, because in the course of it he had done something which no one but himself had known about, and the consequences of which, in terms of human happiness or unhappiness, were so small as to be almost invisible. . . . That single lapse had broken the continuity of a long period in which he had been striving to become a "better man." The only effect of his struggles had been to build a dam behind which the muddied waters had risen and gathered force until nothing, human or divine, could hold them back. Convinced though he might be that to attribute importance to such incidents was the merest folly, he could not help but suspect that for *him* they *were* important. The least of his set-backs struck a hollow echo from the deepest levels of his consciousness. He was perfectly prepared to admit that others might be free from this particular kind of self-torture, and even rejoiced that it should be so: but he judged himself by the law of his being, which was a hard law and unforgiving.

It was raining as he crossed the Place de la Madeleine with its crowd of horse-cabs and taxis. He had no umbrella, but felt too restless to go back to his hotel and spend what remained of the evening in his room. It was humiliating to realize that he had utterly failed to people his life with new faces, and was incapable of forgetting those he had denied. He answered more affectionately than ever before the beseeching letters which reached him from his mother and from Robert. Only with Denis did the bond of friendship seem to have been irremediably broken. But he still had news of him through Rose.

Had he gone home this evening by way of the Rue de Tournon, he would have sauntered past the railings of the Luxembourg, stopping now and again to press his face to the grill and smell the damp earth. No longer did Atys and Cybele roam the marshy landscape of his childhood, but suffered the fate of prisoners confined within this old garden of the Latin Quarter trodden by the passing generations of the young.

The rain came on harder, and he turned for shelter into the first music hall he came to, which happened to be the Olympia. 'It's the fault of the rain,' he told himself, but added, 'that's merely a trumped-up excuse for idling, for looking at a lot of vacant faces, and listening to what the women perched up on their bar-stools are shouting to one another. . . . Not another drop will I touch tonight.'

He paid two francs for a promenade ticket. 'This is no place for you,' he reflected. He looked at his image in the mirrors—a strapping fellow with a red face and scarlet ears, in a crowd of anæmic creatures. In the thick, smoke-laden air, the audience was singing the words of the tune which the orchestra had just struck up. The "turn" marched on to the stage, a man in a tight-waisted evening suit with a flower in his buttonhole. He reminded him of a pig. He wore a toupet which had the effect of making his lard-like face look abnormally long. His eyes were quite expressionless, and his pug-nose looked like the backside of a capon. His head and his hind-quarters were completely symmetrical. He picked up the tail of his dress-coat as though it were a skirt, went through the motions of carrying a band-box, and removed invisible pins from his hair. Every song he sang ended with a reference to "nine months later" or to chemists' prescriptions. Each time he left the stage the audience clamoured for their idol to come back, and yelled for their favourite songs. It occurred to Pierrot that there was not, really, so very much difference between the squalid obscenity of these ditties and the lust of his Atys and Cybele.

He had a feeling that someone was looking at him, and turned his head slightly. Where had he seen those bright eyes of periwinkle blue?

"Don't you know me, Monsieur Costadot? I suppose it's because I've shaved my beard, and because in Paris one is better dressed. . . ."

"Why, it's Landin!" said Pierre to himself with a shock of recognition. . . . The sharp-featured face showing faint traces of powder, and shaded by a soft hat pulled well down over the eyes, was indeed Landin's. He tried to see in this perfumed stranger the bearded clerk who had stood aside so humbly to let him pass that Thursday long ago on the staircase of the Revolou house. He was assailed with questions. Was he just passing through Paris? He was going to settle down there, was he? How very interesting? Taking to literature, no doubt. A little bird had whispered something to him about a certain Atys and a certain Cybele.

"But I see that I am being tactless," he added, noticing an annoyed and mulish look on the other's face. "I only mention it because I happen to be in journalism now, myself. I edit a number of papers which, I must confess, are not primarily concerned with poetry. . . . Still, it's never too late to start a new feature. . . ."

Pierre, suddenly interested, asked for the names of the papers in question. None of those mentioned by Landin meant anything to him, except the *Pie Borgne*, which he occasionally glanced through at the barber's.

"If you'll allow me to give you a piece of advice, you ought to regard newspapers in the light of so many *platforms*, irrespective of what they contain. But what about going downstairs to the bar, it's impossible to hear oneself speak here, and the crowd's a bit too light-fingered for my taste!"

They went down a short flight of stairs. Among the women milling about at the snack-bar, Pierrot noticed a much-beplumed and overripe negress.

"Mumm? Cordon Rouge?"

Pierrot dared not confess that he had already drunk more than was good for him. He was touched by his companion's evident interest in him. Monsieur Landin had the appearance of eagerly awaiting the answers to his questions. He, as it were, pounced on them before they were well out of the speaker's mouth. Monsieur Costadot must have found his first weeks in Paris rather difficult? Nothing affected Monsieur Landin more painfully than the thought of how lonely the young men arriving on the morning train at the Quai d'Orsay from the provinces must be. No doubt Monsieur Costadot often thought about his friend Denis? No? he didn't think about him at all now? That surprised him. . . . Those dear Revolou children! No one, probably, knew them better than he did. After all, he'd been there when they were born. There was a lot he could say about them if he chose! What did Monsieur Costadot think? He must have his own ideas on the subject. . . . As man to man, now, didn't he think they had been saddled with the most appalling heredity?

Pierrot noticed that Monsieur Landin was no longer firing questions at him. Of his own accord, and almost without noticing what he was doing, he had begun to talk, making up at last for two months of crushing solitude. Monsieur Landin had a way of drawing one out, of multiplying one's confidences. He played on sympathy as on an instrument. He wanted to know the real reason for this prolonged stay in Paris. Pierrot had no reason to feel ashamed of his motives. The breaking-off of Rose Revolou's engagement, the horrible behaviour of his brother

Robert, were quite enough to explain his presence in the Capital.

"It really is too bad!" broke in Monsieur Landin. "If only you had been here last month, you would have run into your elder brother Gaston—in the company, I need hardly add, of Mademoiselle Lorati. They are now in Brussels . . . where she has an engagement, though I fear it will not last more than a few days. . . ."

Pierrot protested that he would turn his back on Gaston if he met him. Monsieur Landin refilled his glass. He couldn't, he said, but admire such resolution, though he ought to warn him that it would soon weaken. The air of Paris was not favourable to clear-cut moral judgments. If he had not found that out for himself already, he soon would.

The young man's blush delighted Landin.

"So you *have* come to that conclusion, eh? Well, I must say I'm glad; it makes conversation so much easier, doesn't it?"

He looked straight into the other's eyes. The fumes of champagne dimmed the lineaments of the lurking monster. This was the moment for which Monsieur Landin always hungrily waited, the moment of what he called the "basic confidence." Once reached, almost anything might happen, and on *how* it happened depended his own future relations with the novice.

This particular novice did not need asking twice, though what he said did not make sense. At first, Monsieur Landin thought that the young fool was pulling his leg. He had repudiated both class and money because he did not want to enjoy advantages and privileges, and *did* want to cut adrift from the whole present system. He had even tried to get himself taken on by a printer, so as to learn a trade, but had met with an unqualified refusal. There was no lack of good reasons, he said, why he should give up the whole idea. He might, for instance, argue that his determination to fight against the degrading conditions of labour was not an adequate excuse for himself submitting to them, and that there were better ways in which a poet might serve his fellow

men than by becoming one of the proletariat. But he refused to
profit from such arguments, knowing full well the real motives
for his attitude, which were greed, sensuality and pride.

The young man never stopped talking except to drink. Landin
kept his sharp eyes fixed on him, smiling the while, and hiding
his mouth behind a spatulate hand.

"You've a long way to go yet, Monsieur Costadot, but I
expect you're already making giant strides. . . . Looking back on
the three days you spent in the printer's shop, you must see it all
as a very odd sort of experience for a man with your background.
. . . Between ourselves, working people aren't, well . . . Tell me
what happened. I suppose they made you go to a knocking-shop,
eh? What, they didn't? Then all I can say is that they were very
unlike most of their kind. . . . I expect, though, they put you
through what I believe they call the 'general overhaul'? No? (he
laughed till he choked). . . . D'you mean to tell me that the girls—
there *were* girls in the shop, I presume—didn't try *that*? . . . You
amaze me!"

There had been a time when he, too, had been all for the
people. But that was a thing of the past. It was really quite useless
having *feelings* about them. . . . He had learned his lesson.

"When you've seen as much as I've seen, Monsieur Costadot, I
reckon you'll change your mind pretty quickly. I give you, on a
rough estimate, three months!"

"You like to pretend that you are a cynic, Monsieur Landin,"
said Pierrot suddenly, "but I can assure you that you're wasting
your time. You mentioned something about having *feelings* just
now—well, I happen to know a good deal about your feelings."

"What do you mean?"

A wary and distrustful expression had come into Monsieur
Landin's eyes. He looked suddenly like a trapped animal. . . .
"I'm sure that's just your little joke."

"I've talked a lot to Denis about you, about your case."

The colour went from Monsieur Landin's face:

"My case?"

"D'you know what Denis and I used to call you? Please don't
be angry. . . . We used to call you the '*Sacrifice*'. . . ."

"The sacrifice? Did you really, now."

Again he began to laugh, turning over in his mind the syl-
lables that his companion had just uttered. They had brought
quite other ones to his mind—*sacrifice—sack of beastliness: sacrifice:
sack of beastliness.*

"Old Revolou behaved abominably," went on Pierrot with a
sort of wild fervour, "but you never ceased for a moment to be
his devoted slave. Don't deny that after his death you did everything you could to ensure that his children might suffer as little as
possible. I have never come across a clearer case of rendering good
for evil. I can assure you that both Denis and Rose realize quite
clearly what you did at that time. . . . If they didn't mention it to
you, or write—as I begged them to do—it was because they had
grown accustomed from childhood to accepting your self-
sacrifice as something to which they had a right. My mother
was always telling us how you slaved at that business for a mere
pittance. She was quite sure you would have got Oscar Revolou
out of his last desperate scrape if he hadn't gone and killed himself—'like the fool he was'—she would add."

"Please let us talk of something else, Monsieur Costadot,"
broke in Landin, "I did my duty as his confidential clerk, and no
more."

But the warmth of Pierrot's feelings would not let him stop.
His eyes were shining.

"Your embarrassment, Monsieur Landin, is as good as an
avowal. If I had ever for a moment had doubts about your
remarkable character, these last few minutes would have
silenced them. . . . If you've decided not to make up for lost time,
and to get a little enjoyment out of life, that doesn't in the least
alter the fact that you were an utterly devoted servant. . . ."

Landin could protest no longer. It was he, as a rule, who spoke
of his "feelings," but he was thoroughly disconcerted by the
picture of himself drawn in all innocence by this young man with

a red face, an eye befuddled with wine, and crimson ears, wh
occasionally wiped away with a dirty handkerchief the drops of
sweat that stood out on his forehead.

But Monsieur Landin did not take advantage of the situation.
In fact, all of a sudden, he said something at which he almost
gasped, so amazed was he at the sound of his own words.

"You know absolutely nothing about my life, Monsieur
Costadot—about *me*!"

It occurred to Pierre that there was something odd in this
declaration, though the agonized tones in which it was made
escaped him.

"I don't know the *details* of your life, naturally—but what I've
seen with my own eyes for years and years is quite enough. . . ."

Monsieur Landin interrupted his eloquence to point out that
even what he had seen came from depths of which he was
ignorant.

Pierre seized his hand without the slightest feeling of repulsion.

"Our actions spring from more than one cause, don't you
believe that, Monsieur Landin? It is only the small-minded who
attribute everything to self-interest. Our actions derive from innumerable sources, like the native streams of our countryside at
home. Surely you remember how the water bubbles up all over
the muddy fields, and yet how the main current running beneath
the alder roots manages to stay limpid and lovely. . . . I know you,
Monsieur Landin, as a man who has worn himself out in the
service of a rich employer who thought about nothing but the
satisfaction of his own appetites. . . . It is unnecessary to look
further. . . ."

"Yes . . . but since . . ."

Monsieur Landin did not finish the sentence on which he had
embarked. Instead "I've been through a lot. . ." he said, but
suddenly noticed that young Costadot's attention had been dis-
tracted by a couple sitting at the next table. The girl was very
young, a beginner, thought Landin, or, more likely, some little
shop-girl being given a "treat" by her gentleman-friend. The

latter was paunchy, had a thick neck, hair cut *en brosse*, and tufts growing from his ears. He was studying the wine-list with the help of the wine-waiter, blissfully unaware that every movement made by his companion was deliberately designed to attract the attention of the young man seated on the settee opposite. But Landin, putting out secret feelers, was fully conscious of the web that was being spun by the two young people between the branches on which they sat like birds silently calling to their mates. He knew that there was nothing for it but to watch their pretty game, getting what enjoyment he could from the sight, or to leave the bar and go out alone into the rain. But he was not going to give up without a struggle the chance of confiding, for the first time in his life, of pouring himself out, not, as at other times, to some tough, knowing old sinner, but to someone only just over the threshold of childhood and miraculously able to listen, and, if not to understand, at least to shed an unexpected light on his own sinister existence, to read into it a meaning quite different from the one that at first sight sprang to the eye and filled the listening mind with horror.

The Costadot boy was no ordinary young man. He would be quite capable of explaining to Landin what happens to men when their pet manias, their habits and passions, have been cut away. Landin remembered how Oscar Revolou had always had the ivy in the Léognan copses chopped down, except from the few old elms with which it was so tightly entwined that it was indistinguishable from their own leaves. If *that* riot of ivy had been killed, nothing of the elms would have remained at all: What would have remained of *him* if. . . . The answer to that question would not come from young Costadot this evening. Though the boy was sitting there beside him, his mind was far away. The fat man had gone to the lavatory. The girl and Pierre were exchanging smiles. Words mean so little. The true voice of the blood is in the message that flies between two unsullied beings. They may never have seen one another before, but each recognizes in the other a predestined fate. They sit there, sniffing the scent as in the first nights of the primæval world. Then, suddenly, they break from the underbrush and, naked, trot across the intervening space to meet.

The sight was familiar to Landin, but it did not, this evening, wake in him the usual sense of rancorous and bitter hopelessness. 'Happiness *does* exist' he thought: 'God is good. Youth and purity are blessed states.' He accepted the fact of his own suffering, of his own fate as a piece of refuse thrown out from creation, while the truth flowered in this marvel of two children trembling on the brink of adolescence, motionless and rapt. If ever again he should meet young Costadot he would unbosom himself. . . . For the time being, he would leave him to his happiness.

He settled the bill and got up.

"Please don't think me rude, but I've got an appointment. . . ."

Pierrot, jerked back to consciousness, thought that his companion was annoyed. He protested that he did not want to stay on all by himself in the bar. The girl gazed after him with an expression of disappointment.

It was raining. Landin hailed a cab and gave the driver his address in the Rue Fontaine. Pierrot, still convinced that he was offended, suggested that they might go together. Landin agreed, but in a rather strange voice, and again reminded his companion that somebody was waiting for him.

"I'll drop you at your door," said Pierrot. It never occurred to him that Landin's silence could be due to anything but irritation. He did what he could to bring him back to a more cheerful frame of mind. He breathed in the smell of the cab which reminded him of all the carriages his parents had ever had. They used to stand idle for years in the dark recesses of the coach-house, and he remembered how, as children in the country, he and his brothers had clambered about them playing at "travelling." He was reminded, too, of the Victoria in which he had accompanied Rose back to Léognan. . . . No doubt Monsieur Landin knew Rose Revolou well? Oh, yes, replied the other, certainly he knew her.

She never failed to ask after Mademoiselle Landin. He would always remember her kindness.

"I was in love with her once. As a matter of fact—though I've never breathed a word of this to anyone else—I'm in love with her still, and always shall be."

Monsieur Landin was busy with his thoughts. There *was* a truth to be found somewhere in life: true life *did* exist.

The cab slowed down and stopped. In a husky voice Monsieur Landin said:

"Well, here I am . . . I really am most grateful to you, Monsieur Costadot."

Pierre protested at the use of the word, but the other stuck to his point.

"You have shown confidence in me, Monsieur Costadot: you have spoken to me kindly. You can never know. . . ."

He hesitated for a moment, his finger on the bell, and decided to say no more, because he could see that Pierre, standing there on the pavement, had a far-away look in his eyes, and was not listening.

"I'm glad I've got such a long way to go to get home," said the young man. "I shall walk right across Paris. It has stopped raining, and the air and the exercise will sober me up. I shall sleep like a log."

The cab had driven away. With a wave of the hand Monsieur Landin disappeared through the main door of the building.

Pierre was momentarily tempted to go back to the bar of the Olympia. But the memory of the fat man dissuaded him. Besides, he really must make an effort to control his desires. Did most young men, he wondered, suffer from the same sort of inner struggle between sensuality and a longing for renunciation? It came out clearly in his *Atys*, was, in fact, what would make that poem so peculiarly difficult for most people to understand. He had reached that point in it where Cybele was shown as laying vain siege to an Atys grown newly chaste and radiating the presence of some unknown God. Standing there on the muddy,

rain-soaked pavement, between black buildings pock-marked
with little bright bars where men and stray women of the town
sat whispering side by side, he began to recite the elegiac lines
in which Cybele bemoaned her fate at being thus confronted by
an Atys turned penitent.

> To see thee thus so fragile yet so strong
> Doth make me weep. This soft and grassy bed
> Stains thy bright limbs with greenness. About thy head
> Cicadas shrill, and all the drowsy song
> Of birds has fall'n on quietness. The piny smell
> Of sea-enchanted forests, blown from where
> The wind dies in the limes, speaks to thee here
> Of Sangaris thy love. I weave my spell
> To call that hated rival to my aid.
> I have set round thee all the blaze of noon
> To fill thy sleep with passion. But my rune
> Is powerless. Like a well-tempered blade
> Thy heart stands straight in summer's wilting glare
> How could I guess Atys would prove so firm
> In chastity? The Unknown God, intent to crush the worm
> That at thy heart lies coiled within its lare
> Can call on magic that is all unknown
> To Cybele. No longer will thy blood
> Pulse to the rhythm of Ocean, nor match its flood
> To the thick beat of summer's sap. Now thou art alien grown
> To Nature's deep complicities. The hard core
> Of thy spare body thrills to new delights,
> Sounding a deeper world and scaling other heights
> Than those thy amorous senses knew before.

" 'Deep complicities' is pretty bad," he thought. "I shall have to
do a lot more work on that line."

Still murmuring to himself, seeking new rhythms and com-
binations, he crossed the Seine and reached the Rue de Tournon,
quite unaware of the route that he was taking, moving like some
animal seeking instinctively the shortest way to its familiar
shelter. By the time he reached home he was exhausted. He undressed quickly, and fell at once into a deep sleep.

He was awakened, not by the familiar craving for food, but by
a rending headache and a feeling of nausea. He knew by experience the kind of awful day that stretched before him, and went

back to bed. About seven o'clock in the evening, he dressed hurriedly, and walked along to the small restaurant where he was in the habit of taking his coffee and roll each morning. Tonight he limited his dinner to the same meagre fare, and once more sought the refuge of sleep.

Bright sunshine—too bright for the time of year,"too warm to last," restored his zest for life after thirty-six hours of complete prostration. About noon he went downstairs, bought the latest edition of *La Presse* which the newsboys were crying in the street, and settled himself at a table in the *Taverne du Panthéon*. He was famished, having eaten nothing to speak of for the last two days. He ordered a steak, opened his paper, and saw on the front page a picture of Monsieur Landin. Above it, in fat black capitals were printed the words, "*The Murder in the Rue Fontaine*," and below, "*The Victim.*"

Later, when he tried to live over again in memory that first appalling moment, it was borne in on him that his first reactions had been precisely those of which he would have been conscious had he actually been the murderer. He carefully assumed an air of indifference, and did not look up when the waiter brought him his steak. He was not, at that moment, absolutely sure that he was, in fact, innocent, and had to break off his reading more than once to live over again, minute by minute, his adventure of two evenings back. He was quite certain that he had left Monsieur Landin at his front door. Drunk he most certainly had been, but, equally certainly, he had not gone upstairs with the man. . . . Suddenly his eye fell on the following paragraph:

"The police are looking for a young man whom the victim accosted round about ten o'clock in the promenade of a music hall. The two of them were seen to go downstairs to the bar where they drank a bottle of champagne. Shortly before eleven, Landin asked for his bill. Outside, on the Boulevard, he hailed cab No. 2021, and persuaded the young man to enter it with him. The driver set them down at the murdered man's

house, but did not see them go in. He is under the impression
that the stranger went off alone. His description of the latter
tallies with that given by the box-office attendant at the
theatre, who knew Landin by sight, and noticed the young
man in whose company he left. The evidence of the barman
confirms that of the other two witnesses. Only Mademoiselle
Yveline Chabrat who was sitting opposite the table occupied
by Landin and his companion, differs in her description of the
latter. What makes the whole enquiry more than usually
difficult is that it has to be pursued in a very special section of
the underworld where it is to the interest of too many people
to say nothing. Furthermore, all the witnesses are agreed that
the young man whom the police wish to interview is not a
regular frequenter of the Olympia. No one there is familiar
with his appearance, and it seems likely that he was visiting it
for the first time on the night in question."

According to the stop press, information supplied by the concierge had led the authorities to extend their search in quite a
different direction. It appeared that an unknown man had gone
up to Landin's flat at about nine o'clock, and had let himself in
with a key given him by the victim. The concierge deposed that
Landin had come home about eleven, and that she had heard him
say "good-night" on the pavement to somebody who had then
walked away.

Pierre emptied his glass at a gulp, sighed, and looked about
him. No one seemed to be in the slightest degree interested in
who he was or what he was doing. He closed his eyes and muttered a prayer. Then he re-read the concierge's evidence five or
six times. He was saved.

Should he write to the magistrate in charge of the case? No,
that would be too stupid. The search would be confined to the
hotels of Montmarte or the Place de la République known to be
frequented by "professionals." There was not the slightest danger
that the police would get on the track of a young man of good

family who could be vouched for by landlords of proved integrity. . . . He wandered about the Luxembourg Gardens waiting for the late editions, but these, when they appeared, contained nothing. He passed the night, "the third since the crime was committed," stretched fully dressed on his bed, starting awake every few moments and then dozing off again. At seven o'clock he hurried down to the street and ran to the nearest newspaper stand. He had already pumped the waiter. There was still no news of the mysterious young man of the Olympia whose evidence was so badly needed. It was thought to be extremely unlikely that he would volunteer any information in view of "the excessively unpleasant nature of the case."

All that day, Pierre was dominated by a natural instinct of self-protection. He put on a dark suit and had his hair cut as short as possible. He remained in a condition of miserable nervous tension due now not so much to any fear that he might have to explain his movements in court as to a feeling that he had, after all, played a part in the affair and become personally involved. It was as though *someone* had imposed on him the duty of accompanying the squalid victim as far as possible along his miserable road, up to, in fact, the very frontier beyond which no human aid could be of any avail to Landin, and where no salvation on earth or in heaven awaited him. He was appalled to think that there, ready to the hand of anybody who could afford a penny for a paper, was openly displayed something which was full of deadly danger to the innocent who might, by handling it, lose forever their belief in goodness: that there, for the picking up, was the key to one of those innumerable doors which open on to that hell which, like heaven, is within us.

What had always, in a vague way, been for him the centre and focus of his mind's distemper, took on now a form and substance. Mammon becomes but a secondary and minor monster as soon as he is seen as nothing but the slave of a much more fundamental and terrible power. Of what avail were reforms and revolutions? Sooner or later all such things must come to shipwreck, and those who hunger and thirst after justice are fated to run upon the rocks thrown up by another hunger and another thirst which merely to think of is abomination. No, thought Pierre, the only way to make a beginning was to come to grips with fallen human nature and its morbid growths. But this wretchedness of man's estate, this wound in the soul which might once have prompted his religious instincts to find a solution in the mysteries of faith, worked now in the opposite direction. There was not enough of the theologian in him to rest content with those arguments that seek to absolve the Creator from all responsibility for a creature so abject. Many times in the course of the next week he tried to find escape in acts of faith and confidence in God, only to find that they were not effective save in certain moods, and that he could not, at will, alter the climate of his soul. He remained torn and divided by an inner struggle which was something more than mere intellectual speculation for one who, like him, had been the last companion of Louis Landin on the brink of eternity, whose face had been the last on which the wretched man had looked. He had gone, and thereafter the miserable victim had seen only the terrible expression in the eyes of his murderer. The case, no doubt, was an extreme one, but it bore witness to the existence of something permanent, something variously manifested but indestructible which lay at the very centre of human existence. The unquenchable fires of hell are lit in *this* world, and those whom theologians count as lost are marked for damnation at their birth, and even before it. The road which the boy-poet, his head full of Atys and of Cybele, had been treading, turned out to lead quite simply to the squalid destiny of Landin, to the sheer drop that overhangs the sea of death.

For some weeks Pierre behaved almost like a madman. He visited many confessionals, and came away sometimes with the memory of mechanical answers, text-book formulæ, and the titles of works in which he would find all objections countered, sometimes with the hopeless sense of sheer exhaustion against which the powers of reason beat in vain. But there were times, too, as in the Lady Chapel at Saint-Sulpice, when he felt the call to prostrate himself, if only for a brief moment, at the feet of love. He was in a condition of complete emptiness when men of his temperament are at the mercy of any chance meeting. It was essential that he should make contact with somebody, that somebody should enter his life, take him by the shoulders, and set him on the right path, and that somebody came to him, not in the guise of a friend or a priest or a saint, but of a girl.

In one of the first of the double-deck motor-buses which began, about this time, to run between the Opéra and Saint-Germain-des-Prés he saw the young girl on whom he had first set eyes in the bar of the Olympia. He sat beside her without at first realizing who she was. They fell at once into conversation and got off together at the first stop. Pierre's sole concern was that she should believe in his innocence. "You don't really think that I ever suspected you?" she said. "I've had too much experience not to know a bad lot when I see him!" He was touched to think that she had deliberately given a false description of him. She worked, she said, as a waitress in a tea-shop of the Rue de Rivoli.

What mattered most to Pierre was not the relation that developed between them from that moment, but the kind of life which, almost at once, he found himself accepting as normal. Forced by no necessity to take a regular job, in receipt of a cheque at the end of every month, he began to lead an existence of aimless enjoyment and self-indulgence. That he was a "young Costadot" was borne in on him at every turn. He was reduced to the condition which, when he had noted it in the case of his brothers, had filled him with a sense of horror. But they, at least, had never laid claim to noble sentiments, had never, unlike himself, passed judgment on others. There was nothing now to choose between him and his elders. Like them he floated on the waters of desire, a helpless victim of their ebb and flow. The only difference lay in the fact that the waters, for him, were probably of a thicker, a muddier, consistency. The passion that moved him hither and thither was not mere appetite. All the scents of the earth rioted in his lusts, and his blood moved to the rhythm of the sap in growing things. To him alone faces and bodies were eloquent of a terrifying beauty denied to others.

At one and the same time he discovered the irresistible power which all created existence exercised over him, and his own inability to yield to it without a feeling of despair. Other men lived by the law of their being. For them there was nothing tragic in the satisfaction of a simple physical hunger. They were conscious of no sense of guilt, nor felt degraded by the violence of their pleasures. But he could never get rid of the feeling that virtue was going out of him. Argue as he might, he could not but be convinced that all his satisfactions led to death. The filthy sewage of the world was in his eyes and nose, his ears and mouth. He lived in a constant state of spiritual agony, unable to endure the very pleasures which had become more necessary to him than bread and wine.

Unable to endure . . . and yet the thought of dying was far from him. The ecstasy of life obsessed him utterly. Had he been blind, the mere sound of rain upon the leaves and the odours of drenched earth would still have bound him to it. Had all his senses dwindled into nothingness, he would still have known a fascinated wonder in the movement of his heart, and been absorbed in the splendour of its every beat.

But the thought of what lay beyond death filled him with terror. He believed everything he had been taught. Others could shrug away their fears, but the tiny seed had taken root within his mind and put forth flowers. Cybele and Atys might riot for him among June's high grasses, but still his ears could catch the rustle of an angel's wing in the branches, and still his eyes behold a stable-door and there, within, amid sweet-smelling hay, a seated girl nursing a child on whom the shadow of a cross already lay. While still at school he had seen the pillars of the arcaded playground as a multitude of crosses, and on each a drooping head

7

with eyes that watched him. As he gazed through the windows of the big schoolroom where he sat at work, their tracery against the background of bird-infested trees had shown for him as a pattern of gibbets, even while he yielded to the loveliness of earth.

No less horrible than death itself to his young pagan mind was the idea of dying to this world. Priests he had always avoided, though his heart went out to them. He dreaded the hunters of the Lord with their nets spread to catch the souls of men. Nowadays he haunted them, yet kept his distance, like some young famished fox that scents the hook behind the succulent bait. . . . Then a day came when he discovered a book recently published by Renan's grandson, and also Péguy's *Mystère de la charité de Jeanne d'Arc*.

When we are old we find it hard to believe that the whole direction of our life may have been changed by the reading of a book. Yet such is the truth, and the experience of every day bears it out. Pierre was convinced that the cross and the sword had been put into his hands by others. But the truth was that they had always, though he did not know it, been there within him, as they were within all the young men of his generation and his race. He had to dig only a little way to find them.

He took the simplest course. At his age there is intoxication in resolving all the uncertainties of life merely by signing one's name. So he had signed, and lo!—everything was settled. On a sudden he found that he had finished with Paris, with his mistress, with the life he had been living, finished, too, with his family (for he would go away without a word of farewell to anyone, not even to his mother). He signed his name, and thereafter his fate was in the hands of others, and of Another—of Him who had not without intention sent him one night to the promenade of the Olympia, who had not, without design, set him where a man's life had taken the turning which led to death. It was Pierre's belief that all the contacts of our lives mean something, that they are part of our destiny, and that it is for us to read the message which lies hidden in their strange complexity. Peace came to him with the thought that now he had merely to go straight forward—yes, to the very end of his ordeal, to that spring of 1915, when, at twenty-three, he found the final liberty, and knew that he would see at last with clear eyes the secret of life's happiness for which he had paid so high a price.

XIX

DURING all the time of his mother's illness, until that day in December when she finally died, Julien and his invalidism ceased to hold the front of the stage. He consented to withdraw into the background, where he received the intermittent attentions of Maria Cavailhes. Only when the final act was played out did he resume his position of patient-in-chief. There was nothing organically wrong with him, but he had grown very thin. No special treatment, however, was called for, and Rose found that she could easily look after him in the intervals of what had become the chief concern of her life—keeping the books and coping with the increasing demands made upon her by the exploitation of the Léognan estate.

Julien was now entirely confined to his room. Apart from herself he saw no one except Maria Cavailhes and Louis Larpe (whose presence in the house was a symptom of returning prosperity). He discussed everything that went on at Léognan, and made no bones about speaking of Denis' private concerns. The boy was still living with the Cavailhes, and his brother made it quite clear that, in his opinion, he had, for some considerable time, been carrying on a liaison with Irène. The girl had spent a whole month on her back, and it was not difficult to guess why. Everybody in the neighbourhood knew that she had had a miscarriage. The Cavailhes were only waiting until Denis should be twenty, and freed from the threat of military service, to insist on marriage. Irène's father suffered a good deal from his chest and was anxious to get everything settled soon. He certainly did not lack first-hand information of what was going on.

Rose said very little. She was annoyed by Julien's talk, and pretended not to believe what he said. Since Denis no longer lived in the house, she saw very little of him, and what dealings they had were almost entirely confined to practical matters.

Early in the spring following their mother's death, Julien developed a slight swelling on his lip, to which, at first, Rose attached no particular significance. It is the fate of permanent invalids to be for ever complaining to deaf ears. But in the space of a few hours, the wretched man, whose lips were normally remarkable for their thinness, became afflicted with a mouth which had grown suddenly to the dimensions of a pig's snout. He suffered a good deal of pain which he bore with genuine courage and no little dignity. Faced by the terror of this unexpected crisis, both Denis and Rose believed for a while that they were sincerely distressed on their brother's behalf. What they really felt, however, was the threatening wind of death playing over their own security.

Rose very soon realized that this second fatality, coming so soon after the other, was, to her, a matter of supreme indifference. She had suffered in much the same way when her parents had died, but this time she felt deeply ashamed. This was what a worthless young man had done to her on that gloomy day three years ago in a rain-drenched public park! For a while she had gone on making the gestures expected of her as a loving and devoted daughter. She had prayed, she had offered the sacrifice of her life on the altar of her affection, but, though she did not know it, the old wound had never completely healed, and through it had drained away all the tenderness and passion of which her nature was capable.

Three years—and at the end of them nothing but this aridity, this bankruptcy of all emotion! Three years, during which she had had to live the life of a servant, at the beck and call first of her mother and then of her eldest brother: three years during which she had been shut away from all happiness save that of watching the slow return of prosperity. And even that, she thought, had been gained only at the cost of Denis' future. It was he who had been given as security to the Cavailhes family, his life that had been sacrificed. She did not know how to describe her feelings about the Cavailhes, about Irène in particular, with her coarse red face, her vast protuberance of bosom, and her puffy eyes. She would not admit that it was hatred. It is rare that we give to our passions their true name.

It was not that she felt the jealousy, the sense of physical frustration, which is the fate of disappointed spinsters. She neither regretted nor desired what she had missed. When, at Julien's funeral, she had seen Robert Costadot for the first time in three years, she had been conscious of nothing more intense than a kind of painful curiosity. During the offertory he had stood for a long time waiting his turn while the congregation filed past, and she had had an opportunity of studying his features. They had grown coarser. His hair had receded, but without imparting distinction to his forehead. His eyes were still handsome, but the lashes, once so beautiful, had grown sparse and thin, and the lids were red. 'So that,' she told herself, 'is the man for whom I suffered such agonies, the man for whom I ruined my life!' She felt frightened, and, in some curious way, impressed.

That evening Denis had consented to dine with her.

"You'll come and live at the house, now, won't you?" she had said. "Surely, you're not going to leave me alone?"

He told her it was impossible.

"There's something," he said, "that you ought to know, and I can only hope that you'll forgive me (he hung his head as he spoke). Irène and I are married. It all had to be done very secretly: you see, she's expecting a baby in August."

Rose was not surprised. She had always known this would happen. Her first words were quiet, but gradually she grew excited. Her voice rose, as her mother's had done in the old days, into a sort of chant. .... And so, she said, while she had been working herself to the bone for all of them, *that* was how Denis had been spending his time—with the connivance of the Cavailhes. ....

Very humbly he broke in on this tirade, to defend the Cavailhes:

"We owe everything to them. Three years ago the old man risked all he'd got. The savings of a lifetime were at the mercy of a single frost, one storm of hail. ... We have been lucky, I admit that ... but even you, with your knowledge of the books, can't have any idea what he's made. ..."

She said nothing, and he went on, still keeping his eyes lowered:

"Naturally, I shall not force my wife on you. We shall go on living with her parents. ... This house will be yours, unconditionally, as was originally agreed. ... You didn't really think that I should expect you to live with Irène!"

The idea that she could have thought him capable of such sacrilege made him laugh, and she felt suddenly ashamed that he should rank her so high. Gone was her anger, leaving not a trace. She felt calm now and at peace. Impulsively she voiced a protest:

"And surely *you* don't believe that I could consent to having you and your child live under the bailiff's roof? Forget what I said just now, Denis. Your wife's place is here. The house is quite big enough for all of us to live in it without getting in one another's way. Two rooms will be enough for me."

But he said again: "The whole idea's impossible. You'd hate it!" but the more he protested, the more firmly was she determined to make the sacrifice. The thought of what was involved no longer frightened her. She actually found herself thinking that if anybody was to raise objections, it might well be Irène! She said as much, but Denis only laughed:

"What, *she* object! she'll be only too delighted."

Rose began to reproach him tenderly.

"How could you . . ." and he, with a sigh, replied:

"Well, if it hadn't been Irène, it would have been someone else. . . ."

She pretended not to have heard, and realized with surprise that she no longer felt hostile to Irène. She had a sensation of being lifted, unresisting, to such a height of generosity, that she could look down on all below without bitterness, even without prejudice.

Louis Larpe, in full dress, flung open the double door. Dinner, he said, was served. Brother and sister sat opposite one another in the great gloomy dining-room lit by a fire of twigs. The family silver gleamed on the white cloth. A nightingale was singing in the chilly lilac. It was because of the April moon, Denis said. They would have to burn pitch tonight, so as to smoke the young vines and fruit trees. He noticed Rose's eyes fixed on the napkin which he had tucked into his collar, as Cavailhes was in the habit of doing. He blushed, and transferred it to his knees. What ways he had got into! She scolded him as she had done when they were children: "Don't rattle your spoon. . . . Look where your elbow is, Denis!"

They spoke with detachment of Julien, of their father, of their mother. They could not quite get over the surprise of finding themselves, like this, in the dining-room where Oscar Revolou had once reigned supreme. The fire had died down, and glowed in the vast spaces of the hearth like a little heap of incandescent worms. The cold spring night lay inhospitably about them. From time to time, one or other of them would mention a name —Pierre's or the murdered Landin's, and they realized that there was no longer anything of which they could not speak.

Rose got up:

"I'll walk back with you to the Cavailhes. . . . You mustn't keep them up."

How easy it was to be generous! She would give Irène a kiss, and felt impatient to offer this evidence of her fine forgiveness.

Denis' eyes, as he looked at her, were like those of some night-bird. They were brimming with tears. He took her hand but did not kiss her. They went out. It was the first time that Rose had ever heard a cuckoo calling after dark: three notes followed by a sort of angry hiccough.

XX

"BUT it is only right, Irène, that you should keep the key of the linen-cupboard from now on."

For the first time, thought Rose, she had detected a flicker of interest in the red and sulky face. The piles of sheets and towels ranged in the vast wardrobe were a cause of delighted amazement to the daughter of Maria Cavailhes. She had had her child in a nursing-home, and had been installed in the big house only a few days.

Rose was abandoning her last prerogative, and she was doing so with a light heart. All that mattered to her now was that she should show herself in as generous a rôle as possible in her dealings with Irène. It did not occur to her to wonder why it was that these trivial sacrifices cost her so little. No doubt she had achieved a greater degree of detachment than she realized.

"These sheets were woven on the estate in the time of my great-grandmother—and of yours, too, Irène. They used to sit together in front of the fire with their spinning-wheels."

"The Cavailhes are an old family," said Irène.

"A very good old family," replied Rose, while, to herself she thought, 'She's growing used to her new position at last.'

The young mother took the keys, locked the cupboard door, and began to unfasten her dress, saying that baby must be getting hungry.

"But, Irène, aren't you forgetting what the doctor told you? You're supposed to give Paul just a little rice-water in a

feeding bottle. He was still troubled with a little diarrhœa this
morning."

"D'you think I'm going to let him waste away?"

"Denis will be very much annoyed," said Rose. "It is most
imprudent in this hot weather!"

Irène replied sharply that she didn't have to answer to anyone
but Denis for her actions.

"And I'm going to start little Paul on soup tomorrow," she
added with an air of bravado.

Rose in a fury exclaimed, "We'll see about that," to which
Irène replied, "Is he my child or yours?"

"He's Denis's—he belongs to the Revolous, and I'm not going
to allow . . ."

Irène went out, slamming the door. Rose stood among the
piles of linen for a moment, hesitating. It was stiflingly hot. She
couldn't, she decided, just wait there patiently till Denis returned.
She would take the tram into Bordeaux and fetch him from the
tennis-club where it was his habit to go occasionally for a game
after the office closed (*Léognan Farm* had recently opened business
premises in the Cours Saint-Jean). He would drive her home in
his Darracq. They really must find a nurse this week. The child's
health was at stake, perhaps even its life.

Up in her room she took down a straw hat which gave her the
appearance of a little girl. She looked at herself in the glass. Was
her mourning adequate? The white dress she was wearing was a
little too gay. She discarded the rose which she had stuck in her
belt. The heat did not worry her. She waited beneath a sky from
which all colour had been drained, until the tram came. It was
the same place in which she had been accustomed to watch for
its arrival in the darkness of early morning. A lonely cicada was
shrilling in a dusty elm which had lost nearly all its leaves. She
heard the approaching tram long before she saw it.

She had been carrying about in her bag, ever since the previous
evening, a letter from Pierre Costadot which she had not yet
read. She tore open the envelope and glanced at the first few lines.

". . . A hundred and twenty-two degrees. I suppose that
seems to you almost incredible? But I stick it pretty well. I
am sitting here writing to you with utter silence all about me.
But nobody is sleeping. . . ." She turned the page.

". . . I suppose what I am writing must seem quite idiotic to
you. I am happy, yet unhappy too. There is no one I can con-
fide in, though these men love me and are capable of doing the
most unselfconscious and natural acts of kindness. . . . I am
not so tough as they are, so they put themselves out to help
me. . . ."

She put the letter back in her bag and powdered her burning
cheeks. It was six o'clock, but the light of the setting sun struck
fiercely through the canvas blinds. She got out of the tram and
took a cab to the club. Her open parasol helped her to hide her
face. But Denis recognized her, and broke away from a group of
men to run and meet her. He had not yet become involved in a
game, and suggested going home immediately. They could take
their time and enjoy the evening freshness.

She felt shy about mentioning a registry office or referring to
the subject of a possible nurse. Better not annoy Denis. He had
not changed and was still wearing white trousers and rope-soled
sandals. As he sat at the wheel his face was strangely inexpressive.
His owl-like eyes had a far-away look, and he said nothing. She
was not at all nervous, though he seemed half asleep. The angry
shouts and curses, which followed them in their headlong course,
had no effect on her. Her mood was one of utter indifference.
They smothered everyone and everything in dust. The thought
of death was constantly present to her mind, for death was close
at hand, her own, the cyclist's (in the cloud of dust raised by a
passing car they had not seen him) whom Denis had been able
to avoid only by making a sudden swerve. . . . Their faces were
caked with dust.

"We really must get home, Denis. We shall be late for dinner."

"I'll take the Marcheprime short-cut."

Cavailhes and his wife were sitting in front of their door eating their evening meal by the light of a garden lamp.

"I'm coming to join you," Irène said. "They've not come back yet."

"Better wait: it'll look more polite."

But she shook her head. She would have her meal, feed baby, and then go to bed. Maria went in for another plate and laid a place for her. They had a servant of their own, but Cavailhes could never bring himself to eat while she was hanging round.

It had been dark for some considerable time when Irène saw the quick succession of gleams as the headlights of the car caught one trunk after another on its way to the stables. Hurriedly she undressed in the dark. When Denis entered the room she was pretending to be asleep.

"Are you asleep, Irène? Anything the matter? Aren't you well?"

She made no answer but lay there secretly entrenched in sullenness. Denis could barely see the protuberance of her body beneath the sheets. He would not leave her alone. Wasn't she coming down to dinner? he asked, and, when she still said nothing, added:

"It's terribly hot tonight. I shall sleep on the couch in my study. We shouldn't get a wink otherwise—either of us."

He picked up his pyjamas and took them down to the room in which, one night, Landin had wrestled with his master's ghost. Then he went into the dining-room where Louis Larpe, all shirt front and coat-tails, as in the depth of winter, was waiting behind Rose's chair.

"I have removed one place, sir," he said. He could never bring himself to say "the mistress's place."

Rose came in. She had changed her dress. The white wine was dry and cold. The fragrance of melon filled the room. They could hear, though they could not see, the fluttering moths. There was a distant rumble of thunder.

"Paul's better, but she's feeding him too much. She didn't want to give him his rice-water."

"That reminds me . . . I saw Louise Piffetau at the club. She's got no further use for her nurse—a wonderful woman, she says, and is sending her along some time this week. We'll confront Irène with a *fait accompli*."

Rose resisted with difficulty a sudden savage sense of joy. They spoke very little. The gloomy rumbling darkness seemed to hold the August night in motionless suspense. The room was filled with the flutter of wings attracted thither by the light. They got up.

"If she's still sulking," said Denis, "I shall sleep on the couch."

"No, you must be patient and very, very gentle. It's your duty. . . ."

She was driven to speak thus by an insidious happiness of which she felt ashamed.

"I'm going out for a breath of air," she said, "before bed-time."

She sat in the darkness, her head thrown back, as in the days of her childhood, the better to watch the shooting-stars. The open windows of Irène's room showed as darker patches in the blackness. She could hear Denis's voice raised in rather angry speech, but there were no answering tones. Then the door of the room banged. A minute or so later, he came and sat down on the bench beside his sister.

"She's still in one of her moods. I didn't dare mention the nurse."

Rose said what a riot of shooting-stars there was tonight.

He lit a cigarette.

"How did those lines go that Pierre wrote about lost meteors?"

> The constellations and the ocean surge,
> All the lost meteors diving to the sea;
> Set them against your worn and bitter purge
> Of kisses: what do such things, my Atys, mean to me?

"How does it go on?"

"Something like this":

"Uneasy tides that gnaw a wasting earth."

"It's idiotic not to be able to remember!"

Ranged in thy cheeks embattled Nature stands
All red and white. Food for the hungry heart, yet infinite,
Falling like fruit into my outstretched hands.

There was a short silence.

"I got a letter from him yesterday," she said at length.

"Is he well?"

"I think so. . . . I haven't read all of it yet."

"Poor Pierrot," said Denis. "He was very fond of me, and I behaved so badly. When he comes back I must see a lot of him. Not that he'll care by that time: he'll have ceased to think about me."

They heard a faint sound above their heads. Irène must be leaning on the bar of her window. Rose called up.

"A little fresher, at last, don't you think, Irène?"

The rattle of a venetian blind was the only answer; Rose begged her brother to go upstairs.

"Make an effort," she said, "be nice to her."

He protested. Twice, he said, he had spoken to her and twice she had refused to answer.

"I've thoroughly deserved my night on the couch, believe me!"

"Oh, Denis!" she said, and tried to look shocked. But a hint of laughter lay behind the words.

Furniture creaked in the silence of the empty rooms. Irène had fallen asleep in a storm of tears, and was now faintly snoring, one hand grasping the cradle.

Rose, for the last fifteen minutes, had been on her knees, her head pressed against her bed. But her mind was far from her prayers, wandering down an intricacy of strange paths.

Denis, stretched on the couch, was thinking, though now

without a flicker of fear, that this was the room in which his father had killed himself. The leather of the padded chairs still smelt of the cigars he had regularly smoked. Denis was no longer fearful of the dead. How lovely it was to be alone! Tomorrow they would start sending the white grapes into town. All that mattered at the moment was that his disagreement with Irène should not affect his relations with her parents. He must, at all costs, keep them out of his private troubles. Once the child was safely in charge of a nurse and efficiently protected from Irène's unscientific system of feeding, he would use the first quarrel that came along as an excuse to move out of her room for good and all. How difficult would that be? So far as appearances went, she seemed to be genuinely fond of him. . . . No, he decided on second thoughts, it would be her vanity rather than her feelings that would be hurt. He had never really believed that women could love him. . . . He had a sort of physical horror of himself. Irène bore his name, lived in the great house, and was the mother of Paul Revolou. . . . What more could she want? . . . How wonderfully patient Rose was! But she couldn't go on indefinitely like this. She would grow tired of the life she was living. 'She's twenty-two,' he thought, 'nobody really matters to her any more. But am I sure of that? There is something morbid about this self-sufficiency of hers. . . . Even now she may still meet somebody. It's awful to think that life is in a constant state of flux. Everything changes. One suddenly reaches a stage (as I have done now) at which existence becomes possible and within one's power to control. If only one could call a stop to time. But one can't.'

Rose was listening to the sound of rain on the leaves. How delicious was this quiet downpour, unaccompanied by hail or thunder! Once the worst of the heat was over, and the influence of Irène with her peasant ways neutralized, Paul would be better. . . . Rose could not have been fonder of him had he been her own child. But then, her own child would not have been a Revolou. He would have borne another name. It was odd, the importance she had begun, of late, to attach to these things. . . . She lapsed into a sort of waking dream. A phrase that she had read somewhere kept coming into her mind: "Sacrifice the mother, but save the child. . . ." Whenever it rained at night, her thoughts turned to the dead, but not in pity. She was sorry to think that hers were housed in a tomb of masonry, and could not enjoy the privilege which belonged to the poor, of being made one with the earth, of drinking in, through grass and roots and sand, the gentle rain from Heaven.

"Have you warned her that the nurse is coming?" Denis asked her the next evening, as he got out of the car.

Rose replied that she had not seen her sister-in-law. Irène had had her meals in her room.

"But I asked her mother to speak to her about it. She didn't need much persuading. Maria realizes that Irène is entirely inexperienced, and won't listen to advice."

Irène came down to dinner rather late. Her eyes were red and swollen. Brother and sister spoke about people she did not know. Seeing that her plate remained empty, Rose asked whether she was feeling unwell.

"You must make an effort, you know, for baby's sake."

The young mother burst into sobs and ran out of the room. Rose motioned to Denis to follow her. He got up looking thoroughly annoyed. The moment of crisis had come at last, she thought: but it would pass, and they would settle once more into the familiar routine. Her brother did not come down again and she went upstairs. As she reached the first landing, she heard the sound of Irène's voice broken by sobs:

"I don't mind having a nurse . . . it's not that that's making me cry. . . . I'll do everything *you* want, but I won't have your sister always getting at me! Why can't she marry like anybody else instead of staying on here to plague me? If she tries to steal the child, I'll kill her. . . . Yes, I will. . . . I'll do something awful to her. . . ."

Denis's words came clearly to her ears. He was speaking very calmly, almost unnaturally so, telling his wife not to get into a state, to be sensible. But the latter's references to herself became, if anything, more violent, and she went downstairs again and out on to the front steps, where she stood leaning against the wall.

The sky was overcast. There would be no shooting-stars to watch tonight. She could hear, through the window above her head, her brother's wife screaming in a storm of misery and hate. She could not catch the words, but that mattered little. She knew herself to be the cause of this despair, its sole origin and occasion. Was it really that she cared so much about the child's health? No, she realized only too well that that was a very secondary affair. What was really at issue, she told herself, was the question —whose was to be the dominant influence, the wife's or the sister's? It was the kind of struggle that goes on in the bosom of every family. But why, in this darkness which was so intense that she could scarcely make out the trees, was her heart so heavy? She felt a weight within her breast, a painful tension. Could she have brought herself to move, she would have wandered down the path that was invisible in the blackness. But somehow, she felt rooted to the spot. Her body clove to the wall. Her legs were trembling.

"Where are you, Rose?"

She was conscious of the familiar smell of tobacco. Denis was speaking:

"She's calmer now. I've noticed that she always sleeps like a log when she's been crying. Sooner or later we should have had to have it out. . . . Things will right themselves eventually. . . . It's really all a matter of education. . . . These appalling outbursts come from a lack of early training. They don't, fundamentally, matter either to me or to you. They just work themselves out in a world that is remote from both of us. . . . It's easy enough for me to ignore them, and for you too, I suspect, eh? She goes banging herself against the window pane like a great frightened blue-bottle, while you and I breathe freely in the open air outside. We belong to a different world. It's not only that we share the memories of childhood. Even if we had lived apart, the same current would still flow within our bodies—the current of our common blood. Soon the poor bluebottle will grow tired, and find somewhere she can stay still. . . . When all's said and done, she's been lucky. She's got much more than she could ever have hoped to have. I give you my word, you shan't be bothered any more, Rose. Your happiness matters a great deal to me."

"There is no more happiness to hope for."

He imagined that she was thinking of Robert Costadot, and asked her whether she still loved him. She gave a little laugh that was half a sigh. "Oh, gracious no!" She would never love anybody now. All that was a closed book to her. He protested, but she shook her head.

"People no longer exist for me. Their world is a world apart. So far as I am concerned they are faceless, and they speak a language that I have forgotten."

"I feel much the same," said Denis. "All day long I go through a mechanical series of gestures, discussing prices, signing letters. And then, suddenly, at six o'clock, as I sit at the wheel of the car, I resume my real self, I become again Denis, your brother."

The words were simple. Why, then, should they sound so oppressive? The echo of them hung in the air, stifling her mind. She must not yield to this sudden terror, she thought: that way lay madness.

He was speaking again.

"I'm going to say something, Rose, that will seem very extraordinary to you. I believe that tonight, for the first time in my life, I am really happy. Yes," he repeated. "I am happy."

They heard somebody moving about in the billiard-room, knocking against the furniture. A figure appeared in the french window. Irène's hoarse voice sounded in the darkness.

"Aren't you coming to bed, Denis?"

He replied that he would wait a bit longer. Rose was foolish enough to urge him in a low voice, to go up with his wife.

"So it's you, is it?" cried Irène.

Rose was leaning against the wall. An iron table stood between her and the possibility of attack. She was subjected to a stream of filthy invective levelled at her from the window. Much of it she did not hear, because Denis had clapped one hand over his wife's mouth. How dare she say such things? She must be mad to bring such charges against her! The outburst was quickly over. It had lasted, perhaps, a few seconds. But one flash of lightning in a dark night is enough to show a limitless stretch of countryside. In those few short moments, Rose saw revealed a panorama of passions to which as yet, she was a stranger, a stretch of waste land pitted with extinct craters, sterile and empty.

For most men the road of life is a dead-end, leading nowhere. But there are some who, even in childhood, realize that they are moving towards an unknown sea. At the very beginning of their journey they are amazed by the bitter violence of the wind and taste the salt upon their lips. On they go, until, at length, when the last dune has been surmounted, they find themselves in a world of spume and blown sand which seems to speak to them of an infinity of passion. That is the moment when they must choose their path. Either they must take the final plunge, or they must retrace their steps. . . .

Denis tried to push Irène towards the stairs, but she was stronger than him. Only at last did he manage to get his arms about her, because by that time she was half fainting, and did not fully recover until she had almost reached the top of the first flight. He supported her to her room. She groaned as though in pain. "Don't leave me! Don't go downstairs again! If you do, I shall throw myself out of the window! . . ."

"I'll stay with you: I'll lie beside you on the bed."

"And you won't move all night?"

He reassured her. He would stay with her all night. He held her hand in his. Through the window he thought he could hear Rose breathing, but it was only the sound of the wind in the trees. He heard her shoot the bolt. By now she must be in her room.

Rose sat down on her bed, and remained there motionless.

A few heavy drops splashed on the leaden surface of the roof. She would take no more than her dressing-case, and buy what linen she needed in Bordeaux. She had plenty of time in which to decide where she should go, and her clothes could be sent after her. All that mattered was that she should relieve the house of her presence. She must "flee and be no longer there". . . . She would send Denis a reassuring note to the office. She would tell him that she had gone away for a short time only. How far she was now from the road she had expected to travel on that evening, three years ago when he had first learned of his failure. . . . What would happen in the future she did not know, but only that she must find her way back to the point at which she had left it. Whether she prayed she could not then have said, but surely prayer alone could have shown her what, at that moment, she must do. Her mind did not see beyond the present. She knew that she would creep downstairs shortly before six, that she would walk down the little lane that led from the stables, that she would hear the approaching tram long before it came into view. It would be light by six, and, unless there was a thick mist, she would not see the single headlight glowing like a cyclops' eye. But deep in her heart it burned bright and enormous as in those dawns of long ago.

MC.